SOME GLAD MORNING

A NOVEL

GARY C. HORTON

BLIND TIGER PRESS

SOME GLAD MORNING
Gary C. Horton

Printed in the United States of America.
Blind Tiger Press
1098 Daralynn Dr.
Lexington, South Carolina, 29073

For more information about this book, visit www.blindtigerpress.com

Edition ISBNs

Trade Paperback: 978-0-9855776-0-5

E-Book: 978-0-9855776-1-2

First Edition 2012

This edition was prepared for printing by The Editorial Department
7650 E. Broadway, #308, Tucson, Arizona 85710
www.editorialdepartment.com

Cover design by Carol Ruzicka
Cover photo: "Sunrise for Keitt" by John Hane at www.flickr.com/photos/johnhane/
Book design by Christopher Fisher

To my parents, Les and Vi

"No act of love is ever wasted."
—Geneen Roth

Acknowledgements

Many people helped me bring this story to life. First and foremost is Kathy Kendall. I am eternally grateful for her steadfast encouragement and support. Also, special thanks to Earl and Sarah Baker whose gift came at just the right time, and to their lovely daughter Cassandra Baker McCleod whose charm never fails to lift my spirits.

I am forever grateful to Susan Parks Myer who read my first attempts at fiction a lifetime ago and was there for me in my darkest hour. Thank you to Jeri Collins who talked me off the ledge more than once. Thanks too to Captain Hank Flood who understood why I left a career in Special Forces to follow my heart. I am grateful to Peggy Voorhees who masterminded a hilarious caper to snag a literary agent with fake wedding invitations. With deep appreciation, I thank Lezlie Nelson for her strength, encouragement and generosity.

Thank you to Esther Williams whose kindness meant everything. I am grateful to Mrs. Eliza Shockley for her friendship and inspiration, and to her son John and daughter Ellen Story.

And a heartfelt thanks to charming Marilynn Maddox for her warm encouragement. Finally, my deepest appreciate to Michelle Rinaldi, Charles Evans and John Gary Evans who, when all was lost, reminded me that sometimes the only sane response is to love.

SOME GLAD MORNING

1

"HE'S DYING, AIN'T HE?" The scrawny, bare chested little girl said.

"I don't know." Ransom tucked a blue ledger book beneath his arm. He wore a dirty work shirt and trousers frayed beneath the knee. He had no shoes.

"His name is Mister Evans, 'cause I found him at Mister Evans' store," she said. The two looked down on a gray tabby kitten lying in the dust outside a sharecropper shack. "He didn't have no mama, so I brung him home. He's dying, ain't he?"

"Maybe not." Ransom scooped the kitten up in both hands and felt the tiny ribcage rise and fall with each labored breath. Delicate clumps of sand stuck in a line of moisture along its lips. He could feel bones through the skin and it weighed hardly anything at all. Ransom plucked a sandspur from the kitten's fur and gently brushed the sand from its lips. Although dirt subdued his gray tabby stripes, Mister Evans had the markings of a dignified kitten. He had white boots and a white bib that spilled down from his chin and widened into a broad triangle across his chest. The kitten looked up to Ransom with trusting eyes.

On the dirt road, beyond the newly planted cotton, a shiny black Model T puttered by, kicking up a cloud of red dust. A large sign mounted behind the driver read in bold letters: *'Join the Army Today.'*

"Yesterday the pig tried to eat him," the little girl said, peering into Ransom's hands at the frail kitten.

"What are you feeding him?"

"Nothing. Mama said he's got to catch his own dinner, but he won't do it. I reckon he's just going to starve his self to death."

"You have to feed him something 'til he's big enough to hunt."

"We can't feed the whole dang world," the little girl's mother said from the porch of the shack. The screen door slammed behind her as she leaned a shoulder against a porch post. A soiled dress hung loose on her frame. "We can't hardly feed our own selves." She smoked a pipe made from a clay bowl Charlie Evans sold in his store for pennies. The stem was a hollow reed. She crossed her arms and propped a hand beneath the pipe. Smoke puffed from the corner of her mouth.

"You have to feed him something," Ransom said. "Can't you give him a dab of butter?"

"Butter? I wish," the woman said. "You got butter at your house?"

"Sometimes," Ransom said. He looked past the woman and across the vast field of newly sprouted cotton plants to the shack where he lived. His father was marching through the field towards them. "How about some grease? You got any grease?"

"A little," the woman said, puffing a wisp of smoke.

"Mama, we don't need much."

"Come in the house, Pun'kin." The woman pushed away from the post. "I'll get you a smidgin."

When the little girl had run inside, Ransom looked out over the field. Except for a few oaks along the road and the woods along the creek where it stayed wet, the whole world was planted in cotton, right up to the Blue Ridge Mountains rising in a haze against the sky. Spring cotton grew close to the shack with just enough room for a vegetable garden and a hog pen where a spindly peach tree offered the only shade. Every tillable square inch of South Carolina was planted in cotton save for an occasional patch of corn grown to feed the men and mules.

The little girl hurried from the shack, holding a spoon of congealed bacon fat in front of her. In the distance, between the two shacks, Ransom's father strode along a row of tender cotton plants, his shoulders hunched, his head bowed, which meant he was in a foul mood. He was always in a foul mood when he had to talk to the landlord, Mr. Jenkins.

"Make him eat it, Ransom," the girl said as she gave him the spoon of grease.

He carried the kitten to the peach tree, where he placed the blue ledger on the ground and sat holding his tiny burden in the shade, his back against the tree's narrow trunk. The girl knelt beside him.

"What's that book for?"

"It's an accounting of what my daddy owes Mr. Jenkins. My daddy's recollection and Mr. Jenkin's recollection of how much my daddy owes for seed, fertilizer and what all aren't the same. I'm keeping a record so my daddy can't get cheated."

"That's real smart," the little girl's mother said from the porch. With the pipe stem in her mouth, she leaned on the post. "You learn that at the Baptist Mission School? Won't do you no good. Mr. Jenkins will find some other kind of way to cheat your daddy. That's why he lives so fat. He cheats people."

"Yes ma'am." Ransom held the tin spoon with the dab of grease near the kitten's nose. Mister Evans pressed closer. His tongue slipped out in a cautious taste, then came alive in a flurry. When the grease was all lapped up, the kitten kept licking the spoon and then Ransom felt the tiny rough tongue licking his finger too.

"Feed him bacon grease every day. He'll soon get strong enough to hunt on his own."

"I sort of hoped he'd die," the mother said. "Be one less thing to worry about."

"He'll earn his keep," Ransom said. "Once he's feeling better and a little bigger, he'll keep the mice out."

"Want me to get him some more?" The little girl said smiling up to Ransom.

"Not yet. Let his tummy rest."

"What else can I feed him?"

"You just have to give it to him and see. I had a cat once that'd fight you for corn on the cob."

The kitten curled in a ball in Ransom's lap, closed his eyes and began to purr. Ransom rubbed the kitten's tiny neck and felt each beadlike bone. He picked sandspurs from the soft fur. When a spot of sunlight spilled into his lap, he held the sleeping kitten there for the sun to heal.

"He'll get better now, won't he?"

"I think so." Ransom took a light brown nut from his pocket. As big as the end of his thumb, it looked like a large hazelnut. "Here," he said, passing the nut to the little girl. "Rub my lucky buckeye to be sure." She rubbed the nut between her palms, then rubbed it some more.

"Boy, where the hell you been?" Ransom's father walked out of the cotton field. "You got the book? We got to have the book."

Ransom passed the kitten to the girl, stood up and showed the blue ledger to his father.

"What you messing with kittens for?" Ransom's father said. "You're seventeen now. You need to put that sort of thing behind you and start acting like a man."

Ransom followed his father through the cotton. The green plants were not yet knee-high. The two passed barefoot into the pecan grove surrounding Mr. Jenkins's white house.

"I dare that fat son-of-a-bitch to cheat me now," his father said.

Mr. Jenkins had the only painted house in that part of Pickens County. It glared white in the early morning sun. Mr. Jenkins had a telephone and electricity too. Ransom had never been inside the house and had not seen the phone for himself, but at night, when he sat on the porch of their shack, he could see the electric lights glowing in the windows.

The closer they got, the more he could feel the tension mounting in his father.

"He can't cheat us now," Ransom said. "We got the numbers."

"He better not," his father said.

They found Mr. Jenkins behind the house, at the door of his commissary where a hired man unloaded cases from the wooden bed of a Model T truck. Mr. Jenkins, round and soft-bellied, cocked a straw hat to the back of his head and put his hands on his hips as Ransom and his father came up the cinder drive.

"Mister MacTavish," he said. "What do you want now?"

"Cornmeal, scratch, and coffee."

"Against my better judgment, I credited you seed and fertilizer last month. That put you more behind than you were already. You haven't come out ahead in three years."

Ransom and his father stepped up to the Model T. The hired man kept his head bowed and continued to unload the truck.

"That's what I can't understand," Ransom's father said. "Ever' year we pick more sacks off the fields I farm than any other place, and the price of cotton is higher now than it's ever been in my life, but I still can't come out ahead."

Mr. Jenkins took his hat off and wiped the inside band with a handkerchief.

"Maybe you're not as good a farmer as you think. Numbers don't lie and that's all I got to go on. Your numbers are steady marching backwards. You need cash money if you want to come out ahead."

"We don't have cash money," his father said. "But my boy knows numbers as good as you. We got our own book now." He drew Ransom up closer. "Show him the book."

"Your book doesn't mean a thing here," Mr. Jenkins said. "The commissary book is the only book that matters." He turned his back and went into the weathered barn made of rough sawmill lumber.

The hired man stacked wooden crates inside the door and refused to make eye contact with any of them. A single bare light bulb hung from the ceiling and cast a sickly yellow glow on the shelves of work clothes, hardware and foodstuff. Hundred-pound sacks of cornmeal and scratch feed stood upright, all but choking the middle aisle. At the counter, below the empty scales, shiny tin pails of lard were stacked three high. An open keg of roasted coffee beans filled the place with a rich aroma. Mr. Jenkins picked a single bean from the keg and popped it in his mouth. Sucking loudly on the coffee bean, he opened the commissary ledger book and spread it wide on the counter.

"Ransom," his father said. "Get up here and look at these figures."

Ransom studied the numbers Mr. Jenkins had written in his father's account. He opened his own ledger book and compared.

"What's this?" He pressed a dirt-stained finger at the bottom of a column in Mr. Jenkin's book. "We don't have those numbers. Where'd they come from?"

"You know," Mr. Jenkins said. "I was against the Baptist Missionary School coming here to teach you kids how to read and write and figure. I knew it would only lead to misunderstanding. A little education is a dangerous thing. It can make for hard feelings. If you had as much education as I do, you'd know straight away what those numbers mean. It's not my job to educate you. I'm just trying to make a living, same as anyone else. I own the land you farm. I own the house you live in. I even credit you what you need. But, Mister MacTavish, you have continually tried to take advantage of my generosity."

"What is it? Ransom, what's he trying to pull?" The cords in his father's neck grew tight. His cheeks flushed red. The muscles stretched across his jaw flexed in hard knots.

"He added three dollars to last month's numbers," Ransom said.

"It's a surcharge on the balance you owe. Long as you owe me, I can add a surcharge. That's the law."

"It might be the law, but it ain't decent." Anger charged the air. Ransom grabbed his father by the waist and tried to turn him around. "You're already taking everything I got," his father said, leaning across the counter. "You ain't got to cheat me too."

"Daddy," Ransom tried to pull him away. "Daddy, come on. Let's go."

"Are you calling me a cheat?" Mr. Jenkins said. "Keep pushing me and I just might forget my Christian principles."

"Daddy." Ransom tried to pry his father from the counter. "We got cotton in the ground. We can't start over, not this year. Think about that."

"You don't like it here?"

The hired man passed a double barrel shotgun to Mr. Jenkins who raised it over the counter. Ransom's father took a step back.

"You got cotton in the ground. I can have you out and get a new man in there by the end of the day. I'll give your place to a colored family. They won't complain like you."

"We like it fine," Ransom said, pulling his father toward the door, his eyes fixed on the shotgun. "We like it fine."

With his finger on the trigger, Mr. Jenkins watched Ransom and his father backing out the door. He laid the shotgun barrel across the counter so the muzzle aimed belly high. Ransom felt it in his gut.

2

THEY HURRIED DOWN THE CINDER DRIVE and through the pecan grove. Neither of them said a word until they were again in the cotton field. Ransom looked behind them, but did not see Mr. Jenkins or the hired man.

"We need to move the hell away from this place," his father said, "but we got no money to move on and no place to go. Cotton's in the ground. We can't leave all that work, but the longer we stay here the more my numbers just keep right on running backwards." He paused and pressed a dirty palm to his forehead. "Your mama's expecting me to bring back some cornmeal and coffee, but I can't give that son-of-a-bitch another cent, not one more cent." He spit in the dust and searched his pockets for a plug of tobacco, but there wasn't any. "We need cash money and a lot of it."

A cloud of anger stayed with them all the way home. Outside their shack, his father paced at the edge of the cotton and cast nervous eyes toward the creek.

"Tell your mama I'm at the branch." He headed through the cotton toward the distant oak and poplar trees along the creek and took the angry cloud with him.

Ransom made his way out to the road where tiny wildflowers grew. Honey bees worked the blossoms, buzzing from one to another and flying off towards the woods. Ransom didn't know the names of the flowers, but they smelled so sweet and he liked their colors, blue and yellow and white. There was never enough color at home. When he had a fistful, he arranged them in a clumsy bouquet then padded up to the house and through the back door.

He found his mother kneeling on the kitchen floor scrubbing the bare boards with wet creek sand. She looked up and smiled when she saw him. In spite of the cool breeze blowing in through the open windows, her face glistened with sweat. She looked tired and worn. Ransom held up the ragged bouquet.

"They're not as pretty as Mrs. Jenkins's garden flowers, but they smell sweet as sunshine."

"The prettiest flower ain't always the sweetest," his mother said. With a sigh, she pushed herself up from the floor. She took the flowers and brought the small blue and white and yellow blossoms to her nose. "Sweet as sunshine." She gathered her lanky son in her arms, hugging him close so their hearts touched. "You're as tall as your daddy," she said, resting a cheek on Ransom's shoulder.

She released him but cupped a palm beneath his elbow and looked into his green hazel-flecked eyes. The sun had lightened his brown hair and darkened his skin. She felt the bone in his upper arm.

"Wish I could get some meat on you," she said. "You're narrow as a fence rail."

"But, I'm strong." Ransom thought he saw a tear in the corner of her eye as she turned away and busied herself at the sink. "Once I stop growing up, I'll fill out. You'll see." At the sink, his mother dipped a canning jar in the bucket of well water then arranged the flowers in it as if the squat jar was a fine vase. She placed the jar and flowers on the sill of the open window above the sink and stepped back to admire them.

"Mr. Jenkins cheated us again, didn't he?" Sunlight graced his mother's cheek as she turned to look out the window.

"Yes ma'am. Daddy's down at the branch."

"You'll have to take him supper." She stared out the window over the jar of flowers. She gazed on something far away, past the vegetable garden and the chicken pen and beyond the endless rows of cotton. Sun streamed through the window and washed her face in tender light. For a moment, she looked young and beautiful.

"Your daddy knows not to come home 'til he sleeps it off." She turned from the window and went to the flour bin, a large compartment under the kitchen counter lined with tin that held fifty pounds of white flour. It tilted out. Every morning she made biscuits right there in the bin, mixing the buttermilk, lard, salt, and baking soda directly in the flour.

Ransom watched his mother tilt the flour bin open and dig her hand deep into a corner until she came up with a pint canning jar. After dusting off the jar and letting the loose flour fall back in the bin, she popped open the wire latch, lifted the hinged glass lid, and drew out a few coins. It was her egg money, the only money they had. She gave Ransom some change and kissed his cheek.

"Run down to Charlie Evans' and get some coffee and cornmeal. The chickens will have to fend for themselves a while longer. When you get back, go down to the creek branch and put a fishing pole in your daddy's hand. See what y'all catch me to fry."

Outside Charlie Evans' store, Ransom paused at the shiny black Model T he'd seen on the road that morning. It was brand new and the recruiting sign bolted on the back looked freshly painted. Ransom walked around it twice. Everything about the machine was new. It smelled of leather and oil, and the black metal shone so bright road dust couldn't dim it.

"You like my automobile?" Someone said behind him.

Ransom turned to see a man in a sergeant's uniform, complete with wrapped leggings and campaign hat.

"Does everybody in the Army get a new Ford?"

"You don't need one if you're in the Army," the sergeant said. He sounded like a Yankee. "The Army loaned me this one to drive up here so you farm boys can join up. We're getting a brigade together at Camp Jackson."

"It's a mighty nice automobile," Ransom said walking past the sergeant to the steps of Charlie Evans' store.

"Let me buy you a soda and we'll talk about it," the sergeant called after him.

Ransom stopped at the door. "If you want to buy me something, you can buy me a sack of chicken scratch. Mama's chickens have been eating nothing but bugs since the last freeze."

"Done," the sergeant said and followed Ransom inside.

Charlie Evans met them at the counter and measured out a pound of coffee beans and two pounds of cornmeal. The sergeant hefted a bag of chicken scratch onto the counter and paid for the whole lot. He also bought two short Cokes.

"Not much to this town, is there?" He said as they walked out.

"A church, a store and the mission school," Ransom said. "That's about all you need."

"It might be all you need, but if a fellow got out of here and looked around, he might find he wants a whole lot more."

"I can't pay you back." Ransom sat down on the bench beneath the bright red *Drink Coca-Cola* sign painted across the outside wall of Charlie Evans' store. "My daddy already owes more than he'll make in his lifetime."

"All I ask is a few minutes of your time." The sergeant sat down beside him. He pried the metal caps off the drinks with the bottle opener of his Army-issue pocket knife then passed one to Ransom.

Ransom took a sip and savored the dark sweetness. He didn't say another word and the sergeant didn't either. They sat side by side and sipped from the small bottles.

Ransom belched and it surprised him. "Excuse me," he said.

"You don't get much soda, do you?"

"You mean Coke?" Ransom shook his head. "This is my first one."

"You're a real quiet young man," the sergeant said. "Humble. You're humble, I'd say. That's alright. It takes humility to know who you are." The sergeant turned on the bench to face Ransom. "Listen," he said. "The Army can be a good thing. It's work and it's not all fun, I promise you that, but it can get you out of here. You'll have boots and clothes and a bunk. You'll eat three square meals a day, ham for breakfast, chicken for lunch and beef for supper. Give the Army two years then see what your options are. You can always come back here and pick up again."

Ransom thought for a minute, took a sip from the short bottle and thought some more.

"Does the Army pay cash money?"

3

NIGHT HUNCHED COLD over the muddy trenches of France. Eight to ten feet deep and wide as a man's outstretched arms, the trenches sprawled for miles like some mad hallway to hell gouged into the earth. Black mud, two feet deep and dense and heavy as mortar, filled the bottom of the trenches. Everything was wet and foul. Soldiers slept in flat caves dug into the trench walls. With only enough room for two men to stretch out side by side, the sleeping caves looked like shabby catacombs of a poor man's mausoleum.

Shivering in his cave, Private Ransom James MacTavish lay beside his buddy. The wet blankets held no heat and lice crawled in every tender place on his body. Images he had seen on the march up from Paris three days ago haunted him. The French soldiers who had occupied these trenches had been blown to shreds by German heavy artillery. Each time he closed his eyes, the silhouettes of broken corpses scattered through the treetops rose in his mind. From the moment he saw the bodies in the trees, he had begun to tremble, a constant falling apart that loosened everything inside him.

On this clear night, Ransom could see the sky and the star he had come to think of as his own. It gave him comfort. He knew this star looked down on him and down on his home in Issaqueena. Its light touched his daddy and his mama, and the creek branch and the Blue Ridge Mountains and all things familiar to his life.

"I ain't never going to get warm enough again," his buddy said through chattering teeth. "When this is over, I'm going to find a warm place that's quiet, where nobody will bother me and I'm going to stay right there for the rest of my life."

"When I get home, I'm going to buy some land and farm my own place," Ransom said, still looking up at his star. He could almost believe it changed colors from yellow to green to blue and back again. "I'm saving my pay, every penny. Mama's keeping it in a jar at home. And I'll find a girl to love who'll love me back. We'll start a family. We'll have our own house too, on our own land and grow our own cotton that nobody can cheat us out of. I want to hear crickets at night and rain on the roof. I want to watch my babies grow up."

A headquarters runner slogged past. Runners had been coming and going all day and into the night. Ransom heard the soldier breathing hard as he ran toward the cave where Lieutenant Pinckney slept.

"Something's going on," his buddy said.

Chatter rippled up the trench from the direction the runner had gone. Two men passed by carrying a ladder and leaned it against the trench wall facing the German lines.

Lieutenant Pinckney appeared down the trench. Mud sucked at the young officer's boots as he made his way closer. He wore a wool blanket on his shoulders like a cape and puffed fog with every breath. Bowing in the dark, Pinckney spoke in a whisper where two men lay tucked in their sleeping cave then stumbled onward down the trench. When he came to Ransom, he leaned over him and braced a hand against the trench wall.

"We're going over the top," he said.

"Yes, sir," Ransom said and the lieutenant slogged away to deliver the message to the rest of the platoon.

For a moment, Ransom and his buddy lay in silence, listening to the sounds of soldiers moving through the mud. Tiny, half-concealed, lights flashed against the trench walls as men lit cigarettes. Ransom drew his lucky buckeye from his pocket and kissed it. When he put it back, his buddy tried to speak, but choked instead and faltered into silence. Ransom rubbed the buckeye in his pocket and watched his star change color from yellow to green to blue.

"I heard," his buddy said, pushing back the quiet that had become unbearable. "I heard if you go over the top you never come back. They don't even get the bodies. They just leave them out there to rot."

"I heard the same thing," Ransom said. He drew a chocolate bar from his coat pocket. The cold had hardened it to wax. He peeled the paper wrapper from the chocolate, broke it in two and passed half to his buddy. "I was saving this for tomorrow."

Soldiers crawled from their caves to stand clustered in the trench, their breath fogging the air. Some drew on cigarettes and blew smoke that drifted up into the night. Across no man's land, the Germans sent up illumination flares. One flare after another streaked into the sky until half a dozen swayed beneath parachutes, sizzling brilliantly in the frigid air, their light blotting out Ransom's star.

Savoring the last of the chocolate lingering like sweet paste in his mouth, Ransom forced himself out. He stood in the cold muck and dragged his rifle from beneath the blankets. His buddy joined him standing in the mud. They huddled together, shivering. Along the trench four ladders leaned against the top.

"I'm not scared," Ransom said. "The next world's got to be better than this one."

Lieutenant Pinckney climbed the ladder near Ransom. The young officer stopped a few rungs short of the top and sat down to smoke the stubby end of a cigar while the platoon sergeant herded the men together. A pair of soldiers made the sign of the cross. Ransom rubbed his lucky buckeye.

"The British are on either side of us," Lieutenant Pinckney said. "They're going over the top too. The German trenches are fourteen hundred meters to our front. That's about a mile. When you hear the whistles, get up the ladder, get out and run like hell. The Germans will drop artillery on us as soon as they see what's happening. They won't drop it on themselves, though, so the closer you can get to the German trenches, the better your chances of the artillery missing you."

"Sir," a soldier said. "Once we're over there, what do we do?"

Lieutenant Pinckney puffed on the stubby cigar. The cinder glowed red as a demon's eye as a whiff of smoke chugged from the corner of his mouth. "If you get that far shoot as many as you can." He turned and climbed the final rungs up the ladder, staying low as he looked down the length of the trench to his right then over to his left.

"Dear God," he muttered. "I never dreamed life could sell so cheap."

Beneath him, Ransom stood with his hand in his pocket, his fingers busy rubbing the lucky buckeye. He watched Lieutenant Pinckney draw a curious wallet to his lips. Its silver clasp caught the light of the parachute flares burning in the sky.

"Good bye, my love." Lieutenant Pinckney kissed the wallet. Stowing it away, he muttered a prayer, so softly Ransom heard only, "God have mercy."

Then the screeching whistles blew, loud and desperate, all along the trenches and far off into the distance on either side.

"Follow me." Lieutenant Pinckney rose up on the ladder and scrambled over the top. The night burned with the light of countless illumination flares. Dozens more sizzled into the sky, streaming tails of fire before bursting into brilliant platinum light. Machine guns stuttered across the German lines. Rifles popped and cracked as men raced out into no man's land.

Ransom ran too, as if the rush to death had made a vacuum and sucked every living soul over the top. He ran, his boots pounding the soft ground as he passed tangles of barbed wire and a soldier lying face down. Points of light flickered along the distant trenches. Far behind the rifles, a mountainside erupted in relentless tongues of flame reaching for the sky as German artillery batteries fired every gun.

4

RANSOM WOKE BENEATH A CORPSE, drew a breath, and sank again into darkness. The deeper he sank, the quieter it became. His pain diminished too, until, within the dead silence, he felt the presence of others.

"Breathe," Mama said. Ransom drew air into his lungs and felt his chest rise against some pain he'd forgotten. It would have been easier not to breathe, but he did as he was told. Mama stood over him. Stars shone perfectly above her.

Daddy knelt at Mama's feet. He touched Ransom's shoulder and looked into his eyes as if he might be thinking of calling Doctor Peak. Lord knows where the money would come from to pay him. Daddy said Doctor Peak charged too much and did too little, but when he was scared, he sent for him.

"Breathe," Mama said. "You got to keep breathing." She wore the prettiest dress he'd ever seen on her, blue as a summer sky with tiny white and yellow flowers. She'd wanted a new dress for as long as he could recall, but there was never any money for dresses. All she ever wore were things she made from sack cloth.

Daddy had on new overalls and a work shirt that must have come from the catalog. They weren't that cheap stuff Mister Jenkins sold in his commissary. Brass strap buckles and buttons shone like precious metal, glittering in the starlight.

People crowded behind Mama and Daddy. In the dark, Ransom couldn't make out who they were. When he tried to lift his head and see, Daddy pressed a hand to his chest and made him lie back again.

"Breathe now son," Mama said.

A man stepped closer and peered over Daddy's head, looking down on Ransom. It was Lafayette. Lafayette was old and as black as they come, but he didn't look old now, and he wasn't stiff like Ransom remembered. Lafayette sometimes helped Daddy plow. He had a way with mules no one could explain, not even Lafayette. "Mules just likes me," he'd say. And they did. Mules would work for Lafayette when they wouldn't work for anybody else. When a mule saw Lafayette, it smiled.

"What he going to do?" Lafayette said. He wore the same kind of new overalls as Daddy, and a red flannel shirt that seemed to shine with its own light. "Is he coming with us or not?" Lafayette softened out of focus as he withdrew into the shadow of the crowd. "Make up your mind."

"Breathe now son," Mama said.

Ransom drew air as if a great weight sat on his chest. His lungs didn't want to work. They were tired and bruised and would have neglected their chore if not reminded. Separate and distant from the dry rasp of his breath, Ransom heard his heart beating, slow and rhythmic, like an old time piece buried beneath a quilt.

"Long as you're breathing you got a choice." Daddy wasn't much of a talker, but if he had something to say you'd better listen. He wasn't going to say it twice.

Ransom breathed against the pain, breathed again and wanted more. His chest rose of its own accord as he drank in the air.

"He ain't coming," Lafayette called to the others.

"You're all right now," Daddy said and patted Ransom's shoulder. His mother knelt and kissed him on the forehead. Her eyes met his and in her gaze he saw the depth of unspoken love.

Then she drifted away, leaving only a memory. He lay still, thinking of his mother's face. She had looked so young and so pretty. Gone were the weary lines about her eyes, the exhausted stoop of her shoulders and the ever-present dirt beneath her nails. Her eyes were clear and vibrant. She was happy.

Ransom lay in darkness. Pain burned in his groin and rose through his belly, filling his chest with tentacles of fire. He willed his soul to leave that place and forced himself to rise, as if shoving off the bottom of the blackest mill pond. He kicked for the surface, ascending through infinite layers until finally he broke through to consciousness.

Pinned beneath a lifeless corpse, Ransom woke to a world filled with deafening explosions, storms of whistling shrapnel and ground that bucked and jarred. Parachute flares dangled in the night sky and filled the land with brilliant platinum light and pitching shadows. Soldiers ran in full retreat, sprinting toward the American and British trenches. All around him lay the ruins of young men. German machine guns cut across the terrain, silencing the wounded and mowing down those who ran panic stricken across the mangled ground.

Pain burned white hot between Ransom's legs and in his chest he felt the grind of something broken. Getting out from under the corpse was excruciating, struggling to his feet was worse. He saw an artillery crater a few yards away and tried for that. Stunned and disoriented, he staggered away as machineguns trained their fire on him. Streams of bullets ran in stitches near his feet, tossing up spikes of mud.

In that instant, in the space after a bullet struck near his right foot and before another slammed into the muck, eternity opened before him, as if the veil between this world and the next had come undone. All around him, the wasteland lay still and beautiful. Splintered trees, what remained of them, reached with jagged perfection for the sky, just as they should. How silent the world had become, a deep crystalline silence. He could not hear the sizzle of the illumination flares. They shone bright and quiet as open doors to heaven. The dead were also perfect, sprawled just so. Spectacles on a dead corporal glittered beneath the heavenly light. Behind the broken lenses, half opened eyes watched Ransom frozen in the moment. Another soldier, a private like Ransom, lay on his back, his dead lips fixed in a circle like a choir boy's.

A second bullet slammed into the mud just ahead of Ransom and broke the spell. Bullets, hundreds of them, cracked around him as the German line erupted in rifle and machine gun fire. He dove headfirst into a crater. Overwhelmed with pain, he rolled on his back and found himself with two others, a British captain, sitting up and barely conscious, his legs blown away below the knees, and Lieutenant Pinckney, spread on his back against the crater's wall, gasping, a hand pressed to a belly wound that was bleeding profusely.

Ransom fashioned a pair of tourniquets from the shirt of a corpse and tied one below each of the British officer's knees. The Brit looked old for his rank, older than Ransom's father, and bald. He could have been a bookkeeper forced into an officer's uniform.

"Don't tell Mum," the officer said and closed his eyes. He pitched backwards into the mud and lay still. Above them, parachute flares began to fade. A series of blasts from the German lines sent more sizzling into the sky, flooding that raw place with brilliant light. Ransom pressed an ear to the British officer's chest and heard him breathing, slow and faint, on the verge of stalling. He heard the man's heart too, thudding weak against his ribs. Then, fighting his own pain, Ransom crawled to Lieutenant Pinckney.

"I'll get you back to the aid station," Ransom said. "They can patch a thing like this." He tried to drag the lieutenant to the topmost edge of the crater where bullets cracked the air, but the pain was too much. Lieutenant Pinckney stifled a scream and fell limp and silent. Ransom thought he'd killed him. He hadn't moved the man a foot and the pain was too much. Blood, glistening black, flowed from the lieutenant's body to mingle with the water in the bottom of the crater. He coughed and tried to open his eyes, but the lids merely fluttered.

The lieutenant gathered his hands to his chest and tugged at a gold Citadel ring. Finally it slipped from his finger, but the effort cost him and for a moment he rested with the ring clasped loose in his palm and his eyes closed to the world. The shifting light of parachute flares swayed across the Lieutenant's face. Ransom could feel him drifting away. When he found a thread of strength, Lieutenant Pinckney passed the ring to Ransom.

"Get this to my father." Pinckney's hand fell away. His breathing slowed as blood flowed unrestrained from his belly. Ransom tried to think of something to do, but nothing came to mind except to be with the man and watch him die. Lieutenant Pinckney did not move for a long time and though he breathed, it was the infinitely slowing breath of a man fading into sleep. Then the young officer stirred, as if remembering something vital and tried to reach into the pocket of his great coat.

"Can you read?" Pinckney croaked without opening his eyes. His hand fumbled in the loose folds of the coat tangled beneath him.

"Yes, sir." Ransom reached into the lieutenant's coat pocket and retrieved the leather wallet he had seen Pinckney kiss before the assault.

"Open it."

Ransom untied the wallet clasp and turned back the flap. Neatly stowed inside were several letters, clean and pristine. They smelled of lavender. In the very front of the expensive wallet, just behind the clasp, the photograph of a young woman poised in a garden looked out. She was beautiful.

"Elizabeth." The lieutenant's lips barely moved as he opened his eyes to look on the photograph in Ransom's hand. A smile twitched in the corners of his mouth but faded when he closed his eyes again. Time spread between the dying man's breaths. It took all he had to live another moment. "Read to me," Pinckney said.

Ransom withdrew an envelope, the one closest to the silver clasp. His fingers stained the virgin paper and he flinched to think he had violated something sacred. He opened the letter, feeling the fine linen paper, so out of place there. Struggling against pain, Ransom pressed closer to the Lieutenant. Their shoulders touched as he leaned towards the officer's ear.

My Dearest Isaac,

> *The time is lonely. Mother worries I have too little to occupy my mind and has hired Miss Hazel to keep me company. She is teaching me Latin. Can you think of anything more dreadful? But, I am occupied, more than she knows. I think of you always and I pray you are safe, not only safe, but comfortable too. I*

hear horrible things about life in the trenches. I fear for you. Each night I ask God to break the Kaiser and crush him into capitulation.

My pride in you sustains me. When I go to town, my heart swells to tell others my fiancé is fighting the war to end all wars. The world will one day be a better place for your courage. Of this I am sure. When we are old and frail, with children grown and gone, I will still see you as my handsome Citadel cadet.

Do you remember the first spring morning we walked along the waterfront near your father's house? Salt air blowing in from the ocean made everything new. I recall the smell of coffee brewing in the mansions kitchens. It was your senior year and I was still an Ashley Hall girl. I was forbidden by the school to socialize with cadets outside of formal functions, but your mother made an arrangement to host me on the weekend. God bless her. Do you remember?

We walked in the darkness before dawn, when the Negro fishermen, in their shabby little boats, were heading out to sea. You called them the Mosquito fleet. We watched them riding the current to the mouth of the harbor, some boats lit with meager lanterns, others dark as phantoms.

The sun rose for us. You took my hand for the first time and we walked in silence, safe with each other. You are all I have ever hoped for.

Your dearest,
Elizabeth.

When he had finished reading, Ransom looked to Lieutenant Pinckney and waited for him to breathe again. He never did.

5

IN THE FIRST HOUR OF THE DAY, before it got too hot, color painted the undersides of a few clouds bright orange, but soon the color melted from the sky and flies came out to walk across the dead. Ransom shooed them off the Lieutenant's face until he grew tired and let them have him.

Ransom's pain had turned to stone and when he moved it cracked raw again with screams of light behind his eyes. He crawled from where he lay beside Lieutenant Pinckney and crept closer to the British captain, pressing an ear to the officer's heart. He heard it beating, faint and without rhythm. The man breathed in shallow sucking puffs that came and went.

Daylight brought silence to the war. No man's land lay still and quiet as an empty church. In his pocket, Ransom felt the lieutenant's Citadel ring hard against his thigh and vowed again to keep it safe. He had the leather wallet filled with letters too. With his head propped on a dough-boy helmet, Ransom lay on his back and untied the clasp.

A whiff of lavender spilled into the air as he peeled back the wallet flap and drew out the photograph of the beautiful woman frozen in sepia. Her kind eyes and delicate features drew him in. He could love a woman like that.

Ransom turned the photograph over to see a message on the back: *To Lieutenant Isaac Pinckney, all my love, forever and always, Elizabeth.*

He let his eyes drink in the image of Elizabeth, frozen and beautiful and kind. He studied every detail, her light and neatly gathered hair, her delicate mouth and gentle smile, the smart tuck of her dress about her waist and the modest suggestion of breasts beneath the dark fabric.

He withdrew an envelope, opened it, and inhaled the slightest whiff of lavender. Elizabeth's words flowed across the page, each graceful letter leaning perfectly into the next.

> *At night, when I am falling into sleep, I can almost touch you in that far away place. I dream I put my arms around you, give you warmth and keep you safe. When you come home, I will never again let anyone take you away. President Wilson and General Pershing will have to find some other soul to do their work.*
>
> *I see things every day I want to share with you. How a ray of the morning sun rising through the branches of a live oak shines like an ethereal column to Heaven. It is only there for a moment, a brief golden apparition. I wish to hold your hand and walk together through that mystical light. Magic must be in it. Or, perhaps you are magic and cast the light for me to see. Maybe when I wish to share with you, you are truly sharing with me. The light from Heaven is your gift. I think this must be the case for you are magical. The spell you have cast on my heart is nothing less.*
>
> *Two days ago, a wren entered my room as I lay in bed. I had left the windows open for the breeze and to hear the night sounds. She came to the nightstand mere inches from my nose and looked at me as I looked at her. Such a delicate bird she was and very curious about me. I was glad for her visit and took it as a good omen. I would like to have told you about her visit over breakfast or, better yet, to have snuggled in bed beside you, your arms around me as we both looked on this amazing little creature.*

The day will come when we are together. It will be all the more wondrous too because we have learned how painful it is to be apart.

A loud growling roar came from the sky. Ransom could feel it in his chest as well as hear it. It startled him out of Elizabeth's spell. Engrossed in her letter, he had forgotten his pain and where he lay and all the misery scattered across that wasteland. The growling grew louder and Ransom pressed closer to the unconscious British captain as a pair of bi-planes with French insignia screamed past in an angry blur.

Ransom watched the flying machines point their noses to the sky and separate as they climbed higher, rolling sideways through the air. Guns along the German trenches tracked and fired on the French planes, but the pilots rolled again, slipping through the air as they climbed higher.

The planes seemed to delight in flying loops above the Germans. They rose in graceful barrel rolls and side-slipped down into spins as light and spritely as swallows in sunlight. They circled one last time above the heads of anti-aircraft gunners and then turned toward Pont-á-Mousson.

Beneath the French planes, a third plane flew near a German observation balloon. It skimmed along the trees well below the French flyers. Ransom knew this to be a German scout and from his short time in the trenches knew the German would slip under the French planes and fire up into the fuselage. It was an old tactic. The French would do the same if they had the advantage. But the French planes had vanished.

He searched the sky. He could hear the planes, or more truthfully, he could feel the low guttural roar of their cast iron engines, like the dull thump of a bass drum. The sensation put his teeth on edge.

One of the French planes slipped back into view. The German plane raised its nose and started climbing toward it. The second French plane remained lost in the sun's brilliance until at the higher altitude, the German discovered he was outnumbered and banked towards his own territory, nosing down desperately in a full-throttle dive. A French plane dove on him and together the two planes, German and French, sped toward earth.

Closing on its prey, the French plane opened fire. Tracer bullets cut a blazing streak into the rear of the German plane, which swerved left to right as if the pilot had released the controls. Still, the French plane continued firing. The injured plane plunged, nose first, toward the ground. It curved slightly to the left and circled a bit south, then leveled out. For a moment, Ransom hoped the German pilot might have recovered, but then at the edge of some woods, it crashed.

The two French planes waved their wings at each other, rejoicing in barrel rolls and slides, until again they skimmed the trees and laughed across the wasteland.

"It's not right to kill people in the sky," Ransom said to the unconscious Brit. "They ought to leave the sky alone."

6

RANSOM WAITED IN LINE. He had waited in line all morning and into the afternoon. Finally he was summoned into an office where he faced a sour-looking woman in the uniform of a British captain. Even behind the desk he could see she was built broad as a man and nearly as wide as she was tall. Whiskers bristled above her upper lip. Her salt and pepper hair was also short and combed in the fashion of a man.

"Aren't you the perfect Yank soldier?" she said, smiling as she looked him over from top to bottom. "Healthy. Strong. Young. Ready to mount anything what don't get out the way. I know you."

Ransom began to quiver just a bit as he stood looking above the captain's head to the wall behind her. He dared not look at her. He wanted his orders for home and he wanted out of there.

"Be at ease." She bent to inspect his papers. "You want to go home? What? You don't like it here in England? Miss your dear old mum? Very well, then, you're on your way." She put his papers to one side in a shallow wooden tray marked 'Hold.'

A broad smile spread across his face as he snapped again to attention. "Thank you ma'am, when can I expect to leave?"

The British captain did not look up. "Four to six months at the earliest."

Ransom's shoulders drooped.

"A disease is getting spread about by soldiers," she said. "Spanish Influenza is what they call it. Kills people through the lungs. We have orders to keep everyone right here until it passes. The British Army has its procedures and the United States Army has theirs. All the papers must be in order, triplicated, signed, stamped, recorded and filed. It all takes time, my luv. I *could* shorten your departure to thirty days, but it will require effort on your part in your off-duty time."

"Whatever it takes," Ransom said.

The captain smiled.

"I'm glad to hear that. Private MacTavish, you're to visit me in my quarters each evening for the next thirty days. After which, you will be released from your duties and shipped home to the United States."

"What about those boys ahead of me in line? You gave them all a pass straight home. They told me."

"What those Yank boys ahead of you? They've all got syphilis, can't keep a man here if he's got syphilis."

That evening, in the hospital's janitor's closet, Ransom sat on the edge of his bunk. Overhead, cast-iron water pipes knocked endlessly. On the only other bunk in that tight space a very large middle-aged nurse lay with her legs splayed out.

"Would you give me syphilis?" Ransom said. "Please."

"I'd love to, sweetie, but I don't have syphilis and I wouldn't be half the fun of some tart on the street." As she spoke, her great belly waxed and waned like a breathing mountain. "You know, a lady might take offense to a line such as that."

"I mean on paper," Ransom said. "Give me syphilis on paper."

"It'll stay on your permanent record. You wouldn't want that."

"But the only Americans getting sent home are the ones with syphilis."

"That's because the queen don't want you Yanks contaminating our wholesome English girls." The nurse threw her fat legs over the side of her bunk until she sat facing Ransom. Their knees touched. She drew a glass bottle half-filled with a purple liquid from under her pillow and pulled out the cork stopper.

"How much of that have you had today?"

"Worried for my health, are you?" She glared at him. "You can bugger off with that kind of thinking. You, a man what wants to have syphilis worried about my health."

"It's only on paper."

"What would your girl think about your paper syphilis?" She pointed to the photograph of Elizabeth tacked to the wall above Ransom's pillow and took a long pull. "She looks a little snotty today. I think she don't approve of your paper syphilis. You want a snort?"

Ransom stood to go.

"Maybe if you were wounded," she said.

"I *was* wounded."

"In the bloody balls," she said. "And you still have your balls. You're one of the few men that still has arms and legs. You're bloody lucky you can't make babies. That's a blessing. You raise kids up, and for what? So they can break your heart and get killed in some bloody war when they're not hardly old enough to piss standing up. And don't think the war we just had is the end of it. There'll be another one and another one after that. If we'd all stop making bloody babies they'd stop making bloody wars."

"I'm sorry," Ransom said. "I'm sorry you lost your boys. I just want to go home." She was beginning to cry again. "There's alcohol under my bunk."

"I can't drink it straight," she said, wiping her eyes with the back of her hand. Her round cheeks had flushed crimson and she could not stop herself from weeping. With a stifled cry, she stretched out on the bunk and covered her face with her pillow. "I can't bear it," she said, her voice muffled. "Bring me some juice, Sweetie, would you please?"

Ransom left, and then returned from the kitchen with a bottle of grape juice. The nurse watched with the eagerness of a child as he poured juice and alcohol into the small bottle she kept in the pocket of her uniform."

"You're a good lad," she said. "I'd miss you if you left."

She took a long deep slug from the bottle.

"Read to me," she said. "Read to me one of your girl's letters. Maybe I could sleep. It's awful living with a broken heart"

"It's private," he said. He sat on his bunk and turned a shoulder while she drank and cried, creating a protected place for Elizabeth's letter as he read quietly to himself.

Do you hear me when I speak to you from my soul? Does my heartbeat reach that far?

Today, I walked White Point Gardens by The Battery, where, I am told, the pirate Stede Bonnet lies in an unmarked grave, hanged two hundred years ago. Beneath the moss draped oaks, I spoke to him and learned his secrets. It seems the world has grown no better since his day.

And then, as if to remind me to be more cheerful, I heard The Jenkins Orphanage Band marching in town. I hurried up Meeting Street as fast as I could to see them. The Negro boy's music positively stirs my soul. Who can resist their ragtime beat? My spirit soars to hear them. They are so good and so much fun. And their uniforms, cut down from Citadel castoffs, I'm told, made them look smart as musical soldiers. Some danced a gawky thing of swaying legs and crossing arms, completely irreverent and outrageous, a lesson in light heartedness. If only you could have held my hand, I would have been in Heaven.

When I returned to the carriage house, I immediately felt your presence. Your things were on the dresser, your tortoise shell comb, the one you told me to toss out, the jaw harp you toyed with and played horridly, the sharks teeth we gathered from the phosphate tailings when we picnicked and the Confederate coins you saved as a child. On the wall above the dresser, your painting watches over this shrine I have made to you.

I feel your presence in this place, but I cannot feel your warmth or see your eyes, the very things I ache for.

Ransom looked up from the letter to see the nurse sleeping in a heap, slumped half against the wall and half on her pillow. As he left, he closed the door softly so as not to wake her. He made his way across the grounds of the sprawling Edinburgh Hospital to visit Captain Archibald Sterling.

"Hello, sir," Ransom said as he pulled up a chair. A bouquet of spring flowers stood upright in a vase on the night stand. Beneath the silver ribbon adorning the vase, a formal card with the heading of Sterling & Sterling Cotton Brokers wished the captain well.

"Greetings to the bloke who saved my life," the captain said.

Ransom turned the chair around as he brought it near the bed. He sat in it backwards with his arms crossed over the back.

"If a man wanted to be a cotton broker like you," Ransom said, "how would he go about getting started?"

"It's a dangerous time," Captain Sterling said. "Now that the war is over, the bottom could fall out of the market any day. A man could lose everything."

"But if a guy like me wanted to take his chances anyway, how would he get started?"

"Oh, I see." Sterling looked down at the white sheet covering the stumps of his legs. "You want me to help you become a cotton broker."

Ransom nodded.

"A reasonable request," Sterling said. "It's in the numbers. You buy cotton at the local price and sell at the world price. Taking into account storage and shipping, the difference is your profit. Really, all you need is an understanding of the value of cotton and the money to get started."

"How much money are we talking about?"

"Far more than you're likely to have, my friend."

"Will you stake me?" Ransom said.

"As pathetic as my life has been, it's the only one I have and you saved it. Yes, of course, I will do what I can."

7

"It's all a load of happy horseshit," the nurse said and took a drink. She lay slumped against her pillows, one leg off her bunk, her uniform dress bunched nearly to her knees. Across from her, seated on the edge of his mattress, Ransom looked up from the letter he was writing.

"Courting," she said. "Men and women dancing around each other like peacocks when we all know what they're after. It doesn't matter. In the end, we grow old and fat. In the end we die."

"You're drunk," he said and returned to writing.

Dear Miss Lyttelton,

I was a soldier in the platoon your fiancé commanded. I cannot say I knew him, but I was with him when he passed. His courage, his steadfast nature, inspired us all. He cared for us as well as any officer could and we were all made poorer for his passing. Your love sustained him until his last heartbeat.

If it had been in my power to save him, if I could have somehow made him whole and delivered him to you, I would have. Never have I felt so mortal.

In his last moments, he gave me his ring and asked me to return it to his father, which I intend to do as soon as I am able. He asked me to read one of your letters to him and passed from this world hearing your sweet words. He loved you dearly and he knew you loved him too.

We are told there is a great sickness on the world, a fever of the lungs. The doctors tell us that returning soldiers are bringing it home. So, although my wounds are healed, I am not permitted to leave England until this sickness is over. Once I am home in South Carolina, I will bring Lieutenant Pinckney's ring and letters to you.

Sincerely,
Ransom James MacTavish

His letter went out in the morning mail. He passed the days sweeping and mopping the sick bays and corridors, or writing letters for patients who could not write for themselves. Sometimes, he thought perhaps they had all died in no man's land and this was where they went, a monotonous nether world on the edge of hell.

When he returned to his broom closet one afternoon, he found an envelope on his bunk. Familiar in appearance but new and crisp and never opened, postmarked Pocotaligo, South Carolina. His heart raced and for the first time in weeks, he felt alive. Before opening the letter, he brought the envelope to his nose searching for a hint of lavender. It wasn't there. It smelled of sterile paper and his heart sank just a little. He sliced the flap open with a pocket knife and withdrew the folded letter.

Elizabeth Lyttelton
Pocotaligo, South Carolina
January 12, 1919

Dear Mr. MacTavish,

It was sweet of you to write. When we learned the war had ended, Isaac's mother and I rejoiced. Our hearts soared to think Isaac would soon be coming home. Then, in a most cruel vein, within the week, Mrs. Pinckney received that sad slip from the telegraph office. And all the more cruel, a week later, my last letter to Isaac returned to me unopened. Across the top of the envelope someone had scrawled "killed in action."

The news came shortly before Thanksgiving and its shadow darkened Christmas as well. Even now, in this new year, when I think of Isaac, I cannot believe it is true. I feel it just cannot be true. Surely not. Such things should not be.

Although I know many have had the same sorrow, it is impossible for me to realize the truth. The pastor tells me that God moves in mysterious ways. He tells me to lean upon Jesus and that the most perfect life was but thirty-three years. Some speak of glory and how a noble cause is greater than the individual. I want to scream. It all seems so terribly hard to comprehend. How little we know.

Everyone is very kind, but I want to be alone as many do not understand. Flowers are sent in kindness, but they hurt too. This morning, the sun rose as it always does. Isaac's passing made no difference to that Great War, but it has made all the difference to me. He should have stayed in Charleston. It breaks my heart to know this. He should have stayed.

I grew lonely the moment Isaac left, but I am lonely beyond words now that I know he will not be coming home. There are times when I can feel him with me and, when I sleep, I often dream I am holding his hand. At such times I wish to never wake. Please, if there is anything else you can tell me about Isaac, I wish to hear it.

I was grateful to learn my words were a comfort to him in his final moments and I am thankful for the tenderness you gave him.

Sincerely,
Elizabeth Lyttelton

Ransom sat for a moment with the open letter in his hand. Her letter had ended too soon. He folded it and tucked it away in the leather wallet with the others. Then he gathered his writing materials. With the notepad balanced on his knees, he poised an ink pen over the blank sheet of Army stationary. Above his head, steam pipes knocked.

Dear Elizabeth, he began, careful to shape the letters as gracefully as he could. He paused and drew a breath.

He wanted to tell her everything about himself. He wanted to tell her about his parents, growing up in Pickens County, running barefoot through the cotton, fishing in the branch and about how, in the trenches, he had found comfort in a star.

Dear Elizabeth,

> *It was such a joy to receive your letter. You see, my parents cannot write and I have had no news from home since leaving.*

He paused and read over what he'd written. It seemed common. It seemed stupid. He wadded the paper and dropped it at his feet. He took out his buckeye, gave it a rub, then on a fresh sheet of paper tried again.

Dear Elizabeth,

> *Thank you for writing. I regret the sad circumstances of our introduction. Nonetheless, it was a joy to receive your letter.*
>
> *You asked me to tell you more about Lieutenant Pinckney. I only knew him as my superior. My mind often returns to memories of that time. None of it made sense. I am constantly trying to find an explanation to that madness even as I know there is none. I think when we have had a great shock; the sad tone of it resonates within the mind for years, perhaps forever. I do not understand my time in the trenches, other than to say we were men living in mud. We are told of the glory in war, but I never found it.*
>
> *Lieutenant Pinckney kept us fed and safe for as long as he could. Beyond that, there was little he could do. We served for him as we served for each other. Our little band was all we had. Nothing else remained of the world, only us and the Germans across the way. Any thought of some other time, when life had meaning, came in fragments and was impossible to believe.*
>
> *Please tell me of the news in South Carolina. The Army has stuck me in an English hospital and I think fairly forgotten*

about me. I rarely see an American and never one from my home state.

Some good has come from my stay in England. I recently took the initiative to partner with Sterling & Sterling, a cotton brokerage house in Liverpool. My family has worked in cotton for many generations and once I return, I anticipate expanding our enterprise with the backing of Sterling & Sterling Brokerage.

If I am not too bold in asking, please tell me about Elizabeth Lyttelton. How do you spend your days? If I could peer inside, what would I find in your heart?

I am enclosing a photograph of me taken before I knew the war. To look at it makes me feel lonely for that time. It seems so long ago. I am different now, no better perhaps and hopefully no worse.

Sincerely,
Ransom James MacTavish

He read over the letter and wanted to believe what he had written about his association with Sterling & Sterling. It felt cold, not a lie exactly, more like a dream beyond his grasp. He folded the letter, and before sealing it, slipped his picture inside. The picture had been taken at Camp Jackson the day before they shipped to New York.

That night, Ransom lay in bed thinking of Elizabeth. He had studied her photograph so often, he saw her beyond the darkness of the steam pipes over his head. The great emptiness he'd carried so long inside had taken shape. Now, he knew who he ached for.

His days remained unchanged. He swept. He mopped. He mixed juice and alcohol for the night supervising nurse and visited Captain Sterling in the evening. Once a week he stood in line to plead before the out-processing officer. Days rolled into weeks and he waited through each eternal second for a letter from Elizabeth. When it had been too long, he began to doubt himself. Perhaps he had been too familiar. Perhaps something in his letter had given him away and she saw him as a barefooted son of a sharecropper. But then a letter did come and it smelled of lavender.

His heart thumped in anticipation as he sliced the envelope open. He was alive again.

Elizabeth Lyttelton
Pocotaligo, South Carolina
February 24, 1919

Dear Ransom,

This is a quiet time of the year. I sit at the window as I write. A fire warms the room. Still, an outside chill comes through the glass. I can feel it on my shoulder. My father's fields lay silent, waiting for spring. Men are hunting rabbits in the woods. I can hear the dogs. Above us all, a gray sky conceals the sun.

I was both surprised and delighted to get your second letter. I could not be sure if you would write again. I am grateful that you did and pleased you replied so quickly. Your letters are a good thing for a lonely heart.

You asked about Elizabeth Lyttelton. I'm afraid she is a rather dreary girl and not very interesting at all. My father owns eight hundred acres. I grew up on this farm and it has forever felt like a foreign country, isolated from all others. The language here is rice, corn, peanuts, sugar cane and cotton. No one utters a sentence without mentioning one of these. Unless it is hunting season, during which time, a man is expected to also be fluent in quail, duck and deer.

I supposed if you were to meet me, you would first notice my blue eyes. I am told my eyes are kind. I hope so. When I look in the mirror, particularly when I am mussing with my hair, all I see in myself is that stubborn cowlick near my right temple. Boys should have cowlicks but never girls. It is a curse.

Thank you for your photograph. You are a handsome soldier and I am sure by now you have caught the eye of some pretty nurse. Are you enjoying England? Tell me about the people there. Are they so different from us?

After I post this letter, I will shell pecans and make a pie. If you were here, I would serve you pie and coffee, or have you taken to drinking tea like the English?

Ransom, your kind letters ease my broken heart. Some spark still burns within me. If you were here, I am sure your comfort would be all the more. If you were here, I believe I could find my way past the pain. Please visit soon.

Sincerely,
Elizabeth

He sat dumbstruck in disbelief. She wanted to meet him. He had to write her. He gathered his writing tablet then tossed it again on the bed. Letters weren't enough. He had to see her. He had to find a way home.

Ransom hurried across the hospital grounds to the out-process-ing office. The line of soldiers wasn't long and he talked his way to the front. His urgency appeared to annoy the out-processing officer, but she motioned him in.

"You're disrupting the system," she said. "We have a system and everyone is expected to mind it. This isn't a carnival."

Ransom snapped to attention, saluted and presented the form duly signed by the night supervising nurse. The scent of fresh ink wafted between them.

"What's this?" She snatched the form away. "Syphilis? You Yanks are all the same, every bloody last one of you. Not a gentle-man in the bunch." She pounded the form twice with a rubber stamp. "You ship out in the morning."

Dear Elizabeth,

I'm coming home. The paperwork went through today. I will be shipping out in the morning and cannot receive any more letters at my England address. Please write to me general delivery Issaqueena, South Carolina. I will check my mail as soon as I arrive and write to you straight away.

You have said how my letters comfort you. Please know your letters comfort me as well. You have come to fill my thoughts and, dare I say, my heart.

Please forgive my boldness, but now it seems I have always known you, since before I was born perhaps. I know that must sound strange to you, but it rings true with my spirit. But then, I am drunk with excitement and eager to leave the business of war. I am ready to live, now that I know what living means. I feel I can do anything.

I want to touch you. I want to hold your hand and look into your eyes as we speak soul to soul. My spirit is with you now. We must only wait for my body to be shipped like so much freight.

Your faithful soldier,
Ransom

8

Ransom had been on the train since New York. He wore his service uniform, a wide-brimmed campaign hat and leggings bound to his calves. Strung across his shoulder, he carried an Army satchel that at one time had contained maps but now held Lieutenant Pinckney's leather wallet with Elizabeth's letters and photograph, and a letter of credit from Sterling and Sterling. In his pocket, in a change purse he had made as a child, he carried his lucky buckeye and Lieutenant Pinckney's ring. These things and the little money the Army had given him for travel were all he possessed.

He'd slept most of the way but woke in North Carolina hours before dawn and could not go back to sleep. North Carolina looked almost like home. The sun rose as they pulled into Charlotte. The train emptied and filled again. Then they continued on, stopping briefly at a small depot in Cowpens, South Carolina.

On the boarding platform, a redheaded girl in a dark blue dress stood between a stern-looking man and a sobbing woman. The girl's hair, tightly braided and wound about her head, shone with a touch of gold in the early morning light. Rigid as a prisoner between the two, she had a single suitcase at her feet. The mother clearly did not want the girl to leave. The father clearly did.

She boarded at the back of Ransom's car. When she stepped into the aisle to look for a seat, he stood and offered his. Her indigo dress hung loose from her shoulders to her toes, concealing her body. When Ransom rose, she sat down where he'd been sitting and did a most peculiar thing.

As the train pulled away, she plucked pins from her hair, freeing the single long braid wrapped about her head. It fell down her front like a serpent, the tail resting in her lap. With her fingers she undid each braid until the hair came alive. Then she gathered it in her hands and combed it back so it draped between her shoulder blades. The elderly woman seated beside her, took offense and moved further down the car.

The young redheaded woman patted the now empty seat beside her at the window. Ransom had been so captivated by the spectacle that he remained standing in the aisle.

"Sit down," she said. Ransom hesitated. "*Sit.*"

He stepped over the suitcase and settled in the seat beside the unusual young woman. For a moment he looked out the window at the countryside rolling past, but then she did another peculiar thing. She plopped the suitcase in his lap without so much as a "Pardon me" and opened it to reveal folded clothes, a cotton rope, and a tattered felt hat.

She pressed the old hat onto her head and finger-combed back a few loose strands of hair that had wandered into her face. Next, she withdrew the length of cotton rope, stood up and wound it twice around her middle, tying it in a knot that cinched the dark dress snug around her waist.

"Thank you," she said when she sat down again. She closed the suitcase, drew it from his lap and placed it at her feet. "I mean for giving me a place to sit."

"Was that your mama and daddy back there?"

"Not no more. They sent me off to a Christian home for girls, but I ain't going. If I'd known it would play out this way, I'd of planned it better. They got no right to stick me in God's jailhouse." She sat with her eyes fixed straight ahead, her spine too rigid to touch the back of the seat.

"Then where are you going?"

"Don't know," she said, "Columbia to start."

"A woman shouldn't be traveling alone," he said. "You don't know what you might run into."

"Anybody who runs into me is running into trouble," she said. "I got my lucky buckeye. I don't need nothing else."

"You might be all right if you have a lucky buckeye." He pulled his out and held it in his palm for her to see. "Mine got me through the war."

"You wore all the brown off it." She touched the place where the shell's dark outer layer had worn yellow and thin as paper.

"It took a lot of rubbing to make it back."

"See?" She smiled for the first time. "Told you I'd be all right." She drew her buckeye from the pocket of her dress. "Mine's not worn out like yours. It's still got a lot of luck in it."

"Mine's still plenty good." Ransom held his worn buckeye next to hers.

"What happens if two buckeyes touch?" she said.

"I don't know, but I bet it's good."

She took Ransom's and rubbed both buckeyes vigorously between the palms of her hands. Then she passed them to him.

"You do it too. Give 'em a good rub then we'll both have good luck." Ransom rubbed them, paused, and rubbed them some more.

"Now," she said when he returned her buckeye, "your luck is mixed up with mine. I wonder what'll happen."

"It'll be good," he said and offered his hand. "My name's Ransom."

"Amelia Rose." She gave his hand a solid shake.

They rode together to Greenville, where Amelia Rose got off to catch the train to Columbia. Ransom continued south another hour until the train stopped at the bridge crossing the Twelve Mile River, just outside of Issaqueena. He got off and took the shortcut home.

Hurrying down a cow path through the trees, he stepped around a bunch of Indian turnips growing in a low wet spot. Spring blessed the hills of South Carolina with gold and delicate greens, and the finest warmth and sunshine. He passed under a robin's nest swaying on the end of a cedar limb. Behind him, in the thicker oaks, a woodpecker drummed. He crossed a mud flat and made his way through a thicket of alders that were just breaking out into bud. Passing through a grove of red maples, he came to the creek where his father camped and kept his jug.

He paused on the edge of the creek and looked across to the cold fire pit banked with creek rocks and to his father's lean-to made from a rusted sheet of roofing tin. Grass grew undisturbed throughout the camp. A large black and yellow spider spread motionless in the center of a web woven across the opening of the lean-to. Ransom's heart started racing. He searched the creek for his father's moonshine jug but couldn't find it.

Fear crept up his spine with tiny prickling claws until it reached his brain. Behind his eyes, panic erupted in a blinding light. He ran from the camp but his legs could not outrun his fear. His heart pounded like a fist inside him. Hard branches of river birch and buckeye whipped his face and tore at his uniform, stripping away a button and plucking at the wool.

Sprinting from the woods, the map case slapping his back, he broke into bold sunlight and the green wheat field that belonged to Mister Jenkins, startling a blue-tailed lizard sunning on a rock. At last, beyond the wheat, he could see a field of young cotton and the roof of the shack. Nothing had ever looked better. He found new energy and ran even harder.

Racing through the spring wheat and into the field of tender cotton plants, he saw a young woman standing on the back porch. A hand shielded her eyes from the sun. At her feet, a naked child clung to her dress. Between the cotton and wheat lay a freshly plowed field not yet planted. Pushing himself, he came to his mama's vegetable patch. Weeds instead of vegetables filled the rows. Mama would never have let it get that far ahead of her. And there were no chickens in the hen house, not one. Ransom hurried past it to the woman on the porch.

"I ain't seen you before," the woman said, drawing the words out long and slow, like it pained her to think. "You that MacTavish boy went off to war?" She was all bones. A dirty cotton dress fit her loose as a gray dish rag. Ransom slowed to a walk and approached the back steps, breathing heavy.

"Who're you?" he asked when he caught his breath.

"Folks said you weren't coming back."

"Where's my mama?"

"Dead."

Ransom staggered, then lurched forward and grabbed the porch post. The woman pulled the naked child up to her hip.

"What?"

"They dead, your mama and your daddy too." She turned and went inside the house.

"No," Ransom said, following her.

The house looked the same, but it wasn't the same. He'd been born beneath this roof and lived every day of his life here until he left for France. The same newspaper Mama and Daddy had glued to the walls with flour paste continued to keep out the weather. The same short piece of scab wood Daddy had nailed to the wall beside the sink was still there with Mama's butcher knife, forks and spoons tucked behind it. There stood Mama's cook stove and those were her pots and bowls. But his mother wasn't there. The place smelled foul as chitterlings and the floors needed scrubbing. Mama never would have stood for it.

"You need to talk to Orin," the woman said. "He'll tell you about it."

A little boy, maybe six or seven, sat in the middle of the kitchen floor. In his lap rested a Sears Roebuck catalog opened to its only colored page. Stiff card stock displayed the choice of paint colors in rows of squares. Ransom stood dumb, lost in a nightmare, unable to find a known point.

"That there's red," the boy said, pressing a dirt-stained finger on the appropriate square. "This here one is blue. That's yaller. That's green."

"What color do you see in this room?" the woman said as she jostled the toddler on her hip. The boy looked all around. He studied the yellowing newsprint that covered the walls. He studied the gray translucent drapes made from feed sacks. His eyes rested on the broken window pane stuffed with un-ginned cotton.

"Ain't no color," he said.

"That's right," the woman said. "There ain't none."

Orin Boone came through the front door, crossed the room and offered his hand to Ransom. He was older than Ransom's father and had been farming on shares below the Hog's Back when Ransom left. The Boones were known for laziness and loafing, if not worse, and drifted from farm to farm, never staying anywhere for long. Now one of them lived in Mama's house.

"Folks thought you might of got killed," Orin said. The few teeth in his mouth were jagged and tobacco-stained, dark as rusted nails. "A sickness come through here and took a lot of folks. It took my Mattie and my two youngest boys. Got your mama and daddy too, they all died about the same time. Mister Jenkins can tell you more about it. I married this here girl to help out. She's dumb as a stump but she takes care of the place."

Ransom wasn't listening. He went to the flour bin, tilted it open and dug a hand in the corner where his mother kept the money jar.

"What the hell you doing?" Orin said "You can't go messing with our stuff like that."

"There was a jar of money in here." Ransom dug his hand in each corner of flour and searched again. "I sent money home every month for two years. Where's my money?"

"I don't know nothing about that. We just moved in here 'cause Mister Jenkins needed a white man to work the place. Go talk to him."

Ransom stepped toward the back door, not sure of where he was headed. He passed the little boy sitting in the middle of the kitchen floor with the catalog still in his lap.

"Mister Man," the little boy said, "I can count too." And he started counting, numbering each of his fingers.

Ransom stumbled out the back door and into the sunlight, his head spinning, his insides aching. The mule shed, corn crib, outhouse and barn, the house itself and the way sunlight fell on this corner of the world were the things of his life. They were part of him. They were home. He couldn't leave them, but he couldn't stay.

He made his way around the house toward the front porch where he saw a pair of young mules teamed to a wagon and sporting new leather harnesses. The wagon, though scarred from work, looked fairly new.

"I'm sorry," Orin said when he saw Ransom come around the corner of the house. "I wished it was different. I wished I hadn't been the one to tell you. We all lost people."

Ransom continued away from the house, following the same ruts he had followed every day of his life before leaving for the war. At the road, a small bird, the same color as the sky, watched from a sweet gum limb. Ransom stopped and took off his boots and socks, tied the laces together and slung them over his shoulder. He needed to feel the earth beneath his feet.

He crossed the road where wild plum bloomed white in a thicket and headed straight for the Jenkins place, taking the shortcut through the pecan grove. It wasn't right to give his home away, the one piece of ground he thought belonged to him even if it didn't. The house might have held something of his mama's spirit if Orin and his imbecile wife hadn't moved in. He had to find something of his mama's, something he could touch and believe in, something that would tie him again to this world.

As he walked through the pecan grove, he saw a new International Harvester high-wheeler automobile parked beneath the shelter of the carriage porch at the side of Mister Jenkins's house. Open like a buckboard, the wooden car had wheels as large as a wagon's. When he emerged from the pecan grove, he saw Mister Jenkins sitting on the front porch, smoking a factory-rolled cigarette and swatting at flies with a folded newspaper.

"Ransom. Ransom MacTavish." His jowls shook when he spoke. "It's good to see you, boy. We all thought you might've got killed over yonder. You know a lot of boys did." He met Ransom at the bottom of the steps, put an arm on his shoulder and ushered him up to the porch then waved him into a chair.

"Mary!" He called through the screen door to his wife. "Ransom's here. Bring him something cool to drink."

"What happened to my mama and daddy?" Ransom asked.

"I sent you a letter. The Spanish Flu came through here and killed a bunch of folks. I thought you knew. It took coloreds and whites alike. It took that colored mule skinner, Lafayette. It got the whole Cox family, every last one of 'em. And it got Miss Eli Blassingame, the school teacher. Orin Boone lost his wife and two smallest boys. It touched us all." The screen door opened and Mrs. Jenkins passed a glass of water to her husband who passed it to Ransom. A chunk of broken ice floated in it.

"There was money in the flour bin," Ransom said. "Two years of Army pay."

"Your daddy owed me," Mr. Jenkins said. "He still owes me for fertilizer and seed. I paid to get them buried and I paid for headstones for each one of them like they were my own. Now, you know I didn't have to do that. There's not a soul in this county would have taken care of them the way I did. I did a lot for your family. Your family was good people."

"You took my damn money."

"Hold on now. Don't say things you don't mean."

"It's my money. The one thing I had to make a life and you took it. You got so much. You're fat and getting fatter, living easy in your painted house and sucking the blood out of anybody who gets close. You won't let anybody get ahead. You keep them down and take every good thing they got 'til they're dried up and gone. Give me my money. It won't make no difference to you."

"I'll tell you what I can do, if you're aiming to farm. My thirty-two acre piece doesn't have anybody on it. It's rocky but it'll get you started. There's a dozen coloreds who'd kill to farm that land and they won't squabble. You could make something of that place. The house is in pretty good shape, too. I'll advance you some lumber to patch the floor in the front room. Find yourself a girl, and before you know it, you'll have a family coming on. If you don't want that, you don't know what's good." Mister Jenkins adjusted his oversized frame and leaned closer, dropping his voice to a hush. "Son, you might be poor, but at least you ain't colored."

"Don't talk to me like I'm nobody." Ransom stood. "You treat me like I don't matter, like I'm invisible. I'm somebody and I want my money."

"I don't have your money, son."

"The Army taught me to shoot men I don't even know and who never done me wrong. You know what I can do if you don't give me what's mine?"

"Mary," Mister Jenkins called to his wife. "Hand me out the shotgun." The screen door opened and his wife passed him a double-barrel shotgun like she was handing him a broom. Mister Jenkins held the gun low to his hip and aimed at Ransom's chest. "Don't threaten me, not on my land, not ever. There's buck shot in here, both barrels. You'll be dead before you hit the ground. I got what I got because I'm smarter than you and because God favors me."

Ransom took a step backwards off the porch, but kept his eyes on Mister Jenkins. "I want my money. I want what's mine. I've seen more of this world than you ever will and I'm going to broker me some cotton."

"You do that, son." Mister Jenkins laughed and shook his head, like he knew a funny secret.

9

RANSOM SAT CROSS-LEGGED at the foot of his mother's grave. At her headstone he'd laid a loose bundle of wildflowers he'd picked along the road. A great oak shaded this corner of the graveyard and dry leaves rustled across the ground, stirred by a slight breeze. Behind the parsonage, the preacher split firewood.

"Mama," he said, "I didn't know why you came to me in France, but I do now. It was the only goodbye we got."

He looked at the modest headstones of his parents' graves and waited. The breeze picked up and dandelion fluff drifted across the graveyard. One delicate parachute passed so close he could have caught it in his hand, but he chose instead to watch it fly away. At the edge of the woods, young trees bowed while the hard chop of the preacher's ax resounded from behind the parsonage and marked the end of time as surely as an execution.

"The money's gone." Ransom picked up an acorn that lay beside his knee and tossed it away. "I got nothing. I don't know what to do. I feel like I'm lost in some dark place and can't find my way out."

He sat at his mother's grave until the sun left the sky and the things of the earth went quiet. At times, he read Elizabeth's letters aloud and at other times, he lay beneath the oak, stretched out on the hard clay. He heard his mother's voice as a memory, not words precisely, but the song of her voice, a melody that stirred in him an unbearable loneliness.

Darkness came and brought the stars. Ransom put the letters away and stretched out again beside his mother's grave, resting his head in the crook of his arm.

He spent the night dozing and waking and struggled in his mind about the money. It was a lot more than he'd ever had, but as he grew weary, this worry faded and came back less and less. Memories of his mother softened too, until the only comfort he could find were thoughts of Elizabeth.

He rolled onto his back, the hard clay beneath him. Dark limbs of the oak made a lattice overhead. In their shadow, he recalled the image of Elizabeth in the garden. He saw in his mind her kind eyes and her gentle mouth smiling only for him. She spoke in the same nurturing melody as his mother, not with words but with gentle music that went beyond the ears into the heart.

Night squatted on the earth so long that surely dawn would soon be coming

"Mama," Ransom said as he looked into the dark branches of the oak. His mother seemed far away now and he could hardly feel her presence, only the emptiness of where she had been. His heart ached for comfort. "On the way home, I couldn't wait to tell you about the girl I found. She's a pretty girl with kind eyes. I wish you could see her picture, you'd know she has a good heart, like you. That's the best thing, she has a good heart."

Ransom sat up.

"Mama, God brought Elizabeth into my life for a reason. The only peace I have is knowing she's waiting for me. I'm going to do whatever it takes to make her my wife. You'd be proud. I won't let nothing stop me."

By dawn, he had composed a letter. He only needed the light of day to write it. When the sun rose, he drew his tablet from the map case and began forming each word with new and honest familiarity.

Dear Elizabeth,

I am home. I say I am home, but I truly do not know where that is. The house I grew up in is no longer mine. My parents

have both passed. This came as a shock. And all the money I sent home is gone. Maybe going off to war isn't the hardest thing a man can do, maybe the hardest thing is coming home.

The grief I have for my mother is beyond words. I find her passing incomprehensible. I can't grasp it.

Elizabeth, when I left home for France, I carried with me a deep loneliness, a hunger to love and be loved. Until I read your letters, I did not know for whom my heart ached. Now that I have seen how true you love, I know my life would be a dismal thing without you in it. This letter will arrive long before I do, but rest assured, I am on my way and nothing short of death itself will stop me. Like a compass seeking north, my heart is drawn to you.

Sincerely,
Ransom

He took his change purse from his pocket. Made from the leather of a Billy goat with the stringy white hair still attached, the change purse looked like the tuft from an old man's beard. Ransom opened the draw strings and pushed the buckeye and Citadel ring to one side. He picked through the change remaining from his travel pay. He had a few dollars, but not enough for the train.

For pennies he bought a handful of hardtack biscuits at Charlie Evans' store and put them in his pocket. He gave Charlie the letter to Elizabeth and paid him for the stamp. Charlie carried the letter to the back corner of the store that served as the town's post office and placed it in the pigeon hole for outgoing mail.

"There's a letter here for you." Charlie read the return address aloud as he brought it to the front of the store. "It came general delivery from Pocotaligo. Who do you know down that way?"

"The woman I aim to marry," Ransom said as he took the letter.

"Well now," Charlie said, scratching his head as he watched Ransom step out the door. "Ain't that something?"

Ransom sat on the same bench he'd shared with the Army sergeant two years ago. A gray tabby with a tattered ear sniffed the bench, and then settled at his feet waiting for a handout. He broke the corner from a piece of hardtack and tossed it to the cat, then opened Elizabeth's letter and began to read.

Dear Ransom,

You are safely home and, I pray, making plans to soon visit me. Waiting has become unbearable.

I am told things happen for a reason. I want to believe this is true, but the old heartache still resonates with sadness. I am so eager to be rid of it. Miss Hazel tells me your presence will ease my pain and urges you to hurry. If only I had wings, I would come get you.

Like you, I am starting over. And while no bombs fell on me, the devastation was just as thorough. I miss Isaac beyond words. There is nothing left of the life I had chosen. I must build again. If things happen for a reason, what is the reason we have met and why at such a cost?

Miss Hazel, who has seen so much, tells me each life has ten thousand sorrows and ten thousand joys. Losing Isaac is my worst sorrow and finding you my greatest joy. I have never known a man with a heart so kind as yours. You give me hope. I am waiting.

Affectionately,
Elizabeth

When he finished the letter he read it again to be sure he wasn't dreaming. It was real. *She* was real. Whatever it took, he would find her and win her heart.

"She's waiting," he said to the cat staring up at him, eager for another handout. He would have hugged the cat if it had let him.

When he walked to the edge of town, he stopped to look back on Issaqueena. Growing up it had been his world, but now that he had seen France, it wasn't all that much, a store, a church, a school, and two dusty roads crossing in the shadow of the Blue Ridge Mountains. With his family gone, Issaqueena was just another place. On a gray rock, half buried beside the road, he knocked the dust off his boots. Then with nothing but the clothes he wore and the map case slung over his shoulder, Ransom walked away.

He walked through the morning, stopping to drink from wells when he was thirsty. A farmer with his wife and a wagon load of kids gave him a ride into the afternoon then let him out when they turned off the road. He walked into the early evening until the sun set. Then, with an empty belly, he found a place to sleep among pines where the ground was soft and carpeted with straw.

The next morning, he ate the last of the hardtack before he got to the upper Saluda River at Murder Creek ford. Outside of the wheel ruts, the water looked to be only ankle deep. Ransom waded across, startling a frog sunning on a flat stone. It sprung with a slight croak when he passed and belly-flopped into the swirling current. Downstream a short distance, a blue heron stood on a sandbar, its head hunkered down to its shoulders as it watched him.

On the other side, the road curved and followed a narrow valley. To his right, the land lay low and wet. Large poplars stood in glassy pools. Beyond the woods, the shallow Saluda ran parallel to the road. To his left, the ground rose into a slight hill where oaks and privet and catbrier formed an impenetrable wall. Ransom plucked the new growth from the tips of briers and nibbled the fresh greens.

He spent the morning walking, the river his only companion. Through the trees, he watched it grow wider, sometimes splashing over boulders and sometimes running deep and silent. When he was thirsty, he drank from it.

A man driving a Maxwell touring car stopped to give him a ride. "Where you headed?" he said as Ransom climbed in.

"Columbia. Then down to the low country around Hilton Head."

"You plan to walk the whole way?"

"If I have to," Ransom said. "I walked across France and it's a lot bigger place."

The man took him a few miles and left him on the side of the road before heading off in another direction. Along the way, the Saluda River had meandered beyond the trees and Ransom could no longer see it.

Hunger slowed him down. He struggled to pick his feet up and keep going. An old farmer wearing a straw hat with an unraveling brim drove a wagon pulled by a mule just as old. A back wheel wobbled as the wagon rolled along at a pace nearly as slow as Ransom's.

"You want a ride?" the farmer said, rolling beside him. Tall and slender, the old man sat on the bench seat with his knees drawn up near his chest. His cheeks had the pallor of wax. Ransom climbed aboard as the wagon rolled on without stopping. "I'm Ira Massey." The farmer offered his hand and Ransom shook it, nodding his appreciation.

"You done shook the hand that shook the hand of Jefferson Davis. You ain't but two shakes from the war. Son, you look wore out. You been sleeping in the woods?"

"Yes, sir."

"You hungry?" They rolled past a thicket of blackberry blooming white. "You look hungry."

"I could eat something," Ransom said.

10

THE FARMER TURNED OFF THE ROAD and followed two narrow ruts through a low place where trees crowded on each side, lush and green. Just off the road, the trees opened and Ransom saw a small farm where a band of oaks circled a modest house in deep shade. Fields of young cotton grew nearly to the river but weeds choked every row. As they approached the house, he saw a dinner table on the front porch dressed with a blue checkered cloth and set with plates and tall glasses.

"You can't get where you're going on an empty stomach," the farmer said as they rolled to a stop beside a smokehouse. "Eat here and sleep in the barn. You'll feel better in the morning."

"Much obliged," Ransom said.

When he had washed and shed his boots at the back door, Ransom padded into the kitchen where he met Mrs. Massey, a plump woman whose breasts rolled right into her belly. Smells of fried fish and onion lingered in the kitchen, so rich he could have feasted on them alone.

"When it's hot like this, we eat on the front porch," she said. Sweat glistened on her brow. She took a platter of fried green tomatoes from the counter and motioned for Ransom to follow her. They passed from the kitchen into the sitting room, where photographs and paintings of all sizes filled the walls. Some of the photos were from before the War Between the States. Women, men, and children posed frozen and faded, staring back at the camera

On the porch, the table offered fried catfish, fresh baked bread flanked with little dishes of butter and jelly, green beans cooked with fatback and a dish of sauerkraut. A metal water pitcher sweating condensation stood on a smaller table by the door.

"Let us pray," Mr. Massey said and reached out on either side to grasp Ransom's hand and the hand of his wife. They bowed their heads and Mr. Massey thanked the Lord for watching over Ransom and bringing him to the farm. He thanked the Lord for the food set before them and for their many blessings and ended with a soft "amen."

Ransom managed to butter a slice of freshly baked bread without cramming it into his mouth. He even gave it a thick coat of fig preserves before taking a bite.

"It's good to have you with us," Mrs. Massey said.

Mr. Massey broke a piece of bread. "What would I have to do to get you to stay on a couple of days and help out? My health ain't what it used to be and the weeds are taking over my cotton."

"I can't stay. I got to get down to the coast."

"What's the hurry?"

"I aim to set up a cotton brokering business before the price drops and I hope to win the heart of a certain lady as she has surely won mine."

"You love her, don't you?" Mrs. Massey said. "I know you do. I can see it in your eyes. Tell me about her."

"She has yellow hair with this cowlick on the side of her head. Not every girl has something like that." Ransom paused to think then said, "I haven't actually seen her. We've been writing to each other since I was in France."

"Love letters." Mrs. Massey sat back in her chair and clutched her breast. "My goodness." Her face flushed. "She hasn't even seen you, how romantic."

"Help me chop my fields clear of weeds and I'll give you a ham," Mr. Massey said. "I make the best smoked hams you're ever likely to taste. You can give it to your girl. That'll impress her. You can't meet her empty-handed."

"Ira's hams win at the State Fair every year," Mrs. Massey said. "I got to keep going."

"We won't have *no* cotton if the weeds get it," Mr. Massey said and looked to his wife for help.

"Besides," Mrs. Massey said with a glance to her husband, "you can't show up at your girl's door looking like something the cat drug in. Stay here a few days and help Rudy. That'll give me time to sew a proper suit of courting clothes for you. You have to look your best if you want to win her heart.

After supper, Mr. Massey took Ransom to the smokehouse, a small log building chinked tight with red clay. The last of the day's light shone through the open door and illuminated the interior which smelled of sugar and hickory smoke. Hams, more than Ransom could easily count, hung from the rafters. Lengths of sausage hung from the rafters too. Three open barrels, topped with rock salt, stood inside the door.

"That's side meat and fatback," Mr. Massey said, nodding at the barrels. "You can have your pick of any of the hams on the front rafter."

"You have a lot of weeds in your field," Ransom said as Mr. Massey shut the smokehouse door and fastened it with a wooden latch.

"More coming up every day," the old man said.

Setting low, the sun painted the horizon in broad swathes of pink and orange as Ransom and Mr. Massey rested on the bank of the Saluda. Mr. Massey lit his pipe and exhaled a cloud of cherry-scented smoke that drifted off with the river.

"After Lee surrendered," Mr. Massey said, "I come back from the war and helped my daddy clear this land of virgin timber. Carpetbaggers took the home place. We come out here. It wasn't worth nothing. Nobody wanted it, but we made it into something. It's pretty now and peaceful."

The Saluda ran deep. In a flat place near the river, where tree trunks bore the high water marks of flooding, several skinned pine logs lay tossed in a pile.

"Did you drag those logs out?" Ransom said.

"They wash down when it floods."

Ransom nodded, thinking. Mr. Massey puffed on his pipe.

"Normally," Ransom said, "I'd chop your cotton for nothing just to be neighborly. It's the way I was raised. But right now, I'm in need too. I could sure use some of those skinned logs to make a raft. I'll need some other things too, some rope maybe and some nails, a board or two."

A smile broke across Mr. Massey's face and he took the pipe stem from his lips. "You help me clear my fields and you can have what you need off my place to float the river."

They shook on it.

In the barn, Mr. Massey gave Ransom a pair of worn overalls. The seat had been patched several times with sack cloth. The most recent patch said Adluh Flour in bold red letters. He dressed in the old overalls and a work shirt and gave his uniform to Mrs. Massey to make into a proper courting suit.

That night, Ransom slept in the barn with cats watching him from all quarters, but none of them came near. An old tom slept high in the rafters. Ransom rose before light when he heard Mrs. Massey in the kitchen and drank coffee until Mr. Massey joined them for breakfast. By dawn they were in the cotton.

They went to work in neighboring rows. Slicing the hoe blade beneath the surface of the ground, Ransom severed the weed from its root and left it to dry in the sun. The sun burned him and stooping over the hoe strained his back, but once he found a rhythm, the work became meditative. He chopped to thin the over-planted cotton and he chopped the tender shoots of dandelion, chickweed and nutgrass, and the first prickly shoots of catbrier and blackberry. They all fell under his blade. In that place, the world consisted of just two things: orderly, righteous cotton and legions of invading weeds.

The farmer began to hum. At first the melody was too soft for Ransom to recognize, but as the old man grew happier, he began to sing softly to himself, *"Blessed assurance, Jesus is mine."*

Ransom had heard his mother sing that song when she worked the cotton. He straightened up to look back over the field and see how far they had come. In the old man's song, Ransom heard his mother's joyful voice and, for a moment, he saw her working the cotton beside his daddy. He bent again over his hoe and, with the hymn in his ear, returned to chopping the endless weeds.

"*O what a foretaste of glory divine.*" Mr. Massey's voice cracked, but the melody came through sweet and tender.

At noon, Mrs. Massey brought them lunch to eat in the shade beneath an oak. Afterwards they napped for a bit. Then they returned to the field until supper time. That evening Mrs. Massey measured Ransom's legs, shoulders and waist, blissful to have such a project as a courting suit. In the final hours, Ransom rolled logs down to the water and lashed them together with rope. Finally, well into the night, he laid his weary back on a pile of hay, covered himself with a horse blanket and went to sleep. Each day unfolded like the day before.

After three days, Mrs. Massey had Ransom try on the suit. The pieces were pinned together and not yet sewn.

"Go into Columbia and buy yourself a hat," Mrs. Massey mumbled through the straight pins she held between her lips. "A gentleman wears a hat."

"Yes ma'am," he said.

"And join her church. Don't marry a girl who don't belong to a church and she shouldn't bother marrying you if you don't belong."

"Yes ma'am."

"You got a Bible?"

"No ma'am."

"You do now," she said. "I expect you to read it."

On the morning of the fifth day, with the field chopped clean of weeds and the courting suit completed, Ransom prepared to leave. In the barn, he cleaned and oiled his boots and fashioned a backpack from a burlap sack and rope. Dressed in the worn overalls with the Adluh Flour sack cloth patch, he wore a straw hat with the crown busted out of it. He was winding fishing line on a stick when Mr. Massey entered the barn and presented him with a smoked ham wrapped in brown paper and tied with string. He set the ham beside Ransom's pack.

"You can't go empty handed. Let them know you're a man of substance."

With his hands in his pockets, Mr. Massey shifted from one foot to the other.

"Me and Phoebe have been married fifty-two years." The old

farmer spoke with his eyes cast shyly to the floor. "I never would have made it if my daddy hadn't told me what marriage really is. When you're married, remember we all do foolish things when we're young and even when we're not so young. Marriage is a journey of two souls, a journey of love and loyalty and forgiveness. You got to always reach out to your wife. Most men don't know that. No matter what she does and no matter how mad you get, you got to always reach out to your wife. The tie that binds is a fragile thing."

"And you'll need to plant a garden," Mrs. Massey said as she entered through the barn door. She gave Ransom a paper sachet tied with cotton string. "There's enough vegetable seed in there to get you started and some flower seed too. You know how to garden, don't you?"

"Yes ma'am."

Ransom put the seeds in his pack along with the courting suit. Mrs. Massey left and came again with a lard tin full of coffee, fatback and cornmeal. He packed these things too. On top where he could easily reach it, he put the map case with Elizabeth's letters and the small Bible Mrs. Massey had given him.

They walked Ransom out to the river, where the raft tugged against the current. Mr. Massey shook his hand and wished him luck. Mrs. Massey hugged his neck hard enough to pinch his head off and made him promise to come back with his bride.

"You've been good to me," he said.

He boarded the crude raft and untied it from a tree leaning over the water. The river pulled it away from the bank. Ransom poled into the middle of the Saluda and turned back one last time to wave to the old couple who had given him so much.

11

THE RAFT DRIFTED FREE IN THE CURRENT. Ransom stretched out with nothing to do but surrender to the river. It felt wonderful not to work and not to march and not to have anything to do. Muddy water lapped at the logs and smelled of earth and fish.

Resting his head on the pack, he pulled the busted-out straw hat over his eyes. He waved a lazy hand to an old woman and little girl fishing from the bank. The woman sat on a stump with a cane pole between her legs and nodded.

Near the end of the day, the river grew wide and shallow. The raft entered rocky shoals, below which lay the city of Columbia. Passing the ruins of an old mill, he picked across the shoals, maneuvering through mild rapids and around large rocks until he came to where the Saluda joined the Broad River to form the Congaree.

On a hill beyond the bank, he spotted the dome of a large government building. Occasionally, he caught a glimpse of fine houses.

He poled closer to the bank, where a young woman in a soiled indigo dress stood on a narrow strip of beach. A rope was wrapped twice around her slender waist and cinched tight at her belly. Although she was white, her freckled skin had burned and browned to a dark hue, as if she lived out in the weather. Glorious red hair splayed wild from beneath a tattered felt hat and cascaded down her shoulders.

"Is this Columbia?" Ransom called to her.

"This here's Scabtown," she said without lifting her eyes. Swishing a toe in the river, she spoke to her feet. "You can get to Columbia from here."

He couldn't see her face, but there was no mistaking that red hair flashing golden in the sun. Ransom drifted closer.

"You're the girl from the train."

She raised her eyes and a smile broke across her face. "You're my buckeye soldier. Where's your hat and soldier clothes?" Her green eyes were full of mischief. "Where are you floating to?"

"Down to the low country to court a woman and get married. I'm going to be a cotton broker."

"A woman?" Space opened between them as the river carried him away. "You got anything to eat?" She said.

"Cornmeal," he said. "I can set some lines for catfish."

He scrambled with the pole to force the raft aground, but he'd slipped too far downstream. Amelia Rose ran after him, wading to her knees. Muddy water soaked the hem of her dress even though she had gathered it in a fist and pulled it higher.

"Look up in those trees," she called, pointing to thick tree limbs reaching over the river. "There's a place to hide the raft in there. Columbia's running over with thieves and cheats. Float down a hair. You'll see a little cove back under the trees. I'll come get you."

She stepped onto a trail and disappeared into the woods. Ransom watched where the brush had closed behind her as the current drew him farther downstream. A short distance below the sandy beach, the bank pulled away from the river. Old trees leaned far over the water, far enough to almost hide a tiny cove.

"That's it!" Amelia Rose called from somewhere in the brush. "Go up in there."

Ransom poled the raft beneath the overhanging branches and had to kneel to slip under them. Nearby, a creek spilled down a slender waterfall. Branches closed behind him like a curtain as the bulky log raft filled the secluded place. The cold remains of a fire lay on a spit of sand beside a shallow dent where someone had slept.

Amelia Rose appeared at the top of the high bank near the waterfall. She'd pulled her hair back with a piece of vine and tucked a cluster of yellow jasmine above one ear.

When she joined him on the raft, Ransom baited several fishing lines with tiny cubes of fatback and dropped them in the water. Wiping his greasy fingers on the thighs of his overalls, he shouldered the pack and felt the ham thud against his body.

"You know where I can buy a courting hat?"

"When do we eat?" She said.

"We got to catch something first. We can eat after I get my hat."

Amelia Rose led Ransom through the brush along a trail skirting the river. They came to a flat place grown over with nettles. The woods opened onto a shanty town of several dozen shacks built with sawmill scabs and driftwood and roofed with rusted tin. The village lay in a low place, and judging by the muddy water-line stain on tree trunks, it tended to flood.

"Why are you living on the river?" he said.

"I was supposed to go to a Christian school for girls to restore my virtue," she said over her shoulder as she led Ransom through the village. "But I'll go to hell before I let a bunch of do-gooders get hold of me."

Behind a shack, a sow rooted for acorns while a troop of piglets jockeyed for her teats. Laundry of many colors, blues, whites, reds, greens and yellows, hung from makeshift clotheslines propped on poles. More laundry lay over bushes and draped from tree limbs. Old people, black and weary, sat on front stoops or pieces of cordwood set on end. Little dark children ran naked through the village. Ransom and Amelia Rose were the only whites.

"I don't see why you want to throw your money away on a hat," she said. "We ought to buy something to eat. I know where there's a bakery with these cinnamon buns just dripping syrup. If they taste half as good as they smell we'll be in heaven."

"I'm about broke," Ransom said.

"That's what I'm saying. We can't eat a hat."

"It's a courting hat," he said. "I don't expect you to understand."

"What kind of woman needs her man to wear a hat? A man don't need no hat to court *me*."

They crossed through the village and climbed the embankment twenty feet up to railroad tracks. A concrete storm-drain jutted from under the tracks and spilled into an open ditch running behind a row of shacks. Children played in the drainage ditch, turning over rocks in search of crawfish.

Once Ransom and Amelia Rose had climbed above the ditch and crossed the tracks, they passed between warehouses and industrial buildings until they came to Gervais Street. Gervais led straight up a hill toward the domed government building and the city of Columbia.

"I'd take you to the white man's hat store, but he only sells to rich people," Amelia Rose said. "We'll have to go to the colored man's hat store."

Following Gervais Street, they passed the Adluh Flour Company, where men loaded wagons with sacks of flour. Gervais crossed Assembly Street, a busy brick-paved avenue lined with shops. Mules and horses plodded along, pulling wagons full of produce and wares. A colored man wearing a vest, his shirt sleeves rolled to the elbow, pedaled a bicycle around an idling Model T truck. Ransom had never seen so many colored people in one place. He and Amelia Rose were the only white people in sight. Colored people, men and women and children, walked leisurely from shop to shop. Some were dressed elegantly. Some were as shabby as he was.

Amelia Rose took Ransom by the hand. Her boldness surprised him, but it felt good. He tightened his hold and caught her smiling at him.

On this block of Gervais Street, the colored world of Assembly Street met the white world of Main. Outside a candy shop, an elderly Negro man danced on the sidewalk, all loose and gangly like his joints were made of rubber. He played a pair of rib bones the way Ransom had seen white men in the mountains play spoons, drumming them on his thigh and between the palm of his free hand, rattling a tap-tapping rhythm, energetic and joyful.

"Jump down, turn around, pick a bale of cotton," the man sang. *"Jump down, turn around, pick a bale of hay."*

A woman came out of the candy store trailed by the aroma of

chocolate and mint. She dropped a coin into a coffee can at the dancing man's feet.

"You smell that?" Amelia Rose said. "Peppermint. I could live on peppermint."

"We can get a little something," Ransom said. "I got money for penny candy, but not much else." He wanted to impress her. He wanted to watch her too but he'd grown careful in his watching. When her green eyes met his, it made his brain spin and his face flush hot. It wasn't just her eyes either, but the way she moved fascinated him too, the way she marched right up to life like there was nothing to be afraid of, the way she smiled at everything.

He dug into his pocket for his change purse then opened the door for Amelia Rose. They stepped inside and looked around.

"Don't it smell good in here?" she said.

Jars of brightly colored hard candy lined the counter, peppermint and lemon drops and horehound and crystals of rock candy that looked like rough diamonds. Lollipops, swirled with bright colors, stood upright on wooden sticks. Beneath the glass, lay platters of chocolates.

A woman, so fat her jowls drooped in layers, sat on a stool behind the counter scowling at Ransom and Amelia Rose. In front of her, a windup toy monkey crouched on the counter, poised to strike a drum. Amelia Rose picked it up and wound the brass key sticking out of its back. It sprang to life. The monkey's head turned side to side as one hand and then the other struck the toy drum.

"Don't touch nothing," the woman said. "And hurry up." The toy monkey wound down, beating the drum slower and slower.

Ransom pointed to the jar of peppermints. "How much?"

"Five for a penny."

He pulled the leather change purse covered with stringy white goat hair from his pocket.

"My word," the woman said. "What is that?"

"It's a money purse," Ransom said. "I made it from the nut sack of a billy goat."

He passed a single penny across the counter. The woman counted five peppermints into a piece of wax paper then wrapped the paper tightly before passing it over to Ransom.

Outside, sucking on peppermint, Ransom and Amelia Rose walked the short distance to the corner. On Main Street, two trolleys passed one another going in opposite directions. Horses, mules, wagons, cars, trucks and bicycles filled the street. Pedestrians walked among the cars and livestock, stepping around the occasional pile of manure. Many of the shops that lined the avenue had canopies. One building towered ten floors high.

On the far corner stood an elegant brass clock, twice as tall as a man. Beside the clock, a lone preacher waved a Bible above his head and shouted to people as they passed, "Abandon your dreams and follow me." No one seemed to listen.

At the hat shop, an immaculately dressed yellow-skinned Negro man met them as they came through the door. Lanky and with straight hair, the man smelled of talcum powder. Hats filled the tiny shop from floor to ceiling: fur hats, felt hats, feathered hats, straw hats and hats that didn't look like hats at all.

"You want a courting hat," the man repeated after Ransom. "We should let your lady friend decide which she prefers."

Amelia Rose went straight to a derby hanging on the wall and placed it on her head. The derby sank to her ears. The gray felt framed her face and accented her high cheek bones. She smiled, posing like a little girl.

"Perhaps you would prefer a crusher," the man said, drawing Ransom's attention away from Amelia Rose. "It's more suitable for travel." He demonstrated how the crusher rolled neatly for storage then unrolled without a wrinkle.

"I believe I'll take the one she's got on," Ransom said.

The door opened and a boy stuck his head inside. "They caught a bootlegger down the street!"

12

OUTSIDE THE STORE PEOPLE SCURRIED along the sidewalk in the same direction as though drawn by a great magnet. Ransom paid for the derby and settled it on his head. He grabbed Amelia Rose by the hand and they hurried out the door to follow the gathering crowd.

Down the street, at a mule-drawn hay wagon, white men gathered in a crowd, colored men bunched some distance behind them. Amelia Rose was the only woman. Ransom sauntered up to the white crowd, walking tall with his new derby cocked to one side and holding tight to Amelia Rose's hand.

A pair of police officers stood over a grizzled white farmer who sat dazed on the curb. Beside him, more than a dozen clay jugs were arranged in a line near a storm drain. Policemen continued to search through the hay and passed down more jugs as a Model T rolled to a stop beside the wagon. The police chief, his cheek packed with tobacco, stepped from the passenger side. Big and thick-chested, the chief walked like a man used to bullying. He spoke loud enough for all to hear.

"You want to go to prison?" He paused for an answer, but the farmer kept his head bowed. The chief turned to read the crowd, meeting the gaze of each white man. He ignored the others.

"It ain't like it used to be." The chief stepped up to the farmer until he towered over the man. "This here's a federal crime now.

Lord help you if the federal boys catch hold of you. Where you from?"

"Pelion," the farmer muttered, still refusing to look up.

The chief spat a stream of tobacco juice on the street. "How many jugs you got on that wagon?"

"Twenty-five."

"We got twenty-five," a sergeant said.

"With that kind of evidence against him, a man could go to prison for a long time."

"I got a family," the farmer said. "I got eight kids. Who's going to feed 'em if you put me away?"

"They might have to go hungry," the chief said. "Your wife might have to find herself another man, somebody smarter than you. Boy, what's your name?"

"Cecil Owens."

"I tell you what, Mr. Owens, I'm not doing this for you. I'd just as soon lock you up. I'm doing this for your eight kids and your poor wife. Against my better judgment, I'll let you bust up this evidence here and ride out of town. I don't want you back in Columbia, not while I'm living, not ever."

"Yes sir." Cecil Owens nodded.

"Leave him alone," Amelia Rose called out. "He's just trying to make a living same as you." Ransom jerked her hand to try and hush her, but she only jerked back harder and gave him a stink eye look.

Laughter rolled through the crowd of whites and someone said, "The little lady's right."

"Cecil," the Chief said, leaning close, "this ain't the way to take care of your family." Cecil nodded and hung his head like a shamed boy. "All right now, you got to bust up these jugs here and put this day behind you. Go on, now. Do it."

The chief stepped away.

Cecil Owens rose slowly to his feet and looked out at the crowd. He was all bones and strings of muscle, his face thin, his skin sunburnt leather. Snuff stained his lips. He looked like a man who worked from the time he crawled out of bed before sunrise until he fell back in it long after the sun had set. Fat won't settle on a man like that, no matter how much grease and grits his wife feeds him. He was a working man and it was killing him.

Cecil Owens turned his back to the crowd. He lifted the first clay jug over the storm drain and let it drop. It burst into pieces of glazed green and brown, instantly filling the air with the biting odor of corn liquor. The whittled pine stopper fell through the grate along with five gallons of premium moonshine. The crowd moaned.

Tears welled in Cecil's eyes, spilled down his cheeks, and dripped from his chin. He wiped his nose on the back of his hand and raised a second jug over the grate. The colored crowd slipped away unnoticed. Only the whites remained, but soon the farmer's sadness moved Ransom and Amelia Rose to leave too.

"That police chief don't know what it's like when you can't hardly get by," Amelia Rose said.

"There aren't any jobs," Ransom said, "and farming on shares keeps you worse than broke."

They walked downhill past industrial buildings and trains parked on sidetracks. A colored man, carrying an empty canning jar, hurried past them towards Scabtown. Three more colored men passed Ransom and Amelia Rose, each carried empty jars as they crossed the tracks and disappeared down the embankment where the storm drain emptied. Men and women and children, all with empty jars, walked the tracks from both directions towards Scabtown.

The sun had begun its final descent and would soon set. Brilliant red and orange and violet burned a sky streaked with thin spring clouds.

Ransom and Amelia Rose crossed the tracks and climbed down the embankment into Scabtown. A group of men clustered around the storm drain spilling into the ditch. Two men held a wash tub beneath the storm drain pipe and caught the corn liquor as it spilled out. Two other men dipped the moonshine from the washtub and poured it, a dipper at a time, onto sack cloth stretched over a lard bucket. Bits of leaves and debris gathered in the center of the filtering cloth.

An old man seated on a rock supervised the collecting and

filtering. Someone handed him a jelly jar with half an inch of clear liquor in the bottom. He took the first sip.

"That's smooth," he said and smacked his lips.

The men at the pipe cheered and called for more jars. A shout went out across Scabtown and moonshine rationing began. Women hurried from shacks with arm-loads of gourds and cans and Mason jars, anything that could hold a drink.

"Y'all want some country water?" The old man said to Ransom and Amelia Rose.

Before he could answer, a big woman pressed a pint jar in Ransom's hand. He took a sip. Fire exploded in the back of his throat. Amelia Rose took the pint as he stood gasping for air and thumping his chest to start breathing again.

"You try it," Ransom managed to say.

Amelia Rose took a sip. Her eyes flared wide and she clutched her stomach. Her face went white and then red and redder. Beads of sweat formed on her brow. She passed the pint jar back to Ransom to keep from dropping it.

"I ain't never had nothing like that before," she gasped. "Have you?"

"Not like that," he said.

With their pint jar of moonshine, they slipped from the village as the party grew louder and followed the trail down to the river, gathering sticks for a fire along the way. After tossing the wood on the sand beside the raft, Ransom helped Amelia Rose down the clay bank into the cove.

"Check the lines," he said and knelt to make a fire.

Amelia Rose pulled in the hand lines, soon two small catfish lay thrashing on the back of the raft. She dressed the fish and tossed the heads and skins in the river, saving the entrails to bait the hooks again. When the fish were clean, Ransom threaded them on sticks and propped them over the flames. Fire filled the tiny cove with dancing light that glittered in the eyes of Amelia Rose.

Ransom thinned the liquor with river water and took another sip. It still burned when he drank it but not as much. Along with the moonshine's slow burn, it now had an earthy taste of clay.

Amelia Rose made dough from the cornmeal Mrs. Massey had given Ransom and flattened it into cakes she cooked on a rock nestled in the embers. While they waited for dinner, she nibbled on bits of raw dough and watched spellbound as Ransom twirled the small fish on sticks over the fire.

They passed the pint jar between them, and with each sip, their eyes grew softer and their differences seemed less important. With some liquor in him, Ransom didn't care if Amelia Rose caught him looking. It gave him pleasure to watch her move around the fire, tending to their supper. When she did catch his eye, she smiled at him as though he was the only man in the world. Her smile made him laugh. It was an honest laugh that began deep inside like a healing spring and bubbled right up through his heart.

When the final corn cake had been eaten and the fish bones picked clean, they passed the jar between them, taking ever smaller sips. Ransom felt the hard angles inside him soften. His worries floated off unnoticed beyond the edges of his mind. Amelia Rose washed her hands in the river, her back to him as she knelt at the water's edge. Ransom took in the curves of her body, the feminine lines of her waist, the strength of her hips. When she turned around, her breasts jostled firm beneath the dress. Above them in the village, the shouts of celebration grew louder and more chaotic.

"Tell me about the woman you aim to marry," Amelia Rose said.

Ransom dug the photograph of Elizabeth from the wallet of letters and passed it to Amelia Rose. Seated at the fire, she studied the picture of Elizabeth smiling in the garden.

"She looks like a prettied-up kind of girl. Why you want to mess with somebody like that?"

"I just do," Ransom said.

Amelia Rose gave the photograph back to Ransom and stood up. "I believe we need some more of that country water," she said, looking down on Ransom. "We ain't quite right yet."

She climbed up the bank past the waterfall. And when she was gone, morning glory and jasmine vines closed behind her. Ransom sat alone and listened to the river and to the bullfrogs and crickets, and to the distant call of a bird he didn't know. Night settled black outside the tiny cove and crept to the edge of the fire's light. He gathered more driftwood and dropped it in a pile on the sand, then sat dreaming into the fire.

Laughter and shouts rang from Scabtown. A guitar played and a banjo picked, twanging high through the night, followed with the lonely sound of a harmonica trailing off on melodies of its own. These were sounds of another people, another country.

Vines parted at the top of the bank and Amelia Rose climbed down, clinging to a root with one hand as she lowered herself to the beach. In her other hand, she carried the open pint jar filled with slightly muddy moonshine. She settled next to Ransom on the sand.

"You ought to see the bonfire they got going up there. They're dancing wild as June bugs." She held the jar before the fire, peering through the glass at the grit settling to the bottom.

"I bet this would taste all right if we sucked on a peppermint," she said. Ransom dug the candy from his pocket, gave her a piece and put one in his mouth. Amelia Rose held the bit of hard candy to her nose and breathed in the light peppermint scent.

"Someday, I'll have bath soap that smells like this and I'll sit in the bath all day long, just soaking and getting beautiful."

"You're beautiful now." Ransom took a sip, straining the debris with his teeth. His eyes watered, burning with the alcohol's fire and the mint's intensity. Sucking in air, he passed the jar to Amelia Rose.

She took a sip. Her eyes flared wide and she gagged and coughed and cried. Fanning her mouth, she looked to Ransom with a grin then scooped river water in the palm of her hand and drank it.

When she sat up and had dried her mouth on the hem of her dress, Ransom gave her the last peppermint. It seemed to him that the liquor had smoothed out her roughness and softened her harsh corners. In the firelight, she looked weary and worn and lovely.

"How old are you?" he asked.

"Old enough to eat cornbread without getting choked. You ain't so old neither."

"I'm nineteen," he said. "Why'd your daddy think you weren't Christian enough?"

"My family's nothing to talk about." She took the jar from Ransom and held it in her lap.

Ransom looked across to Amelia Rose. Her eyes were amazing in the soft light.

"How come you don't have a man?" he said. "You're too good-looking to sleep alone at the river."

"No man don't want me," she said. "I'm going to hell just as sure as Christmas." She took a sip of liquor and when the fire in her throat had eased, she looked to Ransom. "Did you kill anybody in the war?"

"I hardly fired a shot, just ran out into no man's land and got blown up."

"That's all you did?"

"They taught me how to shoot and soldier and all that mess, but in the end, it didn't matter. You can't stop a bomb from falling on your head."

"I thought war was different than that."

"I did too," he said, taking the jar from her. "I liked the Army at first. They fed me good and gave me better clothes than I ever had, boots and jackets, good things. You wouldn't know it to look at me now, but they fattened me up. The bad thing is they got in my head somehow and made a prison in there. It got so if they weren't mean enough to me, I'd be mean to myself."

Mesmerized by the fire, they drank and listened to Scabtown's jubilee. In the village, a man preached loud and cursed the devil. Voices sang as a banjo and guitar staggered through separate, disjointed tunes. Softly, as though off by itself, a harmonica played a tearful melody.

"I know what you mean," Amelia Rose said, "about how the Army put a prison in your head. The church makes me feel like that. The church makes out like it's a sin to do what you want or to feel things in your heart. They make out like we're born lousy and don't deserve to be good to ourselves. You know that wind-up monkey in the candy store? That's the way the church makes me feel, like I'm some kind of wind-up monkey. Only instead of beating a drum, when the church winds me up, I beat my own self."

"That's no way to be." Ransom broke a stick and fed it to the fire. "Folks beat on us enough as it is, we don't have to help them."

"That's what I mean." She eased back on one arm, stretched her legs across the sand and leaned her head against Ransom's shoulder. "I don't care if I have to live under a rock, it's better than what

I had. My daddy was a preaching man and he wanted me to marry a preaching man. I felt like I was sliding down a mill sluice with God on my back, Mama on one side and Daddy on the other, and a preacher man at the bottom, waiting to marry me. They acted like my life didn't belong to me. I had to lay up with a guitar picker to get God off my back. Now, I got a baby coming on."

13

RANSOM WOKE LONG AFTER SUNRISE and found himself floating down the Congaree River. Amelia Rose sat at the raft's stern, steering with a short piece of flat board. She wore Ransom's derby adorned with a crown of morning glory blooms, blue and pink and white. Even with his eyes closed and an arm draped across his face, sunlight pained him.

"Drink some water," Amelia Rose said. "You'll feel better."

"You got no right to be here." Ransom moaned and struggled to rise to his knees.

He drank from the river. The Congaree flowed dark, taking its color from the red clay banks and the black water swamps. He checked the double knot he'd tied in the pack's drawstring the night before. It was his knot, but he felt through the burlap to be sure.

"You think I'd steal from you?"

"You stole my raft and me on it," Ransom said. "A woman who'd do that is likely to do anything."

"That's not stealing."

"It's not right," he said. "I never asked you to come along." He snatched the derby from her head and dumped the crown of morning glories in her lap.

She untangled the flowers and placed them back on her head. They looked like a crown on her, a fairy tale princess crown.

"You were so drunk," she said. "I could've done anything I wanted and you'd never know it. Don't bother thanking me for getting you this far down the river while you were laid out sleeping like a dead man. And don't think I need you either. I can take care of myself."

"That's good," he said. "Because when we get to Charleston I'm going my way and you're going yours."

"Then stop looking at me like that."

Ransom stretched out again, resting his head on the pack. "I wasn't looking at you."

They drifted past snowy egrets roosting in the trees. In the topmost crook of a giant cypress, a pair of osprey peered from a nest large enough to hold a child. The river slowed until it seemed not to move at all. Swallows skimmed the water, chasing after bugs and each other. With only its eyes above the surface, an alligator watched them float by.

Time passed in this lazy fashion until late afternoon. Had it not been for the sun's gradual movement, it would have been impossible to imagine time at all. By its nature and with little work on their part, the river carried them toward the sea. On stumps and logs, turtles lay like muddy rocks. A long-legged bird stood contemplating its toes as it floated on a mat of water grass. The banks of the river dissolved and the water flowed off in all directions without restraint, leaving only great bald cypress trees to mark the river's channel.

"Listen," Amelia Rose said.

"I don't hear anything."

"There's nothing to hear," she said. "The swallows are gone. The fish aren't jumping. The wind's not moving. It's not natural for the world to be so quiet."

Ransom sat up, listening. A heavy pall had settled over the river. Ransom wished a bird would fly or a turtle would splash, but nothing moved. Finally, on the edge of hearing, a faint cry came to them in the wind.

"It's a child," she said.

They rounded a turn where a stand of trees stood clustered on a muddy island. The current divided, spilling equally on either side. They heard the cries louder. Drifting closer, they could make out the dark shape of a small naked figure crouched in the reeds, a little black boy. He raised his head and wailed.

Amelia Rose called to him.

"Where's your mama?"

With a hundred feet of river between them, the boy reached for her.

Ransom poled the raft through the shallow water and searched the trees for a village or house, but saw no sign of people. Like the last several miles, there were no riverbanks here, only trees and black water.

The little boy waded into the shallows, reaching for them with small hands as he cried. Struggling against the current, he quickly sank to his chest, staggered sideways and vanished beneath the dark water. A moment later he surfaced, arms thrashing, only to vanish again.

Ransom jumped in and sank to his chest. The boy rose for an instant, gasped and went under. A swirl unwound where he'd been. Ransom fought the current, thrashing on the edge of panic. He felt the river bottom with his feet but found only mud. Then his boot bumped something soft, something not of the river. He sucked in a breath and dove.

Beneath the black water he sprang forward with arms outstretched, but the current had taken the small body away. Ransom swam through the darkness along the bottom of the river and crashed headfirst into the boy pinned against a sunken log. He gathered the little boy to his chest, pushed off the bottom and quickly surfaced.

"I got him!"

Amelia Rose was in the river too, fighting to keep her head above the water. She made for the island where the raft had crashed among fallen trees and met Ransom in the shallows. When she reached to take the boy, Ransom pushed her hand away.

"I got him," he said, gasping. "I got him." He fought to catch his breath as he stumbled into the mud, cradling the boy. "He slipped away, but I got him.

Amelia Rose reached out again. "Ransom," she said. "Ransom, he's not breathing."

On the beach, Ransom held the little boy upside down by his ankle. River water spilled from his mouth. He coughed and vomited, gagged, spat and wiggled. When he cried loud and hard with clear lungs, Ransom handed him to Amelia Rose, who soothed and rocked him.

Ransom stood trembling. "I got him," he said softly.

"Ransom?" Amelia Rose jostled the boy gently in her arms. "Are you crying?"

"I got him," Ransom whispered and turned away.

The boy clung to Amelia Rose. Locking his tiny fingers in the folds of her soaked dress, he buried his head against her bosom.

"Where's your mama?" Amelia Rose said, but the boy only clung tighter. "Where's your daddy?" The boy turned in her arms and pointed behind him to a massive oak leaning out over the river.

Amelia Rose cursed and looked away. Covering the boy's eyes, she splashed through the shallows to the raft. On the farthest reaches of an oak, flies swarmed a black cloud where a corpse dangled from a rope. At the noose, the man's neck broke at an angle.

Ransom shoved the raft into the current and climbed aboard, using the pole to maneuver through the shallows and past the hanging man. Amelia Rose held the boy to her breast and kissed his nappy head.

"Go in the pack," Ransom said as he leaned on the pole and pushed them around the island. "Feed him some cornmeal. Leave the ham alone."

"Ham? You got ham?"

"I'm saving it for Elizabeth," he said.

"You got no sense, walking around starving when you got a prize like that. I bet that prettied-up girl's not starving. She don't need your ham. Me and the boy need it. Look at you! *You* need it."

"We're doing fine on cornmeal," Ransom said. "The boy will be damn glad to have it."

"Ham would be better."

Amelia Rose mixed cornmeal with water in the pint jar and with her fingers fed the lumpy batter to the boy. He ate so desperately she had to pull it away.

They passed smaller islands, no more than mounds of mud grown over with brambles tough enough to survive the river. More alligators appeared, sunning themselves on the mud islets or floating like logs in the current. When the sun had slipped below the tops of the towering bald cypress trees, the boy raised his head from Amelia Rose's bosom and looked around.

"I think he knows this place," she said.

The boy blinked as if waking from a dream and pointed to the left of the channel. Ransom poled the heavy raft to that side. They skirted the tree line as the last of the day's light seeped from the sky. Trees parted where a lesser river joined the Congaree.

"There!" the boy shouted. "There. There."

Ransom poled hard and swung the raft into the mouth of the smaller river. Bald cypress towered like columns on either side, their limbs arching over the water. Massive canopies formed a vast living cathedral where birds flittered a hundred feet above them. In Amelia Rose's lap, the boy bounced and bounced and bounced.

Ransom heard the hard knock of wood on wood, like the sound of a pole against the side of a boat. He stopped and listened, but all he heard was the chatter of birds and the drone of insects. All he saw were shadows swallowing the day.

"Is you lost?" A man asked in a soft melodic voice. Ransom spotted a figure drifting just beyond the trees standing in a boat and poling along at the same pace as the raft.

"We found a little boy up the river," Ransom said. "He knows this place."

"Caleb?" The man called.

The boy squealed, releasing Amelia Rose for an instant only to dash back and cling to her. The man poled his boat out from the trees and floated beside them. Two alligators lay dead and bloody in the bottom of his boat. He was a black man, barrel-chested, healthy and strong.

"Caleb?" he called again.

The boy squealed and said something in a language unknown to Ransom.

"Let me get over there with you," the man said. "If we work together, we can pole you in before it goes full dark, sure enough."

Ransom helped the man aboard and tied his small scow to the raft. The man knelt and touched the boy's shoulder.

"Caleb, this here's River Jim. You know me. Ain't nobody going to hurt you now."

"Mama," Caleb said. He stood up in Amelia Rose's lap and reached for River Jim, all the while speaking a string of words that sounded almost English, but not exactly.

River Jim said something in the same sing-song language. Caleb grew calm and sat down again in Amelia Rose's lap. Quietly he pressed his head between her breasts.

Ransom and River Jim began poling in unison. Together they walked the length of the raft and worked the pole back again, digging into the muddy river bottom. With the men putting their strength into the task, the raft gained speed against the gentle current.

"You see his daddy?" River Jim said.

"Lynched," Ransom said.

"That's what I feared.

They poled in silence as night descended and the trees merged into a single dark body. The cypress canopy blocked even starlight. Ransom could make out little more than the silhouette of Amelia Rose huddled in the center of the raft holding Caleb. A scattering of fireflies blinked on and off, tiny ephemeral points of light floating in the dark.

River Jim moved with Ransom, steadily pushing the raft up the river.

"We're coming into it now," River Jim said, turning the raft into the trees. "Caleb you's coming home."

The swamp grew shallow and tangled with roots. Somewhere behind them in the pitch black, the river flowed, but here in the trees, the water lazed still and warm. They bumped rotted logs and cypress knees, but under River Jim's direction, they maneuvered past them until a black rise of solid ground appeared.

"This here's part of the old rice fields," River Jim said. "That narrow piece of land up there's a dike. Slaves built it, a long time ago, one basket of dirt at a time."

Soon the raft parted a stand of cattails and nosed into the old rice field dike. Behind them, River Jim's boat bumped into the raft and rebounded with a hard tug on its line. River Jim dragged the smaller of the two alligators half out of his boat. With a hatchet, he severed the tail in a single chop then filleted the hide from the underside of it. He tossed the scrap of hide into his boat and shoved the gator's body back as well.

"Here now," he said as he handed the tail meat to Ransom. "Follow the dike. If you's walking in the water, you's off the dike. Caleb's people live about a mile up that way. Ain't no white people know they back in there. They talk the Geechee talk. So you won't understand half of what they's saying. Give them that gator meat and tell them you seen River Jim."

"Come with us," Amelia Rose said.

"I likes people better when I ain't around 'em," River Jim said. He untied his boat, stepped into it, and poled away. Darkness engulfed him and the rising drone of insects soon sang over the knock of his pole.

Ransom shouldered the pack, wiggling some to adjust the weight until it hung even on his shoulders. He could feel the dense ham centered on his spine. He pressed the derby tight on his head and helped Amelia Rose from the raft. As she stepped out, Caleb reached for Ransom's neck and he took the boy in his arms.

"He likes you," Amelia Rose said. She kissed the boy on the cheek and brushed her fingers over his head.

They climbed the slight rise of dry land and began to follow the trail along the earthen dike. Caleb pressed his head into Ransom's shoulder and nestled in the safety of his arms. The boy drifted into sleep, his breath puffing warm on Ransom's neck. In all his years, Ransom had never felt more complete or more alive. Maybe, he thought, this is how it feels to be a daddy.

Fireflies were their only light. Legions of them punctuated the night with glowing spasms of yellow.

When they had walked a mile or so, they heard voices, soft and subdued. The boy heard them too and woke, raising his head from Ransom's shoulder.

A light shone ahead of them and, as they drew closer, Ransom could see the flicker of a communal fire in the center of a tiny village. Shacks made of sticks and palmetto fronds caught the fire's glow. People sat hunched around the flame, speaking softly. Ransom heard the melody of their talk. Beyond the fire, a goat nibbled something on the ground. When they came to the edge of the village, the boy cried out and everyone seated around the fire hushed into silence.

"Caleb?" An old woman called.

The boy squealed and wiggled in Ransom arms. When he set him on the ground, Caleb sprinted to the old woman, yelling all the way.

She threw up her hands to heaven and shouted, "Great Da!"

Everyone gathered at the fire cried out with joy. The matriarch tried to rise from her place, but Caleb threw himself on her. A young man embraced both Caleb and the woman while others pressed close to lay hands on the boy.

"We found him up the river." Ransom stepped forward into the light.

Their laughter stopped in an instant. Their faces turned to stone. They looked with dread on Ransom and Amelia Rose. In the door of a shack, a man held a shotgun at his side. He was dark as the night and bare-chested and the only one in the village wearing shoes.

"River Jim showed us the way," Ransom said. "He said y'all knew the boy."

A young woman, thin and bewildered, stepped from a shack. Her clothes were torn to shreds. Tears caught the fire's light and glittered down her cheeks.

"Caleb?" she cried in the softest voice.

"Mama," Caleb reached for her with one arm but still clung to the old woman with the other.

His mother walked dreamlike. A woman went to her and held her steady by the elbow. When she came to Caleb, he touched her and she fell to her knees, sobbing as she gathered him in her arms. The man with the gun put it away and ventured closer to Ransom.

"You see his daddy?" the man said.

Ransom nodded and gave him the gator meat. Amelia Rose stood nearby wiping her eyes until Ransom took her hand. They withdrew to the edge of the clearing. Tears welled in Ransom's eyes too. He wiped them away, but more came. Together, hand in hand, they watched the villagers comfort Caleb and his mother.

Amelia Rose drew the hem of her dress up to wipe away tears.

"We saved the boy," Ransom said. "We couldn't save the daddy, but we saved the boy."

At the fire, the man in shoes spoke to the matriarch and helped her to her feet. Walking with careful grace, the old woman crossed the lighted circle to Ransom and Amelia Rose. When she spoke, her voice sounded like a mix of languages Ransom could not define, some French perhaps, certainly English and something else. What he did understand was her sincere gratitude. She invited them to stay the night.

"This isn't our place," Ransom said.

"But, please," Amelia Rose said, "may I hold him one more time?" The old woman took Amelia Rose by the hand and led her to Caleb. Ransom followed. He wanted to touch the boy too. He wanted to feel the life inside him.

Amelia Rose knelt and put her arms around mother and son, resting her cheek on Caleb's head. Ransom touched them too. He could feel the boy's warmth, the miraculous warmth of a living little boy. Amelia Rose held to the mother and child as one voice after another fell silent and all the villagers watched the two women, one white and one black, wrapped around the little boy with Ransom standing over them.

"We should go," Ransom said when time had frozen and he knew nothing would continue with them there. He turned to hide his tears.

Amelia Rose kissed Caleb's head. Looking into the mother's eyes, she said, "I'm sorry. I'm so sorry."

Ransom took Amelia Rose's hand. As she stepped back, her fingers trailed across Caleb's cheek and touched his mother hair. Ransom pulled her away. Together they walked from the light of the village and followed the dike into the swamp.

14

Darkness engulfed them so completely Ransom could only find his way by the feel of solid ground beneath his boots. He reached for Amelia Rose and grasped her hand.

"I would have kept that boy if we hadn't found his home," Ransom said. "When I was carrying him, I thought maybe he was a gift to me, like maybe he's the only little boy I'll ever get."

"Maybe not," Amelia Rose said and tightened her grip on his calloused hand.

Together they followed the dike between the black waters. The countless swirling yellow lights of fireflies floated in the darkness like drifting stars and made his head swim.

"The lighting bugs fly up when they turn on their light," she said. "They start out in the dark and dance upwards with the light."

Ransom felt Amelia Rose's hand in his and he felt the solid ground beneath his feet. These were the only things he could count on for sure as the worrisome thought they may be lost crept into his mind.

"It wasn't this far," Amelia Rose said. "We've been walking a long time."

"The raft is right up here," he said. But it was too dark to really know. He looked back in the direction they had come and saw the same darkness and the same endless scattering of fireflies.

They kept walking. Ransom took some assurance in the solid ground beneath his feet until, by degrees, it softened into mud and no matter where they stepped they stepped in water.

"We're off the trail," Amelia Rose said. "Ransom, we're off the trail."

"I know. I know. Go back."

They turned around towards the dry ground they'd stepped from just a few yards back, but couldn't find it. Instead they tripped over roots as they splashed in ever deeper water. Amelia Rose clutched Ransom's hand so tight it hurt. The water and the roots moved against them as if alive. Ransom bumped into the trunk of a tree and had to feel his way around it.

"It's getting deeper," she said. "The water's getting deeper. Go back. Go back where it's not so deep."

But they couldn't find that place either. Wherever they stepped, they sank deeper. All sorts of vines and roots clawed at them. Briars and the saw-edge of palmetto fronds tore at their clothes. Ransom pressed forward through brush and felt the derby fall from his head.

"My hat!" Ransom thrashed about looking for it but found only tangled briars.

Mosquitoes bit the tender flesh of Ransom's face and buzzed his ears. No matter how much he swatted, the buzzing wouldn't stop. They were up to their waists in water now and couldn't see a thing except fireflies.

Ransom bumped into a massive tree. The bark felt rough as oak. In feeling his way around it, Ransom discovered it had thick limbs swaying low and gathering at the trunk.

"Climb up here," he said.

He helped Amelia Rose into the tree. Feeling in the dark, they climbed inch by inch until they came to a cradle formed by the joint of two thick limbs. The branches, each wider than Ransom, formed a shallow dip, large enough to hold their bodies as if nestled in a giant's palm. They were high in the crown where wind chattered through the leaves and kept the bugs away. He could see the stars.

Ransom hung the pack on a limb, stretched out in the cradle with his back to the trunk and drew Amelia Rose into his arms so she rested in his lap, her back against his chest. He couldn't see the ground, only millions of fireflies moving below them.

"How high are we?" she said.

"I don't know. Give me that rope from around your middle."

Amelia Rose untied her rope belt and passed it over her shoulder to Ransom. He wrapped it loosely around them both and tied them to the tree. Safely out of the water and away from biting insects, Ransom felt exhaustion overtaking him. He closed his eyes, drew Amelia Rose closer and breathed in the scent of her neck.

"Ransom?' She said as softly as though they shared a pillow. "You still got your buckeye?"

"Yes." Ransom rested his cheek on her shoulder. "You got yours?"

"I'm rubbing it right now in my pocket. In the morning, we can get 'em together and get our luck running again."

"In the morning–" Ransom yawned and slipped closer toward sleep. He found a soft place where Amelia Rose's neck and shoulder met and rested his head there. "In the morning, I'll be able to find my way back to the raft." He savored the smell of her skin, the curves of her body and how comfortable she was against him. Her warmth drew him to sleep.

"Don't you just love the stars?" she said.

Ransom teetered on the edge of dreams.

"Are you listening to me?" She gave him a firm elbow jab in the ribs. The jolt shocked him awake. He bolted upright with a gasp. If they hadn't been tied to the tree, he would have tumbled out.

"What the hell did you do that for?" Ransom rubbed his sore ribs and backed away from Amelia Rose. A night breeze moved between them.

"You weren't listening," she said.

"I'm wore out."

"Talk to me about the stars," she said. "Don't you just love looking up at the stars?"

"If I talk to you a little bit, will you let me sleep?"

"Maybe."

"All right then," he said. "When I was in France, I had my very own star. You won't believe me, but it changed colors and looked down on me and gave me a peaceful feeling.

"I believe you," Amelia Rose said. "Stars do that for me too. Why do you want to go all this way for some woman in a picture. She's not your kind."

"I thought you wanted to talk about stars."

"But she's not your kind," Amelia Rose said.

"I'll be *her* kind when I'm brokering cotton," he said. "There's people like us in the world and there's people like them in the world. I want to be like them."

"I want to be like them too," Amelia Rose said.

"Go to sleep."

"You shouldn't have to change to be with somebody."

"If loving her makes me a better man, that's a good change," he said. "Maybe that's the way it's supposed to be. Now, go to sleep."

"There's easier women to get. Why are you going to all this trouble for a girl you never met?"

Ransom drew a sigh. He liked the way her skin felt against his and didn't want to move but raised his head just enough to speak into her ear.

"If I tell you, will you hush up and go to sleep?"

"I promise."

"We'd only been in the trenches a few days." He spoke in a hush and remembered it all as if it had just happened. "Lieutenant Pinckney had seen war in Mexico and knew what he was doing, but the rest of us didn't know a thing. The French who had been there before us got blown to bits by German artillery. I saw a bunch of them scattered up in the tree tops, bodies hanging in the trees like laundry blown up there by the wind. That's when I started to get scared, really bad scared. I figured I'd die there and never make it back home. I followed Lieutenant Pinckney over the top. I don't remember hearing anything. I just remember being scared. It scares me now just to think about it."

"Why you scared now?" She turned her head and suddenly her lips were near his. "You're not in France no more."

"It's like the scared gets down inside you and just sits there. It never goes away."

"But you didn't die."

"No," Ransom said, "but I came pretty damn close. I saw the big guns way back behind German lines open up with all they had, the whole mountainside blazed towards the sky, throwing up the big shells. And the ground rose up around me. Then I was some place with my mama and daddy. Other people where there too. When I come to I ran into a shell-hole and saw Captain Sterling with his legs blown off and Lieutenant Pinckney bleeding from a gut wound. He had these letters from his fiancée and he asked me to read to him. When I opened the first letter, I knew I was looking at something special, something a man might only see once in his lifetime, if he's lucky. The letters smelled like lavender and every word was shaped so perfect, like an artist drew them. Most of all, the words showed me she had a loving heart like my mama. I didn't know how I'd live or how I'd get back home, but I knew I wanted to meet this woman and I wanted her to love me the way she loved Lieutenant Pinckney."

"You can't make a woman love you if she loves somebody else."

"Lieutenant Pinckney died in no man's land," Ransom said. "I laid right there beside his dead body and read Elizabeth's letters for days. When I finished reading the last one, I'd start over. When I slept, I dreamed of her and when I wasn't sleeping I read her letters. She was all I had to live for."

"How long were you out there in that no man's land place?"

"Somebody told me five days, but I don't remember." Ransom put his head on Amelia Rose's shoulder, felt her skin on his cheek and closed his eyes. "Now go to sleep."

"Don't you want to know something about me?"

"I want to go to sleep," Ransom said. "We can talk in the morning. Go to sleep."

"I need talking now."

Ransom tightened his hold around her waist and mumbled into her shoulder.

"I never did nothing like what you did," Amelia Rose said. "I suppose I'm just starting out. I know I'm not like other girls but somebody can still love me. Can't they? I want a man who thinks it's a good thing I'm not like everybody else. I thought that guitar picker might love me that way, but he run off."

They sat nestled together in the top of the great tree with stars shining down through the branches and the black ground beneath them alive with the magic of fireflies.

"I didn't want nothing to do with men," she said. "Once, when that young preacher my daddy likes came over to court me, I hit him with a rock right square in the chest and chased him all the way to the road with more rocks. But then, one night when I was in bed, I heard guitar music coming through my window. It came from off in the woods and I could hear a man singing love songs. His songs broke something loose inside me and got it heating up like a little fire. When my mama and daddy were asleep, I slipped out the house and found that guitar picker's camp. He was a grown man, older than you, living out in the woods, just singing love songs. At home, my daddy was always preaching and praying and talking about my virtue. I didn't want no part of that life. I wanted the life that guitar picker sang about."

"So you laid up with him," Ransom said.

"Yep," she said. "And then he run off. If my daddy had listened to me when I told him I didn't want to marry no preacher, I wouldn't of laid with the man. But I had to do something to get out of the box Daddy put me in. Now I'm going to hell, sure as Christmas."

"If children are a good thing," Ransom said, "I don't see why God would send you to hell for making one."

"You ought to give me some of that ham."

"I'm tired," Ransom said. "I'll catch something to eat in the morning." He adjusted his cheek against the back of her shoulder and started again to drift off.

"Talk to me," she said. "Just talk. I want to hear your voice."

"I'll talk in the morning," he said. "Right now, I need to sleep."

"Talking won't do me no good in the morning. I need talking right now, 'cause I'm scared right now."

Ransom pulled closer to Amelia Rose and shifted on the limb, trying to get some blood into his legs.

"In France," he said, "I almost saw Heaven. They were shooting at me and then it all stopped, just for a second, but it seemed longer. It seemed like forever. Everything was quiet and peaceful. Even the dead looked peaceful. And the mud, and everything that looked like Hell most of the time, looked like Heaven. I was right outside the gates to Heaven. I know I was. Then it was over, like it never happened and they were shooting at me again."

"What if," Amelia Rose whispered over her shoulder, "what if there ain't no heaven? What if just being born was some kind of a miracle, no matter if you got a daddy or not? And what if when we die, we're just dead and the miracle is over? I think we'd all be a lot nicer to one another if we thought about it that way. Don't you?"

"People don't think about that stuff," Ransom said. His body begged for sleep but they kept talking. They talked about fishing and farming and growing up. She didn't mind he was a sharecropper's son and he didn't mind she was expecting a baby.

"Army doctors said I can't make babies."

"Well," she said. "It's a good thing I got one coming on."

Eventually they ran out of things to say and even Amelia Rose drifted off to sleep. Neither of them stirred again until birds announced the dawn, chirping and chattering in the branches. Mockingbirds and jays began to sing. The sun rose somewhere beyond the dense cypress canopy, but Ransom couldn't see it. He had just untied them from the trunk of the oak when they heard a tooting sound high in the trees. It sounded like a pair of toy horns, as if children marched through the treetops.

"Toot-toot. Toot." The unusual sound moved behind them. Ransom tried to turn and see, but Amelia Rose held him still.

"They're coming closer," she said. "Just wait." The loud drum of a woodpecker rattled, then the tooting resumed. They held still, too bewildered to move.

A magnificent bird, the size of a crow, maybe larger, landed on a branch of the limb where they sat. It was black with an ivory bill, a brilliant red hood and a large white patch shaped like a shield on its back. The bird considered them with piercing yellow eyes, tilting its head first to one side then the other. It tooted once. Then, almost playfully, the bird stepped closer, flapped its wings and tooted again, "Toot-toot. Toot." Behind them, off in the canopy of vines and treetops, another toy horn tooted and the bird flew away in that direction.

"Some kind of woodpecker." Ransom watched in the direction the bird had flown.

"It's beautiful," she said.

Stiff and achy, Ransom climbed down first. When he turned to help Amelia Rose, she slapped his hand away. "I been climbing trees all my life," she said and jumped the last few feet.

In the new light, Ransom saw a small island nearby and they waded over to it.

"I got to find my hat." Ransom took his boots off and gave them to Amelia Rose who put them on. Black swamp water stained her dress. The fabric, worn thin as onion skin in places, clung to her body. Shouldering the pack, Ransom made his way into the swamp, stepping over rotting, submerged limbs and tangled roots. Amelia Rose held to the straps of his overalls.

The day soon heated up, filling the air with such dense humidity it felt like they were breathing steam. A fog of insects hovered about their faces, biting, sucking blood and sticking to the moist corners of their eyes.

They picked their way around massive thickets of underbrush and over the fallen trunks of defeated giant trees. Cypress knees protruded from the black water, clustered like a gathering of gnomes. A lace of Spanish moss fluttered from the lowest branches, but higher up it grew thick as hay bales.

Ransom recognized nothing. The dike they walked the night before had vanished, so had his new derby.

"We should go back to the tree and start over," Amelia Rose said.

But the swamp concealed every trace of where they had come from. They sloshed onward, startling frogs that leapt and splashed before them.

Noon came and went. They passed beneath a bobcat lounging on the limb of a live oak. It watched them and yawned.

Finally, they came to land, not just a hummock but honest to goodness land that stretched solid and dry into a pine forest. As they stumbled from the swamp and into the pines, they frightened a troop of deer that bounded off, flagging white tails behind them.

They found a place where pine needles formed a thick, comfortable mat. Above them, through the trees, they could see blue sky and light clouds. Amelia Rose lay down and stretched out her battered legs. Ransom arranged the pack beneath her head, fashioning a pillow.

"What're you doing?" She said as he leaned over her.

"Rest," he said and adjusted the pack.

He was so close he saw himself in her eyes along with all the details of their tiny world, the pine trees and brambles, a touch of sky, all of it. His hands, scarred and calloused, seemed too crude to touch her. When he'd made her comfortable, he lay down beside her and together they slept the dreamless sleep of the weary and the lost.

The sun had slipped from the sky when Ransom woke to the smell of something cooking over a camp-fire. He sat up, blinking. Amelia Rose squatted at the fire and stirred the contents of the lard bucket with a stick.

"While you were sleeping, I hunted up some things to eat."

Ransom peeked into the pot. Dozens of crawfish tails floated in a clear broth with pieces of wild onion.

He gathered firewood, breaking off the lowest dead limbs from trees around them. Amelia Rose fashioned a bed of pine boughs and, as the night settled in, they ate from the pot and talked about the strange tooting bird they had seen that morning.

When they had eaten and were satisfied, they lay together on the pine boughs and shared the pack as a pillow. Ransom's head touched hers and they spoke in whispers.

"It ain't so bad being lost," Amelia Rose said. "I like it better than some places where I was found. We could live right here and raise my baby up to be a wild man."

"I have to get to the coast."

"You don't have to do nothing," she said. "We're good together. When I laid up with that guitar picker, he told me some couples are like two candles making one light. You don't know where the light of the man ends or the light of the woman begins. You and me can be like that."

Ransom put an arm around Amelia Rose and pulled her close, his fingers falling not so innocently beside her breast. She let him. Warmth came through the fabric of her dress as if there was nothing there. It occurred to him to undress her, or to at least try, but as they watched the fire die into embers, he drifted off to sleep.

15

RANSOM SLEPT BEYOND TIME. He had no reference to anything, not even himself, until he heard a distant hymn. The song wove through the dark fog of his mind. It sounded happy, full of power and goodness, and made him dream of sunshine on the mountains.

"Some glad morning..." The hymn sounded faint and the singer's voice cracked with age and enthusiasm. *"When my life is over..."*

He had not heard this voice before. His mind clung to it, but he wanted to sleep. He wanted to dream.

"I'll fly away..."

Finally, he realized the song came from outside him. Someone was singing in the woods. He woke so suddenly he startled Amelia Rose. The campfire had burned to embers leaving only a faint glow in the darkness.

"Listen," he said. From beyond the pines, they heard the voice of an old woman, cracking but full of energy.

"It's the middle of the night."

"Hush," he said.

"Oh, Lordy, I'll fly away..."

They gathered their things in the dark.

The old woman drifted further away and her song grew fainter: *"When my life is over, by and by..."*

They hurried after her. Ransom stopped only to listen and once he got his bearings, they hurried off again in the direction of the woman's song.

"*I'll fly away...*"

They stumbled onto an old roadbed, choked with broom straw and pine saplings. It led in the direction of the woman's voice.

"*To some place on God's celestial shore...*"

Up the road, Ransom caught sight of a thin figure among the saplings. She walked bowed and humped, and her voice sounded ancient as the earth itself. The old woman had grown tired and her voice diminished to a slurred jumble until she hit the chorus and sang out: "*...I'll fly away.*"

They followed no closer than necessary, sometimes letting her slip out of sight. The road led to an abandoned field overgrown with wild grass and choked with weeds. Beyond it, straight lines of a large farmhouse were silhouetted against the night sky, its windows black as slate. A split rail fence lay in ruins and the dark mass of a barn towered over the smaller shapes of a corncrib, shed and outbuildings.

"She might be a ghost," Amelia Rose said, "or some kind of spirit person."

The back door of the farmhouse dangled from the top hinge at an angle. When the woman tried to close it, the door wouldn't budge. She stopped trying and disappeared into the black interior. No light appeared in the window. Ransom and Amelia Rose walked through the abandoned field and stood near the well. Inside the falling down house, the woman sang a different, quieter song.

"I'm going up to the house." Ransom slipped the pack from his shoulder.

"Go right on ahead," Amelia Rose said. "I'll stay here 'til you get back."

The house had been falling apart for years. Leaves and debris blew freely past the broken door and into the house.

Ransom stepped inside. The crumbling house had an air of dust and mold. Roof shingles had rotted through and he could see patches of starlit sky through the ceiling of the kitchen. A small table with four chairs stood near the wall. In the corner, a black iron stove sat cold and unused. He rapped his knuckles on the table. The singing stopped.

"Ma'am?" Ransom said.

From somewhere deep within the house, a small voice called back. "Carter?" Shuffling up the hall toward him, the old woman called again, "Carter?"

Her shadow moved into the kitchen and paused. She stood looking at Ransom and he stood looking at her, a shriveled old woman, hunched and frail, leaning on a fence picket she used as a walking stick.

"Carter," the old woman said. Her head bobbed an unsteady jig as she looked on Ransom. "Daddy said Sherman's men kill't you." Leaning on the stick, the old woman strained to raise her head and study Ransom more closely. "The Yankees took everything but the dirt. Get a fire going and I'll scrape something together to eat."

"Ma'am, I'm not Carter," Ransom said.

The old woman jabbed the stick at Ransom's belly. "Hush. That's water under the bridge. Get a fire going."

Ransom slipped out the door, crossed the yard, and joined Amelia Rose at the well.

"She's an old crazy woman. She thinks she knows me."

"Anybody with her?"

"Carter," the woman called from the back door, "get a fire going. I can't cook on a cold stove."

Ransom began searching for anything that might burn. He tore splintered planks from the side of the barn and gathered branches from beneath a scrub oak. When he came up to the house with an armload of wood, Amelia Rose met him at the kitchen door.

"Her name's Annie Banks," she said. "She's got no one to look after her. We can stay and rest up."

Ransom made a fire in the cook stove and left the door of the firebox open so they'd have some light.

"Carter," Miss Annie said, "don't you know, Yankee soldiers came through here right after you left."

At the counter, Amelia Rose opened the pack and withdrew the ham. Ransom rose to stop her but she leveled a butcher knife at his belly.

"She's starving," Amelia Rose said. "She's been starving a long time. She needs fat and meat and pot liquor."

Ransom returned to the stove and nursed the fire.

"I heard somebody shot Mr. Lincoln," Miss Annie said. "Is that true?"

"That's what I heard," Ransom said. "Shot him in the head."

"Kill him?"

"Yes, ma'am," Ransom said. "It did."

"Humph," she said and sat back.

Amelia Rose put a tiny strip of fat in Miss Annie's mouth. She gummed it and sucked the grease.

"My daddy likes ham," she said. Shivers racked the old woman's body. "We ought to tell Daddy when dinner's ready. He'd like this."

"What about your mama?" Amelia Rose asked. "Don't your mama like ham?"

"Mama likes ham fine, but she's dead. She's been dead for years. I don't guess there's anybody who don't like ham, 'cept maybe a pig."

"Ain't your daddy dead?" Amelia Rose said.

With a strip of fat dangling from the corner of her mouth, Miss Annie considered the question.

"Well, now" she said, dragging her words out, "come to think of it, Daddy *was* dead, but I've been seeing a lot more of him lately."

On the stove, ham sizzled in an iron frying pan as the fat cooked out of it. Amelia Rose mixed the last few tablespoons of cornmeal with the melted fat and a little water then left it to simmer into gruel. The kitchen filled with the divine smells of grease and sugar-cured ham.

"Some girls took on four or five sweethearts," Miss Annie said. "Boys were dying so quick, a girl had to hedge her bets, don't you know, but I didn't want nobody but you, Carter."

"Sit next to the fire," Amelia Rose said. She helped Miss Annie to a chair by the stove. "You're shaking like you're about to freeze to death."

"I can't never get warm no more," Miss Annie said.

Amelia Rose pulled up a chair and began feeding her gruel from a mug.

"Don't grab," Amelia Rose said. "Let me feed you. Just a little now and when that settles I'll give you some more." Miss Annie opened her toothless mouth wide as a hungry chick.

Ransom went outside and sat on the steps. His eyes drifted to the dark hulk of the rotted barn and he thought of how the farm had fallen into ruin. Through the open door, he heard Amelia Rose soothing the old woman with childish talk. Then she called out to him.

"Ransom find a washtub and some soap." Ransom didn't answer and she called again. "You hear me?"

He got to his feet. "Don't boss me," he said.

"I ain't bossing you."

Ransom searched the back outside wall of the house for a washtub, but found only a wisteria vine growing through a broken window.

"The washtub is on the front porch," Amelia Rose called from the house.

Ransom crossed through the yard of chest-high weeds and saplings. Elizabeth wouldn't boss him and she'd never live like this. Elizabeth needed a fine painted house and he was going to get her one.

On the front porch, a galvanized tub hung from a nail beside the kitchen window where a gauze drape made a translucent screen. Behind it, he could make out the women's figures in the firelight. Amelia Rose moved with the grace and determination of a dancer. Miss Annie hardly moved at all. Silhouetted by the fire, the old woman looked like a stick figure, her limbs mere lines with knots for joints.

"If you want to wash up, there's soap on the counter," Amelia Rose said as Ransom stepped through the back door with the tub.

"Y'all go ahead." He set the tub near the stove and went outside to think about Elizabeth. Amelia Rose was taking over his life, telling him what to do, helping herself to his things. He didn't like it. Amelia Rose wasn't part of his dream.

Ransom climbed into a tree near the front porch and relaxed among the lower branches. He could easily see the kitchen window and the women's silhouettes on the worn drape. Amelia Rose helped Miss Annie out of her dress and into the tub. Kneeling on the floor, she bathed the old woman. Amelia Rose took particular care of Miss Annie's hair, freeing the braids wrapped around her head and patiently unraveling each one. Ransom saw it all backlit by embers in the stove.

When she washed the woman's hair, the wet strands formed a single long rope. Amelia Rose rinsed it and pressed the water from it with her hands. Finally, she helped Miss Annie from the tub and into a chair beside the fire.

With Miss Annie drying by the stove, Amelia Rose undressed. Her silhouette was so small and so slight, much thinner than Ransom had imagined, just enough flesh to contain a soul and the slightest mound at her tummy. When she turned to step into the wash tub, her breasts showed in profile. Ransom watched mesmerized and, for a moment, did not think about Elizabeth.

Through the window, in the quiet of the night, he could hear the water splash each time she scooped it in her palm and poured it on her skin. When she stood up with water dripping, the fire cast a glowing halo around her body. He saw no details, only silhouette. His eyes traced the outline of her body, the way she held her head and the graceful line of her neck as it played into her shoulders, the tuck of her waist curving into hips and the long stretch of thighs.

When she had dressed, Ransom slipped down from the tree and meandered back to the kitchen. Inside, amid the clean smell of lye soap, he found Miss Annie seated at the table, dressed in his courting suit. She seemed pleased to be so dressed up, even though the suit hung absurdly loose on her frame. Behind her, Amelia Rose stood and worked a brush through Miss Annie's long white hair.

"You can wash if you want," Amelia Rose said, but neither she nor Miss Annie offered to leave the room and give him privacy. When he hesitated, Amelia Rose said, "You got nothing I ain't seen before."

Ransom dragged the washtub from the kitchen and dumped the dirty water on the weeds by the back door. When Amelia Rose had brushed and dried Miss Annie's hair, she braided it. Then she fed the old woman another mug of gruel and helped her to the back of the house and into bed.

Amelia Rose returned to the kitchen and sat near the stove to brush her own hair. The long red strands draped over her shoulder and into her lap, full and thick and alive. There was something else in the way her hair played with the light, something mystical. It was in her eyes, too.

Ransom knew he'd never seen a more beautiful woman, but the thought made him feel guilty. He hadn't even met Elizabeth and already he'd been unfaithful in his thoughts. He tried to push the vision of Amelia Rose from his mind. But the vision remained and so did his desire. He knew the warmth of Amelia Rose's body, the curve of her waist and how she felt when he held her close.

"You gave her my courting clothes," he said, trying to rally anger.

"She was freezing." Amelia Rose focused her attention on the brush passing through the length of her hair. "I wasn't going to let her put the same rags on."

"It's May," Ransom said. "Nobody freezes to death in May, not in South Carolina."

"They might if they're an old woman."

"They weren't yours to give."

"If you're that kind of man, go back there and strip your dang clothes off her."

Ransom sat in silence and watched the fire. Like a salve, the flames drew the anger from him and brought to mind the picture of Elizabeth, her eyes looking out to him. Her words came to him too. He could smell lavender and see the flow of her writing in the last letter she had written: *You give me hope. I am waiting.*

Ransom looked to Amelia Rose, so beautiful in the fire's light, her body glowing, her long hair glistening, and he felt his heart pulled in two. It would be easy to stay, but this was not his dream. Amelia Rose was like him, coarse as sawmill lumber. She was the old life of sharecropping shacks and cheating landlords. Ahead of him he saw his new life, a genteel life with Elizabeth in a painted house full of fine things. Elizabeth was waiting.

16

JUST BEFORE DAWN, RANSOM LAY AWAKE on the kitchen floor with Amelia Rose sleeping beside him. She snuggled close, but he didn't put his arm around her like he had in the swamp.

He was sure he'd violated some principle of love for thinking the things he had last night. If he stayed another day with Amelia Rose, he'd lose his dream and Elizabeth too. If he stayed, he'd slip back into the old life of scratching in the dirt to make a living, getting cheated by people who thought they were better than him, never getting ahead and never having anything.

As first light filtered through the windows, Miss Annie shuffled down the hall and into the kitchen. She lifted the partially eaten ham from the counter and, clutching it to her breast, shuffled out again.

Ransom sat up. Amelia Rose reached for him, trying to draw him back. "Lay down," she mumbled, still half asleep. "It's barely light."

"The old woman stole the ham," he said.

"I seen her."

Ransom stood up and went to the counter where he rummaged in the pack until he found the wallet with Elizabeth's letters. Stepping around Amelia Rose, he made his way to the back door and leaned against the frame.

"Where you going?" she said.

"I got things to do." Ransom slipped out the door. Behind the barn he found an old chopping block. He sat down on it and waited for the sun.

He held the leather wallet in his lap and tried to get his bearings. Dawn came by degrees. Stars retreated one by one. Ransom passed the time thinking of Elizabeth, searching for the feelings he had known. He untied the wallet and withdrew Elizabeth's photograph. He held her picture in both hands, trying to find an answer. In the gray of dawn, he could see Elizabeth's shape and the lightness of her face. He knew her eyes and although he could not see them clearly at the moment, he remembered. He remembered the scent of lavender too and how it kept him alive while everyone was dying. Finally, when the sun crept above the horizon and gave him light, he saw Elizabeth looking out from the photograph. Her kind eyes invited him into her life.

"I have to meet you," he said. "I have to meet you."

Later that morning, Amelia Rose stood at the back door as Ransom dumped an armload of firewood beside the steps.

"Miss Annie had the ham in bed with her," she said.

Ransom straightened his back and drew a breath.

"This is a good place," Amelia Rose said. "We can make a life here." With a nod to the large pile of fire wood Ransom had stacked, she said, "You brought more than enough to see us through the next few days. You don't have to wear yourself out."

"I'm just trying to get y'all ahead. If I'm going to be a cotton broker, I have to do it this year while cotton's selling at the war price. There won't be any money in it after that."

"Oh." Amelia Rose straightened her spine and set her jaw.

"I have to go," he said. "It's what I started out to do."

"But we're good together. Maybe we ain't like two candles just yet, but we will be. Give it time."

"That's your dream, Amelia Rose. Not mine."

Amelia Rose withdrew to the kitchen and Ransom followed. He stood near the stove and watched as she helped herself to his pack. She took the lard tin with the last of the coffee and cornmeal and set it on the counter, then felt in the corners and pulled out the sachet wrapped in brown paper and tied with string. She held it under her nose and smelled of it. Then she shook it gently and heard the faintest rattle.

"Seeds," Ransom said.

Without a word or a glance, she loosened the knot and folded back the paper. It contained several smaller packets, each held a tablespoon or more of seed and was labeled in Mrs. Massey's neat hand: tomato, okra, squash, corn, pumpkin, pepper, watermelon, four kinds of beans, sweet peas, and a packet of tiny seeds marked tobacco. The seeds were better than money in the bank. Amelia Rose stashed them in the lard tin.

Ransom went to the barn and made two rabbit boxes from boards stacked in a corner. He tested the long rectangular traps several times to ensure the door would fall and lock the rabbit inside. He carried them to the open kitchen door where Amelia Rose stood watching.

"These will get you some meat when you need it," he said, walking past her into the kitchen. He put the traps on the counter and began gathering his things. "I saw a rabbit this morning, out at the barn."

"You don't know spit about this girl," Amelia Rose said. "And she don't know spit about you. All you got is letters and a picture. What if she doesn't like you? What are you going to do then?"

"I have to see it through," Ransom said. "I never asked you to come along."

"But things have changed!" Amelia Rose pressed closer to him. "You didn't know we'd meet. I wasn't looking, but if I'd known you were in the world before this, I'd come hunting you. And I'd find you too. I don't know how, but I would. If I'd known you were hurting over there in France, I'd have gone all that way and got you my own self. I wouldn't let you lay out there in that no man's place for five days."

"I believe you," Ransom said.

"Can't you see what we got? We can make a life together. It might not be all that fancy, not at first, but we can work up to it. We don't have to start out in a big painted house. We'll get there in time. I can help with your cotton business right here." Amelia

Rose pointed to the woods." I bet somebody's growing cotton just over those pines there."

Ransom slung the mostly empty pack over his shoulder and felt the wallet and Bible slap against his back. He tried to touch Amelia Rose, but she pulled away.

"We both got lucky buckeyes," she said. "Don't that mean anything to you?"

Ransom reached again, but she would not let him touch her.

"We just went through hell together and we come out okay. Damn it, we come out better than we went in. Your prettied-up girl couldn't do that. You'd still be out there in the swamp, carrying her on your back. You think she'd know how to stew up crawfish to keep you alive?"

"I got a dream," he said. "I can't let it go."

"Don't you feel anything for me?"

"I feel..." Ransom couldn't find the words. "I do," he said. "I do feel something and it's damn confusing. That's why I have to go."

"Ain't there anything to keep you here?"

It took him a long time to answer.

"I have to see this through."

Amelia Rose set her jaw and stepped back.

"All right then," she said. "If there's nothing here to keep you, you should go. Go on. Go find the girl in the picture. Why do I have to work so damn hard just so somebody will love me?"

Ransom wanted to hold Amelia Rose. He wanted to feel her warmth, his arms around her, her breasts pressed against him. He wanted to hold his heart to hers and feel that magic bond again but it had vanished and left him feeling empty and off-balance.

"Goodbye, Amelia Rose," he said. "I..."

"Go on." She shooed him out the back door. "We don't need you. We'll get by just fine. You don't know what you're missing. You don't know the half of it."

He crossed through the high weeds and started down the roadbed leading away from the house. At the woods, he stopped to look back and saw Amelia Rose watching from the kitchen window. He waved, but she only closed the tattered drape. He shoved his hand in a pocket and rubbed his buckeye, hoping to see her at the window again, but she didn't appear. He waited for a sign, for the drape to move or for Amelia Rose to step out the back door. But, there was no sign, just an old farm house rotting into the ground.

Ransom followed the roadbed into the woods. After a short distance, he stopped and looked back. Still Amelia Rose did not come to the window. Finally, he turned and walked away.

17

Soon after leaving the old woman's place, Ransom came to a well-traveled road. The new road led southeast and that was the direction he took. This was low country. Water lay on the ground. Vines and briars tangled in the brush so thick a man couldn't enter the woods without first chopping a path.

Late in the morning, he heard the growl of a machine in the air. It was on him in a rush.

A yellow biplane skimmed the treetops, so close he could have hit it with a rock. In the passenger's seat, in front of the pilot, a woman screamed and laughed. When the plane passed over, it trailed behind it the harsh noise of a cast-iron engine.

Ransom met no one on the road until noon when he stopped for water at a tumbled down house set back a few feet from the road. A young girl, with straight black hair trimmed in a bowl cut, sat on a stack of newly made cedar roof shingles and played with the curled shavings scattered on the ground. Constellations of small red sores covered the girl's legs, the festering bites of chiggers, bedbugs and mosquitoes. At the well, Ransom helped himself to a drink. The girl watched him and carefully arranged curled wood shavings in her hair.

"See my curls?" The little girl said.

"You're about as pretty as they come." Ransom tried to smile.

The girl stared at him, but there was nothing more to say. Ransom managed a quick wave. She waved back and he started down the road again.

Late in the day, he came to a farm on the edge of a small town. He joined a crowd gathered at a pasture fence as they watched the yellow biplane coming in to land. The machine swooped low then circled over the trees as it lined up on the long axis of the pasture. The engine throttled back until it nearly quit.

For a moment, it seemed to hang in the air, its nose pointing skyward ever so slightly. Then, with all the grace of a dropped sack of grits, it fell the last ten feet into the pasture and bounced, its wings tilting wildly from side to side. It bounced again and again, each bounce smaller than the last, until it rolled to a stop in the center of the pasture.

"Can't see how it stays in the air," a farmer said. The last bit of a smoldering cigarette, rolled in newspaper, dangled forgotten from his lips. "I heard about it, but to see it is something else."

In the pasture, the pilot killed the engine and climbed from the cockpit to help the woman passenger out. Bold letters painted on the fuselage beneath the cockpit spelled out the pilot's name: Captain Henry "Ace" Edwards.

"He come in early yesterday," the farmer said, "landed right out there like he owned the place, scared the wits out of Sister Bowen. She locked herself in the pantry for three hours, but she likes the boy now. Women fall in love with him like nobody's business. I suppose there'll be a fight before it's over. Somebody's husband will have to set him straight."

The farmer spit the last fleck of cigarette to the ground and rubbed it out with a boot held together with bailing wire threaded through the sole.

"If you're hunting work," the farmer said, "go up to the house and talk to Eugene Bowen. He can't get no work out of his son on account his daughter-in-law's stupid in love with the boy driving that thing. I bet they'd feed you good."

On his way to the farmhouse, Ransom passed a flock of giggling women. In the pasture, Captain "Ace" Edwards helped another woman into the passenger seat.

Painted pristine white and trimmed in dark blue, the two-story farmhouse faced the road with a wide front porch. Pecan trees shaded a swept yard. Ransom followed the drive to the back, where a windmill pumped water into a cistern raised on timbers. The barn and outbuildings were all painted red. At the gate to the pasture, a middle-aged man in spotless overalls stood cleaning his nails with a jackknife. Beyond him in the pasture, the plane cranked and spewed blue smoke.

"Sir, I'm told you can use some help." Ransom had to shout to be heard above the plane's engine.

"Who told you that?"

"Somebody down by the road." Ransom pointed to the spectators hanging on the pasture fence.

"Somebody ought to mind their own business."

"Yes sir." Ransom turned to go.

"I won't pay you anything, but I'll feed you and you can sleep in the barn." He eyed Ransom's soiled and ragged overalls. "My wife won't let you at the table looking like that. You got anything better to wear?"

"No sir."

"Then you'll have to eat out the back door."

Ransom spent the rest of the day working for the farmer's son. They built a temporary fence out of barbed wire and locust tree posts to keep the cows away from the airplane. The son, who was only slightly older than Ransom, mostly sat in the shade and chewed on his fingernails. Ransom was hammering a staple into the last post when the dinner bell rang. Without a word, the son left his shady haven and marched off toward the farmhouse, leaving Ransom to gather the tools and carry them back to the barn.

Ransom washed in the water trough near the pasture gate then waited at the back steps. Soon the farmer brought him a pie tin piled high with fried chicken, rice and gravy and green beans cooked with fat meat and burnt just enough to give them extra flavor. The door opened again and the farmer appeared with a canning jar filled with coffee and a small mixing bowl of blackberry cobbler. Ransom moved from the back steps to the woodpile.

Captain "Ace" Edwards ate inside at the family table where the women laughed at his stories. Ransom heard the dinner chatter through an open window, just as plain as if he was sitting in there with them. The daughter-in-law laughed the loudest, but the farmer's wife laughed too. Ransom heard little from the farmer or his son, except when they asked for more rice and gravy.

The cobbler was so good Ransom wanted to tell somebody about it and thought of Amelia Rose. She would have loved the cobbler. When he was finished eating, Ransom leaned back against the woodpile to rest his belly.

Captain Ace Edwards stepped from the back door and stood on the stoop picking his teeth. He did not see Ransom and neither did the daughter-in-law when she leaned out the back door and kissed Ace right on the lips.

In the barn, Ace had taken the tack room as his own. Searching for horse blankets while the pilot was tending to his plane, Ransom peered inside the small room and saw a military cot properly dressed with wool blankets. A corked pint bottle of Doctor Clover's Vitality Booster lay on the pillow.

The barn housed two mules and a horse, each in a separate stall. In the center of the barn, near the back, Ransom made a nest in a pile of loose hay and lined it with a couple of blankets, then stretched out to read Elizabeth's letters.

Ace returned to the barn in the last moments of daylight. The pilot walked up to Ransom nestled in the hay and stood over him like a man accustomed to dominating others.

"Where are you headed?" Ace said.

"A little town called Pocotaligo. It's on the coast, just north of Savannah."

"That's not a town. It's a swamp." Ace leaned a shoulder on a post. "I'll fly you there for ten dollars."

"I'll walk it," Ransom said.

"Spoken like a man with more time than money." Ace walked back to the tack room, his boots kicking up little clouds of dust. "It's just as well." Ace paused at the door to the tack room. "The sheriff there tried to kill me once. It seems we're both partial to a certain lady."

Long after the sun had set and the night lay cool and quiet,

Ransom woke to the sound of the barn door creaking open. A figure slipped inside. Ransom could make out the smooth curve of a woman's hip and the translucent fabric of a nightgown. The woman went into the tack room and closed the door. Moments later, Ransom heard giggles and rough knocking. Soon they were laughing.

Ransom couldn't sleep and left the barn to walk the starlit pasture. A dog howled far off in the woods as Ransom approached the biplane. Ropes tied the wings and tail to stakes driven into the ground. A small oil-stained tarp lay draped over the engine.

Ransom touched the skin of the plane with an open hand, just as he would a fine horse. Cables stretched diagonally between the upper and lower wing. He stepped up and peered into the cockpit. The fuselage was like a sculpted basket of wooden ribs covered with taut canvas, hardly more substantial than a kite.

He lowered himself into the pilot's seat and placed his knees on either side of the joystick. He grasped it with both hands and pulled it back. The wings moaned and he stopped, afraid he might break the thing. It felt so alien to him.

He recalled the dogfight he'd seen over no man's land, the scream and whine of engines, the sound of machine guns in the sky. Even now, in this peaceful place, he could hear the sounds of war and feel the dread.

When he returned to the barn, the door creaked opened before he reached it. The farmer's daughter-in-law slipped out. He stood not three feet from her, close enough to catch the scent of bath powder. She gasped when she saw him and hurried to the house.

Ransom lay in the hay and listened to the mice scampering between the stalls. He thought of Elizabeth, but he was lonely for Amelia Rose. He missed her, but he couldn't turn back. He had to keep going.

A plan began to form in his mind. It began with the farmer's daughter-in-law and ended with him in Pocotaligo. When he'd thought his plan through, he carried his pack out to the plane and stowed it behind the passenger's seat. Not sure how long it might be until dawn, he waited on the woodpile for someone to stir in the house.

Ransom had dozed when he woke to the sound of a cock crowing in a nearby tree. A light shone from the kitchen window. He rose, stretched out the tight places in his back then tapped on the back door. The daughter-in-law appeared with a mug of hot coffee which she passed through the door to him.

"We have a secret, don't we?" She said.

"Yes ma'am." Ransom sipped the coffee, so full of cream and sugar it tasted like candy.

"Would you like something special for breakfast?"

"I just eat what's put in front of me."

"This morning, I'll make you something special. What do you like best?"

"Onions," Ransom said.

"Onions?" She looked surprised.

"Fried onions and scrambled eggs is my favorite."

"Fried onions." She hesitated as though she might try to negotiate then said, "Okay."

"And could you chop the onions real fine?" Ransom said. "I like that."

"Glad to," she said, but she didn't look happy about it.

Ransom sat on the woodpile and enjoyed the coffee while across the county roosters crowed. When he thought the time was right, he went to the barn and rapped on the tack room door.

"Go away," Ace said. "I'll eat when I'm ready."

"The farmer and his son know about you and the woman." Ransom tried to sound convincing. He wasn't used to lying. "They caught her sneaking back into the house last night. I heard them talking."

The door of the tack room flew open. Ace stood in the doorway wearing only briefs. In his hand, he held the uncorked bottle of Doctor Clover's Vitality Booster. He turned it up and took a swig.

"The lady's in there now, bawling her eyes out," Ransom said. "These are country people. You can bet they got a shotgun and don't mind using it either. If you want to live another day, you better make a run for it. The sun will be up soon."

Ace dressed and put on his boots but didn't bother to lace them up. With his shirt tail out and his hair mussed, he hurried to the woodpile, where he climbed up to peek through the kitchen window. At the sink, the daughter-in-law stood over a cutting board, her eyes red and swollen with tears streaming down her cheeks.

Ace sprinted back to the barn and threw his things together.

"You have to crank the plane," he said, shoving blankets into a canvas bag. "I need you to turn the prop."

"This isn't my fight," Ransom said. "I like these people. I can't help you get away then eat their breakfast like nothing happened."

"What do you want? I'll pay you."

"If you go, I have to go with you," Ransom said. "I can't stay here, not with them so fired up. They're liable to shoot me if they can't shoot you."

"I'll fly you to Pocotaligo," Ace said. "Will you do it?"

"All right then." Ransom nodded. "But I don't like it."

In a mad flurry, Ace gathered his things and stuffed them in a duffle bag. With light just peeking over the horizon, they sprinted from the barn. Not slowing to open the pasture gate, they scrambled over it. In seconds, Ace untethered the wings and tail, and stripped the canvas cover from the engine before climbing into the cockpit. Ace fumbled with the contact switch then coached Ransom through turning the prop.

Ransom grasped the propeller and heaved with all his strength, throwing his weight into the effort. The cold, damp engine coughed and spat and died.

Ransom tried again. Still, the engine only coughed.

Ace watched the farmhouse and became more desperate with each passing second. Ransom spun the propeller a third time. It spat and sputtered and nearly died before spewing a plume of smoke.

While Ace steered the rolling plane, Ransom scrambled around the wings to climb into the passenger seat. Ace lined the plane up for take-off and opened the throttle. The engine picked up speed, driving the plane faster and faster. It bounced for the sky and settled back to earth, then bounced again, jarring every bone in Ransom's body. Once, the nose pointed skyward but leveled again toward the pasture fence. The woods rushed at them. Another bounce and the nose kept rising. The wheels left the ground and the plane swayed left to right. They cleared the fence, rose above the trees and climbed higher.

18

RANSOM RODE A SCREAMING smoke-spewing magic carpet. Soon they were over a river where a flock of egrets erupted from their roost and scattered like white linen. A brilliant sunrise painted the eastern sky. Fiery oranges and reds set the scattered clouds ablaze and shot golden rays as high as he could see.

Small towns came and went. In the fields, men worked rows of young cotton or sprouting corn. To the east, the land played out into marsh and a few islands before ending in beach and surf. Beyond that, Ransom saw nothing but ocean all the way to the horizon.

Further south, two large rivers flowed into Charleston Harbor. Ships docked along the waterfront. More ships waited in the harbor, dozens more at sea.

They flew over streets bustling with buggies and bicycles, wagons and mules and horses and automobiles and trucks. Ransom could see it all at once: the bare-knuckle neighborhoods and the sprawling mansions overlooking the harbor. On the waterfront, real ladies with slender arms waved lace handkerchiefs and called to them from the wide piazzas of mansions built side-by-side. Little boys in short pants played on manicured lawns.

South of Charleston, a hamlet appeared near vast spreading marshes. The land rose slightly above the water and the roads were all sand. Train tracks cut through the tiny town and past a gray rectangular depot. Ace nosed the plane down until they skimmed above the trees and lined up with the railroad tracks. Ransom read the depot sign as they flew over: Pocotaligo, South Carolina.

Shops and businesses lined the wide sandy main street. Eighty feet across with a covered boardwalk on each side, the street resembled a long, rambling town square with a bandstand at one end. A banner read: Pocotaligo Rose Day, July 4th.

They circled the town twice, looking for a place to land, but all Ransom could see were cotton fields, marshes and black water. The occasional pasture, squeezed between swamps, was little more than grass growing beneath tall pines. Ace banked and circled back.

"There's no place to land!" Ace shouted. He aligned the plane with the road leading into town. "Main Street's wide enough! Have to land there. They won't like it!"

They began to descend. They passed the depot and a large white house across the street from it, then slipped below the rooftops. People scattered wildly as the plane bore down on them. A wagon bolted into a side street with the driver fighting to control a team of panic-stricken horses.

The landing gear struck the ground and sent the plane careening to the left. A wingtip lifted higher, threatening to flip the plane. When the landing gear struck again, it sent the other wingtip up. The plane curved toward a barber shop then drifted toward a general store.

Ace brought the plane back to the center of the street. Another bounce, then another, and the plane settled into a screaming sprint, scattering people, terrifying horses and stirring up a great dust cloud.

Ahead of them, the bandstand blocked their way. They were slowing, but not enough, not nearly enough. Ace throttled back and the engine's terrifying growl subsided to a deep grumble. The plane slowed, but the bandstand stood firm. Finally, the tail began to drag. The plane slowed a bit more and a brown dog chased behind them, barking and baring its teeth.

"Get out!" Ace shouted. "I'm not stopping."

Ransom couldn't believe what he'd heard, but Ace repeated the order along with heated curses. With the plane still in a sprint and kicking up an enormous dust cloud, Ransom unbuckled the lap belt and grabbed his pack from behind the seat. He climbed out holding to the fuselage and stood on the wing.

"Jump!" Ace shouted and spun the plane around. "I'm not stopping. Jump!"

Ransom threw the pack and sprang head first after it. He landed on his chest and belly all at once and rolled until he came to a stop face down.

Spitting sand, he looked up to see the plane charging back the way it had come, facing the brown dog that had chased it. The dog stood frozen for an instant. Then, with a yelp, twirled around and raced wide-eyed down the street. The plane now chased the dog and was quickly gaining on it. Again, people pressed themselves against exterior walls, ducked inside buildings and hid around corners.

The nose of the plane tried for the sky but returned to earth, rolling and bouncing as it gained speed. The propeller spun a halo mere feet from the terrified dog running for its life. Another bounce sent the plane leaping over it. The tail touched down again and the startled dog once more chased the plane.

The wings swayed first to one side and then the other until finally the nose pointed up and continued to climb. Beyond the pines at the edge of town, the yellow biplane banked towards the ocean and flew out of sight.

19

IN FRONT OF THE GENERAL STORE, Ransom sat in the road and hugged the pack. The roar of the plane's engine still rang in his ears. Faces appeared in windows and around corners to stare at the stranger dropped from the sky. A man dressed in an elegant suit cussed as he swept sand from the driver's seat of a Model T.

Down the street, a sheriff slapped his hat across his trousers, knocking off clouds of dust. The lawman marched up to Ransom and stood over him. He was a thin man with a body too long and too narrow, like a stretched out rubber toy. The sheriff appeared to have been snatched from the womb by his ears which were the biggest Ransom had ever seen on a man. The lawman wore two pistols, one on each hip, and he had the soulless eyes of a poker player.

"Now we got drifters falling out of the sky," the sheriff said.

A man wearing an apron stepped from the general store. He stood on the edge of the boardwalk. Leaning on a broom, the storekeeper looked down on Ransom. Townspeople gathered around.

"You could've killed somebody," the sheriff said. "And livestock, too."

"I wasn't driving."

"Don't matter," the sheriff said. "I know the cur in that machine, but you're the reason he landed here and you're the one who's going to clean up this mess."

The storekeeper tossed the broom down to Ransom. Ransom didn't see it coming and the handle cracked him on the head.

"There are thirty-two porches on this street," the sheriff said. "They were clean this morning before you stirred things up. I expect them to be clean by the end of the day. You can get to work or you can get gone."

Ransom shouldered the pack, picked up the broom, and climbed the steps to the general store. Across the street, a colored barber watched from the door of his shop. The small crowd soon dispersed as Ransom began to sweep. When he'd nearly finished the porch of the general store, the barber crossed the street and greeted him.

"Sir," the barber said, "you could use some cleaning up." The barber was a fair skinned black man, a high yellow with wavy hair and gray-green eyes that held a person's gaze. Ransom caught his own reflection in the window of the store and didn't recognize himself. His face was painted black with burnt crankcase oil and his clothes were soiled rags stitched together.

"I used to have a courting hat." Ransom patted his hair. It was stiff with black oil and no matter how much spit he put on it, it would not lie flat.

"Do you have any money?" The barber asked.

"Not much," Ransom said, stunned by the image he'd seen in the glass. "I need it to get some new overalls."

"My son is learning the barber trade. He'll cut your hair for half price and he'll shave that bit of whisker off your chin for nothing. You can wash up in our shop for a nickel. Two bits will cover it. Can you pay?"

Ransom nodded, pleased to have someone speak to him so kindly.

"Come to the shop," the barber said. "We'll get you looking better in no time."

"I have to sweep. The sheriff will probably shoot me if I quit working."

"Yes sir, Sheriff Pate is indeed a shooting man, but if you get cleaned up and wear some new overalls, folks can get used to seeing you at your best before the day's out. You're just scaring people the way you look now. Talk to the sheriff. There's time to get cleaned up and get your work done too."

Ransom walked up the street to where the sheriff sat in a chair leaned back against the front wall of the jail house, which looked more like a converted store. Through the large display windows, he could see two cages inside made of strap iron and big enough to hold a man.

With cold eyes, the sheriff listened to Ransom and did not move. When Ransom finished explaining the barber's logic, he waited for the sheriff to speak, but the man only sat there without expression.

Finally, the sheriff nodded ever so slightly. "Get cleaned up. Then get to work."

It was a slow day for the barber. An old bald white man sat by the window, but the barber chairs were empty.

"Any of y'all know Miss Elizabeth Lyttelton?" Ransom said.

"I live out her way." The bald man chewed a matchstick and studied Ransom. "You don't look like the sort to call on such a lady. Who do I say is asking about her?

"Ransom James MacTavish."

"Are you staying at Miss Wanda's boarding house?"

"Where's that?"

"Across from the depot. You damn near landed on it. You'll find this town interesting, but watch out for the sheriff. He shot a kerosene cook stove salesman in Miss Wanda's bedroom."

"What was the sheriff doing in Miss Wanda's bedroom?" Ransom asked.

"I bet that salesman asked himself the same thing." The man chuckled. "The bullet went clean through his heart and cut his backbone in two. The sheriff thinks Miss Wanda's his girl, but Miss Wanda, she don't see it that way. If she hadn't testified the salesman was in the process of forcing himself on her, the sheriff would be in the state prison this minute. The truth is, if anybody forced anything, I'd say it was Miss Wanda."

Ransom washed his face in a basin at the back of the barber shop and had to change the water twice before it rinsed clean. With a clean face, he leaned over the basin while the son stood on an apple crate and scrubbed his hair. The son was a nervous sort, thin as a willow switch and high strung, but he did a fair job combing the tangles out of Ransom's hair and trimmed it nicely.

"Shave him and you'll be done," the barber said.

Terror filled the boy's eyes.

"It's just that little place on his chin, son. Lather him up."

With a brush, the son worked a mugful of soap into lather and dabbed it over the patch of dark whiskers growing on Ransom's chin. The rest of his face was as hairless as a child's. When the son picked up the straight razor, his hand shook.

"How many men have you shaved before?" Ransom asked, watching the chrome blade waver close to his face.

"You're the first one."

"I saw a young barber nervous like that once," the bald man said. "Shook so bad, he slipped up and cut a man's lips clean off. They just lay on the floor. That man lived the rest of his life with no lips at all. You could see the man's teeth. It looked like he was mad at you all the time. It happened right up there in Robertsville."

"That's just a story," the barber said, but the son shook all the worse for it. "You can get that little bit in one swipe. Just go like you're scraping the lather off."

The son stood on an apple crate and stretched higher on his toes. Light glinted from the straight razor as the boy pressed one hand on Ransom's chin, braced the razor and closed his eyes. Ransom could feel the trembling in the boy's fingers and moaned a protest without daring to move his jaw. In an instant, the razor scraped across Ransom's chin, leaving a cool swath behind it. The boy opened his eyes. His father stepped closer, breathed a sigh of relief, and nodded his approval. Ransom felt for blood, but his chin was smooth and whole.

"That boy might make a barber after all," the bald man said.

"Now, go over to the general store and get some new clothes," the barber said as Ransom paid him. "Get the best you can afford and be nice to people. They'll soon forget you came in here looking like a scarecrow."

At the general store, Ransom bought a pair of heavy denim overalls. They were stiff as rawhide and would chafe the inside of his legs until they were broken in, but they'd last a long time too. He also bought a work shirt and a straw hat. While he was looking at himself in the full-length mirror at the back of the store, he saw a brass bedframe leaning against the wall. It shone golden in the light. A rich man would sleep in a brass bed; he thought and promised himself that just as soon as he was rich he'd sleep in a bed like that.

"You're a new man," the storekeeper said when he saw Ransom admiring the bed frame.

"How much is it?"

"More than you got," the storekeeper said.

Ransom shouldered his pack, went outside and took up the broom again. He crossed the street to a business with a large glass window. A man's name was lettered on the glass: Doctor Lucius Lafitte, Esquire. Below the name, and lettered just as neatly, were the professions of Doctor, Dentist and Attorney. A man wearing a suit stood in the back of the office. He looked up from the open book he was holding and considered Ransom, then came to the door.

The man leaned out so only his head appeared and said, "Do you need assistance"

"May I sweep your porch?" Ransom said.

"May I pull your teeth?"

"I don't need my teeth pulled. The sheriff told me to sweep all the porches in town because he thinks I made that airplane land here and stir up the dust."

"The dust is constantly stirred up," the man said, stepping onto the boardwalk. "It is the nature of dust, and while planes may on occasion assist, dust will on its own, and without the aid of airplanes or any other mechanical device, stir itself into a naturally occurring nuisance. We are powerless against it."

"Should I sweep or not?

"The dust is not your fault," the man said. "However, I think it would be to your diplomatic advantage to humor the sheriff."

"Are you Doctor Lafitte?"

"I am indeed."

Ransom pointed to the window and to the professions listed.

"And you can do all that stuff?"

"It's not what I can do that matters, it's what people think I can do. Therein lies the secret to power."

"Which one is the Esquire, the doctor or the dentist?"

"In my case, both. An esquire was once someone aspiring to knighthood. Later it was used to address a gentleman. Now, lawyers use it to describe themselves because no one in their right mind would call them gentlemen, at least not with a straight face."

Doctor Lucius Lafitte entered his office and closed the door behind him. Then he opened the door again and leaned his head out. "I am also the mayor."

20

ACROSS FROM THE DEPOT, Ransom found the boarding house, a two-story affair with a deep porch dripping pink wisteria. Inside the white picket fence, a pair of massive pecan trees shaded the yard. Magnolias grew at the side of the house, rising as high as the rusting tin roof. Ransom let himself in at the gate and followed the brick walk up to the front porch where a calico cat groomed herself beside the door.

"If you're looking for work, you got to come to the kitchen, around back," a colored woman said when she answered the door.

Ransom walked around the house and past the magnolias. Rice birds flitted in the azaleas growing against the foundation. When he reached the kitchen, the cook spoke through the screen door.

"Miss Wanda don't need no help," she said.

"Temperance?" A woman called from deep inside the house. "To whom are you speaking?"

"That man what flied here."

Footsteps approached. The face of a white woman appeared behind Temperance. She was a mature woman. Long black hair, streaked with traces of gray, flowed down her back. She wore a green silk gown and makeup that drew Ransom's gaze to her lips.

"Nigel didn't take kindly to you landing in his town," she said with the slow, honeyed accent of a Charleston lady. "I think he might have shot you if he hadn't so recently killed a man. I'm Wanda." She turned her back to Ransom and walked away. "Let him in, Temperance," Wanda said over her shoulder. "He's such a man, stupid in a charming sort of way."

Ransom entered the kitchen where several pots boiled on the stove and filled the air with dampness. Steam fogged and streaked the windows. He caught a glimpse of Wanda as she left the kitchen. Her hips undulated beneath the silk robe like a fluid invitation.

"We can visit in the sitting room," she said and motioned over her shoulder for Ransom to follow.

Through the dining room, he negotiated his way around a long table with wooden legs carved like dragons. Ransom stepped into the hall in time to see Wanda go into a room at the front of the house. He found her there, seated on the sofa, barefoot and apparently naked beneath the gown. She crossed one leg over the other at the knee. The top leg kicked the air, parting the green silk gown to her thigh. Ransom hesitated at the door.

"Come in." She rattled the ice in a tall glass before taking a drink.

"You're not dressed, ma'am."

"Yes, I know," she said. "I'm being naughty. Naughty is my nature, Love. I'm as dressed as I'm going to be before dinner."

Entering the room, Ransom forced himself to avoid Wanda's seductive gaze. Instead, he looked at the photographs on the wall. Many were of foreign places and distant seaports.

"That's my husband," she said, "my *late* husband." She pointed to a picture of a distinguished older man in the uniform of a ship's captain. "He was lost at sea seven years ago. We were best friends. I loved him dearly and he loved me. Now all I have are memories. Memories are so important." She tried to get up from the sofa, but fell back into it. "Damn these sinking spells. You have no idea how difficult it is to be a woman." Pointing to the piano bench, she said, "Look in there for my pills."

Ransom moved a bottle of Puerto Rican rum from the bench and lifted the hinged seat. He found only yellow and aging sheet music.

"Pills," she said. "A little bottle of pills."

He leafed through the papers until he found a small brown glass bottle. Wanda uncorked it and tapped a few pills into her hand. Her gown opened dangerously wide and Ransom averted his gaze. When he looked back again, Wanda smiled ever so slightly.

"I see you've discovered that I'm a woman." She tossed the pills in her mouth and washed them down with a gulp of rum. Then took another drink and studied Ransom. "What do you want?"

"I want to stay here, but I'm out of money," Ransom said. "I can work."

"Sit down," she said, patting the sofa cushion beside her.

Her eyes had gone soft and dreamy and her breasts jiggled beneath the green silk each time she moved. No matter where Ransom tried to look, his eyes came back to Wanda's breasts. He sat on the sofa, but not too close, and breathed in her perfume, the scent of roses mixed with a titillating underscore of musk.

"Why on earth would you come to this abysmal town?" She reached for his hand but stopped short, letting her finger tips touch his. "Is it a woman?"

"Business," Ransom said.

"Business? You couldn't come on the train or by motorcar like my other boarders?"

"Miss Wanda?" Temperance called from the kitchen. "John Divine Christopher Columbus be here. He got a letter for that man you with."

"Interesting." Wanda pushed herself up from the sofa. "You haven't been in town a day and already you have a letter."

They went in the kitchen, where an old gray black gentleman stood at the kitchen door. He held a ragged hat in his hand and a crisp, cream-colored envelope. Wanda sat down at the kitchen table with the bottle of Puerto Rican rum and her glass. She motioned for Ransom to join her. When Ransom took a seat, Wanda moved her chair next to his until they touched. She pressed her thigh to Ransom's and took the envelope from John Divine as he settled into a chair across the table.

Wanda brought the letter to her nose. "Lavender," she said. "I'm jealous already." Ransom reached for the envelope, but Wanda slipped it between her breasts. It disappeared somewhere beneath her silk gown.

"Miss Elizabeth give me that letter to give to him," John Divine said, pointing to Ransom. "You the man come in on that airplane, ain't you?"

"Elizabeth Lyttelton?" Wanda looked to Ransom with eyes filled with amazement. "Damn if I haven't heard it all. Her father hires and fires men like you every day. She couldn't be any further out of your reach if she lived on the back side of the moon."

"But," Ransom said. "I'm not like me." His eyes stole back to that tender place between Wanda's breasts. "I met a cotton broker in France. He's backing me in buying and selling cotton."

Wanda looked at Ransom with eyes as dreamy and as sultry as a long morning in bed.

"The truth is," she said, "I have designs on you myself. But, let's not be crude." She placed a hand over her bosom. "Ransom, you and I can work things out between us any time. John Divine doesn't come around every day and he usually has a juicy story to tell. He picks up work all over the county, sleeps in people's barns and hears things along the way. He's got the skinny on everything from Estill to Hilton Head."

"Ain't all of it worth telling," John Divine said. "But, you know them two brothers out by Purrsyburg Landing? They both got a bushel of children, little ones right on up to working size. And last year, they switched wives. Or maybe the wives switched husbands. I ain't sure how to tell it. The wives and the children stayed in they own house, but the mens, they just walked over to the other's place and took up with the other's wife. That was last year. This year, they moved back to the woman and children they started with."

"I suppose one man's about as good as the next," Wanda said.

"Ain't none of 'em all that good, no way," Temperance said. "If a man ain't a drunk and if he don't beat you and if he'll work some and take care of the babies, why, that's a good man."

"I'll tell you another thing that ain't right," John Divine said. "They's a rum runner out 'round Hilton Head, bringing rum up from Puerto Rico."

"Is that right?" Wanda said as Temperance poured rum straight from the bottle into John Divine's coffee.

"John Divine," Wanda said, "don't tell anyone who you saw here.

You know how the sheriff can be." Standing up, she braced a hand on the back of Ransom's chair to steady herself.

"No ma'am," John Divine said.

"I'm feeling weak and wish to retire," she said. "Ransom, you can stay here and work until the sheriff finds out. Nigel tends to shoot the men I find interesting." She reached between her breasts and retrieved the letter, dropping it on the table in front of Ransom.

The letter was warm in his hand. He tore into it as Wanda walked away, her hips slithering beneath green silk.

Dear Ransom,

Thank God you are here. I thought you would never arrive. Knowing you were on your way quickened my heart and raised my spirits. Thanks to you, my days are fresh again and worth living.

I go to Christ Church each Sunday with my parents. Please join us in the morning. I'd like my father to see you, although, I must warn you, he is quite suspicious.

Affectionately yours,
Elizabeth

"Elizabeth wants me to meet her at Christ Church in the morning," Ransom said to Temperance as he folded the letter and slipped it back into the envelope. "I can't go to Christ Church in overalls."

"The only suit we got here is the one what belonged to that kerosene cook stove salesman Miss Wanda was laying with," Temperance said. "It's bad stained but I can clean it up some. Won't nobody know, if they don't look too close. But you got to do something for me if I get that suit ready."

"Like what?"

"Shrimps," Temperance said. "I like shrimps and crabs. Catch me some of them and we'll be square."

"I don't know anything about catching shrimp or crab."

"Go out to the bluff and talk with Froggy. He'll show you how."

John Divine Christopher Columbus left after Temperance

wrapped squares of cornbread in wax paper for him to take. Ransom spent the afternoon at the kitchen table while Temperance scrubbed the suit in a washtub. The biting odor of ammonia filled the air as she worked the wet fabric up and down a washboard. Ransom went to the back door and opened it to let a breeze blow through the kitchen.

Temperance seemed to be about his age. She was very dark with round features, but she wasn't fat like a lot of women who worked in kitchens. She pulled the shirt from the suds and inspected the stain that blighted nearly the entire front. After scrubbing it between her hands, she inspected the stain again.

"Good Lord," she said, "this here is going to take some time."

That evening at supper, Wanda dressed magnificently and played hostess in grand style. She charmed the boarders, all of them men. Two were traveling salesmen. One who'd checked in just that afternoon sold gasoline-powered irons he claimed would revolutionize the care of clothing. Wanda asked for a demonstration after dinner. The other salesman was a veteran boarder who seemed to know everyone. He talked faster than Ransom cared to listen about the wonders of his patent medicines, Doctor Clover's Vitality Booster and Baby Silencer.

"Baby Silencer is a mother's best friend," he said. "It contains only the highest quality opium extract and medicinal grade alcohol. I personally guarantee it will ease a child into sleep. It works equally well on older children and adults."

"I'll take a bottle," Wanda said.

After supper, Ransom carried a red railman's kerosene lantern to the bathhouse and prepared a tub of unheated well water. The day had been hot and he was eager to cool off. He lathered up in the tub and was scrubbing the rust from between his toes when the door opened. Wanda entered with a glass of ice and a bottle of rum, a little unsteady on her feet. Ransom covered his privates with a washrag.

"Relax, my love," she said. "I've led more men to bed than General Pershing ever led to battle." She settled on a stool beside the tub. "You are amazingly naive, even for a man, and helpless as a kitten in a coal bin. If you want Elizabeth Lyttelton and if you want to be a big time cotton broker, you better start acting like something big time, or at least like a man on his way to the big time. For purely selfish reasons, I'll help you. No one knows the interplay between a woman and man better than I do. You made a grand entrance, we can build on that. You're new in town, so keep your mouth shut. Women will think you're mysterious. You smile too much. It makes you look stupid."

She leaned close and placed a hand on Ransom's bare shoulder. Her breath blew warm across his ear.

"Money brings out the worst in people." Wanda pulled a bottle of Baby Silencer from the folds of her dress and sprinkled a few drops in her glass. "Ansel Deadwilder controls every piece of lint grown between Savannah and Charleston. If you take business from him, he'll crush you like a mouse turd. Are you ready for that?"

"I hadn't thought that far ahead," Ransom said.

"You can walk out of here tonight." Now that she was drunk, she did not sound Southern. "You'll just be something for us to talk about for a while. I'll miss you and I'll miss the fun we could have had together."

She wavered on the stool. When she tilted too far forward, she gripped his wet shoulder tightly for support.

"I'm not leaving," he said. "I came here for Elizabeth."

"But is Elizabeth here for you? That's the question."

Ransom didn't answer. She passed him the glass of rum and he took a sip.

"I wish I could be young and foolish in love again." Wanda sighed and took the glass back. "Before I married," she said, "I was a dancer in New York." Her accent slipped and she sounded more like a Yankee. "I was beautiful then and made Charles fall in love with me. He came to every show for three weeks and every time he brought me the biggest bouquet of roses. Within a month, we were married. Then he began sailing out of Savannah. We moved down here and bought this extraordinary house. Charles didn't need people. He had his ship and he had the sea. But I live for others approval. I have to have it or I will die. My Love, a New Yorker is not accepted down here, not at all, not even a little bit. I had to learn to talk like these people. No, that's not right. Actually, I had to learn to talk like their superior. Now, they think I belong here more than they do."

"You have money," Ransom said.

"It doesn't take money." With a smile, she resumed her aristo-cratic Charleston accent. "It takes belief. Tomorrow you'll go to Christ Church and say very little. Do *not* smile. Do not be kind. Then, we see what happens." Rising from the stool, Wanda pressed her weight on Ransom's bare shoulder then staggered out the door.

21

SUNDAY WAS A DAY OF REST. Nobody worked the fields and everyone, except the most incorrigible, went to church. Dressed in the dead salesman's suit and carrying Mrs. Massey's Bible, Ransom left the boarding house about an hour after sunrise. He passed a mockingbird singing from a fence post, greeting the day with its own hallelujah. He could smell the salt air blowing in from the marshes.

The road paralleled a train track leading from town. For the first mile, a crow followed Ransom, flying beside the road from one tree top to the next. But the bird lost interest when Ransom stopped at a vast oak-lined drive where a most unusual short train was parked on a side rail.

The train was no more than an engine and a caboose with three cars in between: A luxury coach, a Pullman car and a car that must have been a kitchen because of a metal smoke stack on one end and the delightful smells of coffee and frying bacon coming from it. Black, and trimmed in brass, every inch of the train had been waxed and polished. It was the cleanest, most beautiful train Ransom had ever seen. An oval brass sign mounted just below the engineer's window proclaimed in flowing letters: Roebuck Railways.

A middle-aged man dressed in the impeccable uniform of an engineer climbed down from the caboose. He motioned to Ransom.

"Are you lost?" The engineer braced beside the caboose and raised his chin in a posture of superiority. He considered Ransom with a stern look of suspicion.

"I was just admiring your train," Ransom said. "It's perfect."

"It belongs to Mister Roebuck, a member here at the Yamassee Club. Whenever he's here, his train and I stand ready. I've driven this train on nearly every stretch of commercial rail in the country. Sometimes Mister Roebuck is on board, but mostly we run empty to deliver documents. I've taken this train to Denver, Detroit, San Francisco, New York, Philadelphia, Boston and Chicago just to get a single contract signed."

"All that for a piece of paper," Ransom said. "It must've cost a fortune."

"An *important* piece of paper," the engineer said, raising his chin to new heights of superiority. "And it did cost a fortune, but Mister Roebuck made an even greater fortune in the transaction. It's the way the members do business when they're here at the Yamassee Club. In the fall, during the hunting season, every member brings their own private train. I've seen a dozen parked along this side rail."

"That's some kind of big money," Ransom said.

The engineer swept a hand toward Ransom, motioning him to leave. "Please go away so I may return to my breakfast and paper. It's Sunday. I have no intention of entertaining you or anyone else."

Walking from the polished train, Ransom looked up the long drive. Crushed oyster shell gravel covered the entire stretch in a brilliant white ribbon. Mature oaks, fifty or more, lined each side. The drive looked to be half a mile long and led up to a massive brick plantation house, mostly obscured by trees.

Ransom continued to follow the dirt road and felt the heat on his shoulders as the sun rose higher. Finally, he came to Christ Church where automobiles and fancy buggies with fine horses gathered in the yard. Christ Church was a surprisingly small building that squatted so close to the ground a cat couldn't crawl under it. It stood on a rise of soil, less than a hill but dry and sheltered beneath the moss-draped arms of ancient oaks.

Ransom paused to inspect his clothes. The bullet had passed through the brown jacket near the top button and out the back just below the collar. The cloth puckered where Temperance had mended the bullet holes and each mended place was circled with the faintest halo of a blood stain. Ransom straightened his tie and smoothed a wrinkle from the jacket. Then, clinging to Mrs. Massey's Bible, he advanced on the church.

Inside the narrow church, the morning sun streamed through stained glass windows, bathing the interior with brilliant reds and blues. The priest wore a white robe trimmed in gold and stood behind the pulpit waiting, not so patiently, for Ransom to find a seat.

He sat on the back pew, beside a thin woman with thick glasses that made her look like an insect. The church had a hushed feel like the great cathedral he visited in Paris. Except this tiny church could have fit in the corner of Notre Dame and gone unnoticed until time to sweep up.

Ransom studied the backs of people's heads, searching for Elizabeth. He looked for blond hair, but all he saw were women's hats. In the center of the front row, directly in front of the priest, an elderly black man sat looking up at the pulpit. He was the only colored person in the congregation and he sat alone on the front pew.

When the congregation stood to sing, Ransom spotted Elizabeth on the fourth row. She turned and whispered something to a woman beside her who Ransom thought must be her mother. Perhaps feeling his eyes on her, she looked back through the congregation, past countless faces. When their eyes met, she smiled. The clean line of her lips and her perfect teeth made Ransom weak at the knees. Creamy skin with the slightest blush on her cheeks begged for his touch. Her blue eyes, clear and innocent, fixed him in place and purged his brain of all intelligence.

During the sermon, the preacher didn't have much to say and what little he did say was rather tame. He didn't threaten anyone with hell's fire and he failed to serve guilt as thoroughly as might be expected. Ransom attributed this to the man's youth and inexperience. Mostly they rose up to sing and knelt to pray, over and over again. It was a lot of unnecessary work for a Sunday morning, but it kept everyone awake.

After the service, people emptied into the aisles and stood around talking. Making his way to the front and closer to Elizabeth, Ransom slipped around and between parishioners. He was greeted cordially by a pair of men who asked who he was, where he was from and what sort of business he was in.

"Cotton," Ransom said.

"Aren't we all," a mature gentleman said with a chuckle. He pointed to the middle-aged man in a black suit who had sat near Elizabeth during the service. "That's Ansel Deadwilder, he's the cotton broker here. You should get to know him. If you get a line on cotton, he'll do business with you." Ransom thanked the man and turned to go. Then the man asked, "Do you know anything about horses?"

"No sir," Ransom said. "I prefer mules. A horse tends to step on the crop."

"I meant race horses," the man said and chuckled again.

The old black man, who had been sitting alone on the front pew, wove his way towards Ransom. His dark skin had aged and weathered into deep wrinkles. He worked his way around the man who owned race horses and fixed his watery eyes on Ransom, smiling a kind toothless smile.

"Welcome to our church." The man grasped Ransom's arm with a calloused hand then patted Ransom's shoulder, saying, "I like that suit." He continued down the aisle, weaving around the white parishioners as he made his way out the door and into the sun.

"Ransom," Elizabeth said as she pushed her way towards him. "I thought you'd never get here." She threw her arms around his neck. "Thank you for coming."

The surprise of her greeting paralyzed him. For a moment, he couldn't think. He couldn't even move. The scent of vanilla lingered about her and he breathed it in. By the time he thought to hug her, she had pulled away.

She took a step back and her soft blue eyes drank him in. Her eyes made him think of angels. Ransom lost himself again and feared he wasn't good enough. A round, elderly woman pressed behind her. Elizabeth took the woman by the hand and pulled her up to Ransom.

"This is Miss Hazel Wintergreen," Elizabeth said. "She's the postmistress in town and my personal tutor."

"I can also be her chaperone should the situation require it," Miss Hazel said with a smile. The short, buxom postmistress hugged his neck and whispered in his ear. "Your letters have cheered Elizabeth up more than you know. Now that you're here, she is positively beaming." Miss Hazel pecked a kiss on Ransom's cheek and released him. "I am so pleased," she said, "so very pleased."

Ransom saw Ansel Deadwilder working the crowd like a politician, shaking the hand of every man he came to until he joined Elizabeth and Miss Hazel. He offered Ransom his hand as well, but when they shook there was nothing friendly in it.

"I recognize that suit," he said, pointing his finger like a pistol. "They should have buried it too."

"I'm told you're in cotton," Ransom said.

"I'm told you want to be."

Elizabeth forced her way between Ransom and Ansel. "What's it like to fly?" she said.

"It's like nothing I've ever done before. I could see everything, the whole world. We flew over Charleston, out over the water and over houses. I could practically touch the people on the ground. It's like being free, freer than you can imagine."

"I've flown before," Ansel said, "but I didn't make a show of it."

"Elizabeth!" Her mother pressed through the crowd to join them. "Your father is waiting in the Ford." She glanced at Ransom then turned back to her daughter. "It's time to go."

"Mother," Elizabeth said, "this is Ransom MacTavish."

"Good to meet you," her mother said. Without making eye contact she pulled Elizabeth away from Ransom and down the aisle toward the front of the church. Miss Hazel smiled uncomfortably and dismissed herself to follow Elizabeth and her mother. At the front of the church, Elizabeth paused just long enough to look back at Ransom. She smiled and Ransom felt his heart reach for her. Then, with a tug that startled them both, Elizabeth's mother pulled her out the door.

"You're wasting your time," Ansel said. "Her parents have raised her to marry a man of substance, a man with resources equal to her father's or greater. I've known Elizabeth all my life and I will not stand idly by while you take advantage of her grief."

"It's not like that," Ransom said and walked away.

On his way back to town, Ransom saw a man on a motorcycle far in the distance and racing closer. A cloud of dust trailed behind the machine and drifted into the trees like heavy smoke. Ransom slipped out of the suit jacket and draped it across his shoulder. In the heat, it had begun to smell of ammonia. He stopped to admire a cotton field, the young plants and the clean rows. The tender leaves had wilted and were drooping in the heat.

The man on the motorcycle was suddenly on him. Ransom recognized the sheriff moments before the lawman throttled down and rolled past with Ransom's pack tied to the seat. The sheriff turned the Indian motorcycle around and came back to stop beside Ransom.

"Where you headed?" The sheriff raised his goggles to his forehead to reveal a mask of clean flesh around his eyes surrounded with dirt stained cheeks. A dust cloud swirled around them both.

Ransom pointed down the road. "Back to town."

"To Wanda's boarding house?" The sheriff said.

Ransom nodded.

"No, you ain't." Sheriff Pate tossed Ransom's pack in the sand. "I killed the last man who wore that suit." The sheriff yanked the goggles over his eyes, revved the engine and headed back to town, spewing dust in his wake.

22

AT PINE BLUFF, a clay cliff overlooking the Broad River, Ransom found an old man with stringy white hair and beard sitting on the end of a dilapidated pier. The old man sipped tea from a bone china cup and wore a soiled hat made of folded newspaper that fit his head as snuggly as a skullcap. Across the river and beyond the marshes, the land rose into sand dunes, beyond which the Atlantic Ocean stretched on forever.

A shack made of salvaged roofing tin and driftwood stood in the shade of a live oak. A scrap of nautical canvas hung where a door might have been. Tea crates were arranged like chairs around a fire pit where steam rose from an iron kettle warming in the embers.

A Bible lay open on one of the tea crates. Many pages had been torn from it and the ragged remains of paper were crinkled near the spine. An unhitched wagon with two large wooden barrels tied upright in the bed was backed up to the pier. Down in a low place and nearly out of sight, a black mule grazed on sea oats.

Ransom stepped cautiously along the rotted pier to where the old man dangled calloused feet off the end. An outgoing tide washed against the ragged pilings and made the pier tremble.

"Are you Froggy?" Ransom said to the man's back and stepped closer.

"Dammit to hell." The old man turned and looked over his shoulder at Ransom. "You run 'em off."

"Who?" Ransom took a step back.

"Didn't you see 'em? Where are your manners? We were visiting."

"What?" Ransom said. "I didn't see anybody."

"The dolphins." The old man spit off the end of the pier. It sailed through an arch before splashing lightly on the water.

Ransom looked for dolphins but saw only dark, muddy swirls flowing past.

"It's Sunday," the old man said. "There's no shrimp on Sunday. No crab, neither. I deliver in town tomorrow afternoon. Go away."

"Are you Froggy?"

"It ain't the name my mama give me, but it'll do." Froggy sipped from the delicate tea cup adorned with ivy and roses.

Ransom judged him to be at least eighty years old. Froggy removed his paper hat and scratched a place on his bald and darkly tanned scalp. His beard hung down to his chest and was white as ash except where tobacco had stained it around his lips. He had but two teeth, one on top and one diagonal to it on the bottom. But the old man's most striking features were the dramatic scar across his left cheek and the remains of his left ear. The scar, shaped like a meteor, began beneath his eye and cut along the side of his head to where his ear had been. Only the topmost portion of that ear remained; a mere sliver of flesh that drooped down in a curled hook.

"Since you run off my company, I'll just have to visit with you." Froggy pointed to Ransom's boots. "You a soldier?"

"I was," Ransom said, standing over the old man.

"In that war over yonder?"

Ransom nodded.

"You don't look no worse for it." Froggy thumped the remains of his ear with his fingers. "That's what a Minié ball will do if you don't get out its way."

Froggy's skin had burnt dark as rust and he smelled of rotted fish. Ransom thought the tea cup and saucer too beautiful for him.

"I need a place to stay," Ransom said.

"I don't take in strays. There's a boarding house in town."

"The sheriff told me not to go back."

"That so?" Froggy raised the china cup to his lips and drained it. "Wanda must've taken a liking to you. That woman's got to turn that thing off before she gets another man killed."

"I owe Temperance some crab and shrimp."

"I ain't going to give 'em to you."

"I'll work it off and I'll work off staying here too," Ransom said. "I just need a place until my credit comes in and I can start brokering cotton."

"Why the hell you want to do that? Didn't you learn nothing in your war?"

Froggy stood up and looked out on the river and marsh. His trousers and the ragged shirt he wore were stained with blood and grease and fish scales. He pointed to the water flowing ten feet beneath them.

"A shipload of slaves drowned theirselves right down there," Froggy said. "They walked clean off the ship and into the water all chained together and drowned theirselves; every last one. There's a lesson in that, if you care to think about it."

Ransom saw only swirling muddy water and marsh grass. Froggy raised his head and pointed south to a distant bluff.

"That's Hilton Head," he said. "The children of slaves live out there. Don't nobody mess with 'em. Sometimes at night, when I'm sleeping, they leave me charms made out of clay and feathers. It brings me luck. They talk the Gullah talk. I can't hardly understand a word. It's like a song, the way they talk, makes me feel good inside, like maybe we ain't all that different."

Froggy walked from the pier and Ransom followed, stepping over and around the rotted places. At the fire, Froggy put the fine tea cup and saucer away and went to the open Bible. A pair of gold wire-framed glasses rested in the crease of the spine and he put them on, taking great care to prop the earpiece over each ear. Then he silently read from the Book of Deuteronomy, tracing a dirt-stained finger tip beneath the finely printed words as he moved his lips. Froggy was a slow reader and Ransom resigned himself to sitting on a tea crate while the old man struggled through the text on both sides of the page. When Froggy finished reading, he bowed his head and closed his eyes for half a second, as though nodding off to sleep.

"Amen," Froggy said when he had finished praying. Then he ripped the page out of the Bible. He folded it and folded it again. Then he tore the ripped page along the folds to make four, nearly equal, smaller squares. Three squares he put in a Prince Albert tobacco tin. The last square of scripture he sprinkled with tobacco and rolled it into a cigarette. He lit it with a stick from the fire, puffing it to life as whiffs of smoke escaped from the corner of his mouth.

"Some parts of the Bible are best understood smoked," he said when he saw the shock on Ransom's face. "You can stay here a day or two, but after that, you better find your own place. I can't take company but for so long."

That night they ate cornbread around the fire while bullfrogs croaked and bellowed. When they'd finished, Froggy sat smoking on a tea crate, listening to the sounds of the marsh and the distant crash and hush of waves.

Ransom motioned to a large chunk of cornbread remaining in the pan. "You going to eat that?"

"That's Sheila's dinner. She'll be around when things get quiet."

But Sheila did not come around and the fire died low. When it was time to turn in, Froggy carried the cast iron frying pan and the remaining cornbread inside the shack where he left it on a table made from the hatch cover of a shrimp boat. Ransom sat on the sand floor in the doorway. With the canvas door pulled back, he could see the embers of the fire and the endless stars over the Atlantic.

"Don't lay in the door," Froggy said. "Sheila's got to get through there."

Ransom moved out of the doorway and lay against the wall. Froggy crawled beneath the soiled quilt of a makeshift bed and began to pray.

"God," Froggy began. "Thank you for this day. It was a good one. Please watch over Sheila. Her leg's hurting her bad again. Amen."

A thud came from outside. It sounded like someone had fallen from a tree. Then Ransom heard a drunken stirring in the leaves and small steps. He sat up and moved further away from the door and away from the sound of something dragging through the sand.

He could just make out a small figure, smaller than a child, hunched and favoring a leg as it approached the doorway. The figure stopped at the door, sniffed and waved small hands in the air.

"Sheila," Froggy called in a sleepy voice, "your dinner's on the table."

Sheila entered the doorway and sniffed Ransom's foot. In the dim light, Ransom could just make out the bandit mask of a grizzled raccoon. Dragging a leg, Sheila attempted to climb onto the tea crate at the table. After several attempts she pulled herself up and sat on her haunches. With a growl, she dug into the cornbread, eating with both paws, shoving a fistful in her mouth with one, while she grabbed more with the other. She growled and smacked and ate until she licked the frying pan clean, then shoved it off the table. She licked the table top too. Finally, she went to Froggy's bed where she nestled under his arm.

"Settle down," Froggy said as he adjusted the blanket under her chin. "Time's beating us to death, ain't it?" Sheila kicked Froggy's arm until it cradled her just so, then yawned, and stretched a paw over his chest.

Soon the old man and the grizzled raccoon were asleep. Slackjawed, Froggy ground out long sawmill snores that filled the shack. Sheila snorted a shorter, softer note. Ransom lay awake.

23

THAT MORNING, LONG BEFORE DAYLIGHT, Ransom pushed the canvas door aside to find Froggy seated on a tea crate and feeding sticks to a growing fire. Flames licked the base of a blue enamel coffeepot, further blackening its sides. Once the coffee was ready, they drank it loaded with sugar and shared a loaf of stale bread. When they'd eaten and finished the last of the coffee, they walked out to the pier and climbed down a ladder to a flat-bottom boat.

Froggy helped Ransom aboard and directed him to the bow. A live well occupied the center of the boat and Froggy maneuvered around it to get to the stern. Three buckets half filled with the rotting flesh of some sea creature were wedged between the live well and Ransom.

"The tide is my timepiece," Froggy said. "It's a good way to live. You'll see."

Froggy settled at the stern with a short paddle in his hand and asked Ransom to untie them from the pier. The tide swept them away on the outgoing current. In a sky dense with stars, the moon shone like a lantern from another world.

Ransom tried to say something, but Froggy hushed him.

"Listen," Froggy said. "Dolphins." A gentle sigh sounded nearby in the darkness. "You can hear them breathe."

A pair of dolphins followed the boat. In the moonlight, Ransom could see the couple gliding to the surface, bowing forward as they breathed. In that moment, the dolphins looked into Ransom's eyes. He could only marvel at their grace as they continued bowing through the water and slipped again beneath the surface.

"The dolphins know me," Froggy said. "And now, they know you."

They came to a glass jug bobbing against its anchor. The dolphins swam away and left the men to do their work. Ransom grabbed the jug and the rope running from it.

"Hold on," Froggy said and cut a large chunk of rotted meat into smaller pieces. He tossed a handful of slimy flesh across the live well into Ransom lap. "Tie bait on every ten feet or so. Work down the line."

Ransom pulled on the rope beneath the jug, making his way hand over hand and shaking crabs into the live well. The crab line stretched through nearly a quarter mile of marsh. Ransom worked it while Froggy cut bait, which he said was a shark he'd caught three days back.

A sea turtle poked its head above the surface. Treading against the current, it watched them for a moment before submerging. By the time they reached the end of the crab line, dawn had begun.

"Now we shrimp," Froggy said when the sun was fully above the horizon. He looped a rope around his wrist. At the other end, a cast net lay in the bottom of the boat, lacy as a bridal train. Froggy stood up, placed a portion of the net's hem between his teeth then draped the rest over his arm.

Twisting and stooping, he wound his old body like a spring then unwound in a burst of energy, flinging the net into the air behind the boat. The net spun open into a disc ten feet across, trailing the rope tied to Froggy's wrist. It splashed flat on the water and sank.

He snatched the rope and pulled. Several small spatters erupted within the closed net as it surfaced. When he lifted it into the boat, half a dozen shrimp the size of a man's finger flicked against the netting.

"It starts out slow," Froggy said. "Most of the shrimp are still in the marsh grass. The outgoing tide will draw them into the creek."

When Ransom cast the net, it tangled in a wad that plunked like a rock in the water. After two more attempts, the net finally opened flat in the air and hit the water with a clean slap. Froggy nodded his approval and rolled a cigarette in a fragment ripped from the book of Joshua.

Catching a few more shrimp with each cast, they drifted past an island beach where odd-shaped horses played; small creatures with round bellies and spindly legs. A trio chased across the sand and into the water. Others grazed on sea grasses that grew between the beach and dense woods.

"Spanish horses," Froggy said. "Their kind has lived here since Spain claimed this land."

As the morning wore on, Ransom's shoulders ached from casting. But with each throw the net became more like a part of him, until he wasn't thinking about it at all, just casting and retrieving as naturally as he breathed. Then the tide began to slow and the number of shrimp in each cast diminished.

"Put it away," Froggy said. "The shrimp are in deep water now." The tide changed and a slow current came from the direction of the ocean, urging the boat back the way they had come.

At the pier, Ransom loaded the catch into water-filled barrels on the wagon while Froggy hitched up the mule. When they were ready to ride into town, Ransom hurried to the shack and got the letter of credit from Sterling and Sterling.

The mule pulled the dilapidated wagon at a modest pace. Water sloshed in the barrels until the level adjusted. They passed large open fields of young cotton, several hundred acres, with four teams of laborers chopping in the distance. On the steps of an expansive brick home near the road, stood a tall, hard looking man with high cheek bones and a pistol on his hip. His dark eyes followed Ransom as the wagon rolled past.

"That's Joe Broke-shoulder," Froggy said when they were out of earshot. "He owns about six hundred acres, right up to the Yamassee Hunt Club. He can't stand Ansel Deadwilder, so he might sell you cotton if he don't kill you first. He's Muskogee and mean as hell. Word is he killed a man in Alabama, did time for it too. See that pistol he's wearing? I seen him shoot the head clean off a cottonmouth thirty feet away. You never met nobody mean as Joe Broke-shoulder."

They passed an old unpainted house set back from the road. Bales of hay were stacked on the porch, and every window had been knocked out. From Joe Broke-shoulder's to this run down house the land grew cotton, but behind the old house a strip of ground seventy-five feet wide and as long as Ransom could see, lay black and barren without so much as a weed sprout. It looked like endless flat rock. A ditch paralleled the stretch of barren ground on one side.

"That ditch is the edge of Joe's property. The rest belongs to the Yamassee Hunt Club."

"What's wrong with the dirt back there? Nothing's growing on it."

"The club dug that ditch to drain the swamp on their side. Big steam powered equipment come in here and tore the place up. That was before Joe got out of prison and bought his place, so he didn't have a say in it. The club dumped the black clay on his side and rolled it flat. Can't tell you why. It don't make sense to me. That clay's baked in the sun for more than twenty years now and it's hard as brick. Rain don't even get through it."

They passed the Little Muddy Baptist Church that backed up to an easy going black water river. Froggy waved his arm at the brush and jungle across the road from the church.

"That land belongs to the Yamassee Hunt Club," he said. "They own about fifty thousand acres, all the way over to the Savannah River. We're coming up to the club house now."

The old mule plodded along, breathing hard against the burden of the wagon, its head slumped low and its gray lip rolled out. Noon was coming on and so was the heat. Ransom pulled his straw hat off to let the breeze cool his brow. They came to the short ornate train parked on a side rail and the manicured drive of crushed oyster shell lined with live oaks.

"I talked to the engineer of that train," Ransom said. "He told me he drives it all over the country, sometimes just to deliver a single piece of paper."

"I don't doubt it," Froggy said.

They stopped first at the boarding house for Ransom to repay his debt to Temperance. She met them at the wagon with biscuits and coffee.

"Blue crab," Froggy sang out as they rolled away from the boarding house and onto Main Street. "Fresh blue crab! Shrimp!"

24

MAIDS AND COOKS WITH BUCKETS and newspaper met the wagon on the street. Froggy reached into the barrel and grabbed a handful of shrimp by their threadlike antennae. Pulling them out, the shrimp flicked water on everyone standing close. He fished the crabs out with a dip net fashioned from a scrap of burlap and a dogwood branch and was paid in coins, which he shared with Ransom.

At the bank, Ransom jumped from the wagon and went inside. He presented the letter of credit to the teller, a wiry man of advanced years who eyed Ransom's mud-caked overalls and drew a breath.

"Are you Ransom James MacTavish?" The teller said.

"Yes sir."

"Ransom James MacTavish as stated here?" The teller tapped a finger on the Sterling and Sterling letter. "You don't look like Ransom James MacTavish."

"How do you know what I look like?" Ransom said. "You've never seen me before."

Another man appeared at the shoulder of the teller. He wore an expensive suit and peered down at the letter, then raised his eyes to Ransom. He looked like a man prone to secret cruelty.

"You smell like bad fish," the man said.

"If you don't want to give me credit, I bet there's a bank in Savannah that'll do it." Ransom reached for the letter, but the man in the suit held it just out of reach.

"That won't be necessary. We merely need to confirm with Sterling and Sterling. Once I have confirmation, I'll gladly issue you credit as outlined herewith."

"How long will that take?" Ransom asked.

"Our letter will go out in today's mail and should arrive in Liverpool within a few weeks. Then, it's entirely up to Sterling and Sterling. I can't speak for them, of course. Once they write the necessary letter of confirmation with the proper signature, it should take another few weeks for their letter to reach us. I would say a month at the earliest, perhaps longer."

"Isn't there a faster way?"

"I'm afraid not. You must also write to Sterling and Sterling telling them where you are now and to expect a letter from Pocotaligo Farmers Bank regarding this line of credit."

Standing outside the bank in the sun, Ransom counted the few coins Froggy had given him then went to the general store. There he picked out a plain stationary set. Before paying, he took a stroll through the back of the store to look at the brass bedframe. It pleased him to see it was still there.

"Hold that brass bed for me," Ransom said at the counter. When he dumped out the contents of his change purse, his lucky buckeye rolled out too.

"A buckeye," the storekeeper said. "That one's worn threadbare. How long you had it?"

"About three years," Ransom said as he counted his change. "It got me through the war."

"You 'bout wore it out, didn't you," the storekeeper said. "When I was a kid, I had a buckeye like that and the little girl from the next farm over had one too. We'd rub them together for luck. You know, if you rub two buckeyes together like that, they make a spell that can't never be broke. Most people think it's foolishness, but I'm here to tell you it ain't. It's real. The girl next door moved away when she was ten or so, but she came right back when she got big enough and we've been married thirty-two years this August."

"It's true," said a woman dusting tins of peaches near the counter. "Rubbing two buckeyes together is powerful stuff."

Ransom paid for the stationary and went out on the boardwalk where he sat to write a brief letter to Archibald Sterling. When he had finished and sealed it in an envelope, he took it to the Post Office.

"Ransom!" Miss Hazel beamed when she saw him come through the Post Office door. "It was so good to see you in church yesterday. Elizabeth was thrilled." Miss Hazel wore a green visor and stood behind a dark stained oak counter where she was sorting mail into pigeon holes. "What on earth have you been doing? You look like you've been drawn through the mud. And my stars, what is that smell?"

"I'm out with Froggy until my line of credit comes in."

"In the marsh? My word, what on earth for?"

"The sheriff doesn't want me at the boarding house."

"Oh," Miss Hazel said, blushing and diverting her eyes to the stack of letters in her hand. "I gather Wanda took a fancy to you. I swear that woman should wear a sign across her forehead warning all men about the dangers of her flirtations. It's sad, really. She wasn't that way before she lost her husband. I think grief has taken her mind."

Ransom passed her the letter and Miss Hazel pressed a stamp on it. "Liverpool, England," she said. "I don't recall ever sending a letter to Liverpool, England."

Ransom left the post office and listened for Froggy hawking shrimp. He caught the wagon as it rolled past the jail house. Outside the jail, a deputy sat in the shade of the boardwalk in a chair leaned back against the wall. He was guarding a half wooden barrel with a sprig of a rose bush growing in the center of it. Between two posts, banana peels dried on a line.

"The sheriff's rose looks kind of puny, don't it?" Froggy said. "He's feeding it banana peels, but it ain't doing no good. Rose Day ain't but three months off. He can't beat Miss Hazel, no-how, not with that little thing. She wins every year. You should see the roses at her place."

As the sun burned down on them, Froggy steered out of town onto the Charleston Road. They passed field after field where men and women and grandparents and children chopped cotton.

They passed a few shacks before they came to a house with

a wide porch wrapped around both sides. The house was larger than any they'd seen since leaving town, but it was more like a fine farmhouse than a plantation. Trees grew around it: pecan, magnolia, mulberry and chinaberry, but few leaves lay on the ground. The sand yard had been swept clean. A Model T sat parked beneath a shed near the smokehouse and chicken coop. A magnificent vegetable garden grew behind a wire fence, rich with blooms and butterflies.

Froggy pointed to a large flat rectangle on the ground beside the barn. A net divided the rectangle in half. "You ever seen anything so foolish?"

"What's it used for?"

"It's a tennis court," Froggy said. "People stand out there and knock a ball back and forth with these paddle-looking things."

A maid appeared from inside the house. She stood at the top of the front porch steps and wiped her hands on her apron. "Mrs. Lyttelton says she'll take all you got."

Froggy climbed to the back of the wagon to scoop the remaining shrimp and crab from the barrels

At the front door, a figure stood behind the screen.

"Hello, Ransom," Elizabeth said.

Ransom jumped to the ground and made his way up the steps to the front porch. Elizabeth wore a simple house dress made of red fabric with small white squares. Her bright hair flowed loose and free down her shoulders. Deep within the house, her mother said something to her but Elizabeth didn't answer. Her attention remained fixed on Ransom. Time slowed. Ransom considered the toe of his boot then looked again to her.

The screen kept them apart, but through that thin barrier he saw her eyes, closer now than ever, blue and kind and inviting. He wanted to touch her and pressed his open palm to the screen. Elizabeth brought her hand to his and he felt its warmth. A horse fly, as big as a nickel, crawled in a tight circle on the screen door, measuring time on tiny black feet.

"When I saw you in church, I wanted to leave with you," she said. Her cheeks flushed crimson. Her breasts rose and fell.

"Me too," Ransom said then realized it didn't make any sense. He felt like he might float away.

"Elizabeth." Her mother appeared behind her. "You are not presentable." She pulled her daughter away from the door, but Elizabeth broke free and rushed back.

"Ransom," she said through the screen. Her mother reached for her again. "I miss your letters." Elizabeth stumbled backwards as her mother forced her from the door. From the dark interior of the house he heard her say. "Write to me."

All the way back to the pier, Ransom composed a letter in his mind and, with Froggy's help, worked out the best way of secretly getting it to Elizabeth. By the time they were at the shack he knew what to write.

Dear Elizabeth,

Please excuse my clandestine means of getting this letter to you. I trust John Divine Christopher Columbus to get my notes to you secretly. Miss Hazel, with her official responsibilities as Post Mistress, and her allegiance to your parents, may not be as discreet.

Today, when I saw you at your house, I wanted to touch you. But, with your mother there, the screen door may as well have been prison bars. I did not know what to say. Maybe there was nothing to say because seeing you and feeling your presence was enough, but I wanted more. I have never been so hungry to touch a woman.

I want to see you now. I want to see you every day. I want to see you every minute. I can think of nothing else. When I am in business, I will have proper clothes and a fine buggy. I will court you in style. But for now I must wait. I am so tired of waiting. I want to live. I want to forever hold your hand, to breathe in the scent of your skin, feel your warmth and hear the soothing rhythm of your heart.

Can you imagine if we had no screen doors between us and no guards protecting us from each other? What are they protecting? They cannot keep me from my feelings. I knew when I first read your letters I had to meet you. I knew, if I lived at all, I would live for you.

Affectionately,
Ransom

Elizabeth's reply came three days later when John Divine stopped Froggy and Ransom on the way to town to deliver their catch. John Divine passed the letter up to Ransom and then climbed on the wagon to ride back to Wanda's.

Dear Ransom,

John Divine brought your letter today. How very clever. You are right to suspect my mother would censor the mail. I am a prisoner here. I have no doubt my parents love me. I know they are concerned with my virtue and want me to marry well, but I am old enough to manage that myself. They have no idea how lonely I have become or how difficult it is. Sometimes, the sadness reaches so deep I fear I will suffocate from its grip.

Ansel dances around and tries to cheer me up. He always says the right thing, but I can tell he doesn't mean it. He has no heart, just a calculating business mind that has drawn my life into his long term plans. Ransom, I cannot believe how you have swooped down out of nowhere and brightened my life. At times I think you must be an angel sent to comfort me.

What a surprise to see you; close up without Ansel or my father standing guard. When you came to our screen door, delivering crab and shrimp, of all things, it was as if you had answered my prayer. I was at that moment thinking of you and fairly wrapping you in a fantasy, a fantasy I will share with you some other time. If there had been no screen door, if my mother was not home, I would have thrown my arms around you and dragged you into the house.

Your Dearest,
Elizabeth

25

THAT NIGHT, RANSOM AND FROGGY roasted croakers on sticks over the fire. As the small fish browned, the moon rose over the ocean and a stiff breeze blew across the marsh, bringing with it the scent of salt and mud.

"Sheila was complaining about you this morning," Froggy said breaking the silence Ransom had come to enjoy. Each time Froggy spoke, his stringy white beard twitched as though alive. He smoked a hand-rolled cigarette to the tiniest ember between his lips. "I didn't want to say nothing about it, but it's got to be said. You can sleep out here by the fire, if you want, but Sheila, she can't rest right with you inside, makes her nervous."

Ransom looked up from the browning croaker he turned on a stick. "She told you that?"

"She talks to me in my head." Froggy tapped a finger to the folded newspaper hat he wore. "I don't expect you to understand." He picked the slight remains of the cigarette from the corner of his mouth and tossed it on the breeze.

"All right then," Ransom said. "I'll move on."

"I ain't saying for you to move on." Froggy took the tobacco tin from his breast pocket. "I'm saying you can't sleep in my place no more. There's a shrimp boat run aground on the other side of the bluff, down in that low place. They busted the back end out when they tried to tow it off the mud and left it sitting. The cabin's still good. You can stay in there and help me out in the mornings. I'll ride you into town to check on the bank money and find John Divine to take letters to your girl. And that thing that's worrying you," Froggy said, tearing a page of scripture into quarters, "you best let it go."

"The bank said it'll take a month or more for me to get my money. Don't you think that's worth worrying about?"

"Not one bit." Froggy sprinkled tobacco in a square of paper and licked the edge. "It ain't your money, no way. You're borrowing it. And when you put it back, you'll have to give more than you took. I've seen a lot of men go belly up 'cause of owing somebody."

"Borrowing is how business is done," Ransom said. "You don't understand business."

"Maybe not," Froggy said and rolled a fresh cigarette tightly between his fingers until it looked like a weathered twig. "But I've watched men struggling for nearly eighty years and I seen every way to do business wrong. I seen men chase all sorts of crazy dreams. I chased some too 'til I learned. Mostly, I seen men piss their lives away 'cause they don't learn a damn thing. Now I'm watching you do it. You think you found yourself some kind of gold mine in cotton, but there ain't no money in cotton. All the money done been squeezed out of it."

"Ansel Deadwilder's making money in cotton," Ransom said.

"Ansel Deadwilder's running rum up from Puerto Rico," Froggy said. "That's where his money's coming from."

"You're crazy."

"No more than anybody else," Froggy said.

"If cotton won't make money, what will?"

"That's the riddle." Froggy pointed the new cigarette at Ransom to emphasize his point then put it between his lips. "I'll think on it some. Maybe I can come up with something. When I got a riddle like that, I like to lie down in the bottom of my boat and just drift under the stars, let the tide take me wherever it wants. You ought to try it. There's a whole lot of good out in the marsh if you listen for it."

"Elizabeth wants to see me and I don't have any way of courting her."

"Don't read too much into that." Froggy lit the cigarette dangling from his lips with a flaming sea oat stalk. The ocean breeze swept away the small clouds of smoke that puffed from the corner of his mouth. "Women got their own reasons for doing things."

The conversation trailed off into silence. Between them, the fire cracked and popped. Glowing cinders rose above the flames in a scattered cloud of sparks that curled on the breeze and died. Beyond the river and marshes and sand dunes, the Atlantic lay black to the horizon. Its dark surface rose and fell like some sleeping beast as waves rolled to the beach and hushed wet across the sand.

When Froggy had finished his cigarette, he stood up, stretched and cracked a tight place in his back. "Sheila will be down directly," he said. "Don't say nothing to her about what we talked about."

"Not a word," Ransom said.

Later, after Froggy had gone to bed, Ransom gathered his stationary from his pack and walked to the pier where he sat with his feet dangling over the end and listened to the dolphins breathing in the dark. A waning moon shone over the ocean bright enough to write by.

Dear Elizabeth,

I think of you sleeping in your bed tonight, comfortable and warm, and wonder what it might be like inside your private world. I intend some day to know your parents and to earn their trust. Ansel Deadwilder will never trust me, of course, but I do not care. In time, he will be forced to relinquish his imagined hold on you.

I wish you could be with me here. It isn't as snug as your home, but I have the moon. It's so bright it throws a wide beam across the ocean and illuminates the whole world. I can see forever, nearly as well as in the day. It's not quiet here either. I have a natural orchestra to entertain me. You would like it and I would like it all the more if you were here with me.

Dolphins swim beneath the pier where I sit. I can hear them sigh when they surface and it sounds to me as if they are waking from sleep. They are never alone, but always in pairs. If you look into their eyes, you will know they are forever bonded to each other. I envy their freedom to love and hold fast to the one they have chosen. To see the dolphins happy with themselves reminds me of my loneliness for you.

We are worlds apart. Not because of who we are, but because of where we find ourselves. I have come so far to be with you and still you are out of my reach. I have so much further to go, not in distance as measured by the eyes, and not in distance as measured by the heart, for I am there already in my heart. Before I can be with you, I must travel the final and greatest terrain, that immeasurable vastness between your father's wealth and my own ungraceful beginning. It's maddening.

Tonight, all I have is your letters and my desire. If my desire could propel me to you, I would be there this instant. And I would bring with me all I have, the moon and the stars and the hushing of the waves. And I will ask the dolphins to teach us how to love as free as the ocean and as eternal.

Affectionately,
Ransom

26

WHENEVER THEY WENT TO TOWN, Ransom stopped at the bank to see if the letter from Sterling and Sterling had come. Day by day, mud, slime and the stench of rotted cut bait worked its way into his overalls and into the pores of his flesh. His hair grew wild again and the sun tanned him dark as buckskin.

Finally, after six weeks, when he entered the bank, sunburnt, and mud-caked and reeking of dead fish, the bank manager motioned for him to enter his office. The manager forced a smile that made his teeth look big. For the first time in all of Ransom's visits to the bank, the man did not seem to notice Ransom's overalls or his odor.

"The letter from Sterling and Sterling came in this morning's mail." The bank manager pulled out a chair for Ransom. "Everything is approved and in proper order." He pushed a paper across his desk for Ransom to sign and pointed to a dollar figure above the signature block.

"That's a lot of money," Ransom said.

"It is indeed. That's why we have banks."

"What do I have to do to get it?"

"Sign here." The manager tapped the signature line. "Then you may take cash from the teller, or, if you prefer, you may have my secretary prepare a legal check. For large purchases or scheduled expenses, such as boarding or livery services, a check is recommended."

Ransom pointed behind him to the teller's booth where the little man with a visor sat.

"You mean I can go over there right now and get some cash."

"That's right."

"How much?"

"Up to the authorized limit of course," the bank manager said. "You understand."

Ransom pushed the chair back and stood up. "I think I'll give this a try." He walked to the teller and leaned towards the black iron bars between him and the little man. "I'd like a hundred dollars."

"Yes sir, Mister MacTavish." The teller began counting out bills. Within seconds, a hundred dollars lay on the counter. The teller then prepared a slip of paper which Ransom signed. "Thank you Mister MacTavish," the teller said. "Is there anything else I might do for you?"

"No," Ransom said, taking the bills and folding them in his pocket. "I think you pretty much did it."

He left the bank and no one shouted for him to stop, so he patted the bills in his pocket and joined Froggy on the wagon.

"I been thinking about your riddle," Froggy said, as they rolled out of town. "Cotton ain't it. I can tell you that." The old mule plodded along, putting one hoof in front of the other as though each step were her last. "I was thinking about after the war when I went out to California to get rich mining gold. Walked the whole damn way, too. Me and some boys staked a claim up in Clipper Gap. All the easy gold had been found a long time before I got there. That's what I'm trying to tell you about cotton. All the easy money's been made. Ain't nothing left in it."

"Did you find any gold?" Ransom said as they rolled past Mister Roebuck's private train, the brass trim gleaming in the sun.

"Sure, but not enough to make anybody rich. We found enough to keep us digging, that's about all. And that's what cotton's going to do to you. It's going to keep you digging but it ain't ever going to be more than just enough."

They passed Little Muddy Baptist Church and the drainage

ditch with the hard packed clay flattened out beside it like an endless black road, and the old house with no windows filled with hay. They passed Joe Broke-shoulder's brick house, but the mean Muskogee was nowhere to be seen. In the distance a thin cloud of dust rose from the cotton fields where laborers worked.

"I'll tell you who made the money," Froggy said. "This ol' boy ran a store down in the valley below our claim. He didn't bust his guts for gold, like we did. He traded for it. Damn if he didn't run a train up there to trade us dungarees and liquor for our gold. He ran track to other mining towns, too. Wasn't long before he had track running down the valley and over the mountains. Before you know it, a damn little ol' storekeeper was running most of the railroads west of the Mississippi River. While we all were breaking our backs, scratching for just enough gold to keep us stupid, he seen something nobody else seen. That's what you got to do if you want to make real money. You got to see something nobody else sees and make a business out of it."

"All I see is cotton," Ransom said.

"Yep." Froggy nodded. "That's the riddle."

27

THE NEXT MORNING, Ransom walked to town. By the time the sun was up, he'd scrubbed the fish smell from his body in the bathhouse behind Miss Wanda's and dressed in the suit of the dead kerosene cook stove salesman. He was the first customer at the barbershop, where he got a shave and a haircut and a generous splash of bay rum aftershave. On his way to the depot, he passed the post office. Miss Hazel hurried outside to hug his neck.

"Why Ransom, you look almost human." A smile dimpled her cheeks.

"I need a place in town to stay," Ransom said. "Some place reputable."

"My front room is available."

At the depot Ransom sent a telegram, then purchased a ticket and boarded the Palmetto Limited north. By noon he was in Charleston where he hired a horse-drawn cabriolet. The day was sunny and glorious and the driver had folded the top back.

"I want to buy a suit," Ransom said to the driver as he settled into the back seat of the open carriage.

"Yes sir." The driver took him to a men's shop on King Street where he bought a suit and shoes and a fine derby hat. By the time the tailor had finished the alterations, the day was easing to a close. Ransom stepped from the store. The newness of his clothes and all the wonderful smells felt strange to him but exciting too. A business man, dressed just as nicely, tipped his hat as he passed. With a tip of his derby Ransom returned the greeting and felt like he belonged among the gentlemen and ladies of Charleston.

As the sun set behind the old town, he walked King Street to Murray Boulevard. A lamplighter went from lamp to lamp along the waterfront, touching his flame to the glass chimneys. A halo of illumination spilled onto the brick walk as each lamp came alive. Lights shone in the windows of the fine houses lining the boulevard.

Ransom found the Pinckney house and rapped on the front door with the polished brass knocker. A moment later, a maid appeared.

"I'm Ransom James MacTavish. I'm here to see Mister Pinckney."

"Yes sir," the maid said. "He got your telegram this morning."

The maid took his derby and directed him to the parlor. A moment later, Mr. Pinckney joined him, a glass of bourbon in his hand.

"Thank you for coming," Mister Pinckney said. He looked distinguished but his face was set and rigid. His eyes were red as if he'd been crying. They shook hands.

"Forgive my wife for not greeting you. She remains overwhelmed with grief. Isaac was our only child." Mister Pinckney motioned for Ransom to sit on the sofa.

He turned his back and busied himself at a table between two electric lamps where a crystal decanter stood half full of bourbon. Matching glasses circled the decanter like crystal soldiers. Mr. Pinckney poured a fresh glass and refilled his own.

"This feels like a funeral," Mr. Pinckney said and passed a glass of bourbon to Ransom. "This whole damn house has felt like a mausoleum since we got the news." He raised his eyes to the ceiling. "Isaac was not supposed to die. He was supposed to marry Elizabeth Lyttelton. He was supposed to join me in my law practice and go into politics. He was not supposed to die."

Ransom dug in his pocket for the Citadel ring and pressed it in Mister Pinckney's hand. "I promised your son I'd give you this."

Mister Pinckney's face turned cold. He looked to Ransom with red, swollen eyes. "Why didn't *you* die?"

"I don't know."

28

LATE THE FOLLOWING DAY, Ransom went to the livery behind Doctor Lucius Lafitte's medical clinic and law office. The livery smelled of a curious blend of manure and machines. Ransom wore the fine suit, shoes and derby he'd gotten in Charleston and, for the first time in his life, the thought of dirt concerned him.

On a side alley, a narrow red gas pump stood higher than a man was tall. The glass tank on top of the pump was filled with a gallon of amber gasoline that lent a horrid smell to the air. Beside the pump, a new bicycle leaned against the outside wall of the barn. Two more bicycles hung on pegs above it.

Ransom walked through the open double doors and through the center of the barn. A young red mule favoring a front leg bandaged to the hock was hitched to a central post inside. It watched Ransom make his way through the barn and out past a pile of manure where a little brown-eyed girl filled a bucket with her hands.

"Hi," the little girl said when she saw Ransom. "My name is Biddy and I'd appreciate your vote on Rose Day for the prettiest rose."

"The Daughters of the Confederacy are the only ones voting on the prettiest rose," Ransom said.

"I know," Biddy said. "You can tell Miss Hazel to vote for me. She's the president."

"I'm not going to tell her how to vote."

"It don't matter," Biddy said. "I'm going to win. Nobody's ever seen a rose like the one I got." With a bucket full of manure, she crawled from the pile and stood up.

"Miss Hazel's favored to win," Ransom said.

"Not this year. This year I'm going to win. My grandma's helping me and she knows roses better than anybody." Struggling with the weight of the loaded bucket, Biddy clung to the handle with both hands and crossed the paddock to the gate.

Ransom found Cooter Acorn with his head in the engine compartment of a 1915 Dodge truck. Dressed in oil-stained overalls, the man had his back to Ransom and cursed as he wrestled a chunk of steel off the engine block.

"I need to rent a horse and your finest buggy," Ransom said to Cooter's back.

Cooter drew his head from the engine compartment and wiped his hands on a rag. "Damn," he said when he saw Ransom dressed so smartly.

After hitching a black mare to a buggy, Cooter walked it out of the barn and into the sun. Ransom paid him with a check drawn on the Pocotaligo Farmers Bank.

"She's gentle," Cooter said as he put the check in a pocket of his overalls. "Be good to her."

"I will." Ransom released the brake and dusted the buggy whip lightly to the mare's hindquarter, clicking his tongue to encourage her. The mare stepped out with a steady cadence and soon carried him onto Main Street.

Ransom drove the buggy through town to Miss Hazel's house; a gray clapboard, single-story Victorian with a deep porch edged with scroll trim. On this block and the next, the houses varied little. The neighboring house was identical except for different trim and white paint instead of gray.

Looking at the velvet roses that grew along Miss Hazel's fence, Ransom understood why she won the competition each year. Nearly every house in town had roses, but none were as magnificent as Miss Hazel's. In the corner of the yard, where Miss Hazel's fence tied into her neighbor's, pea vines grew in a tangle of green haze. The pea blossoms were more delicate than the roses, mere touches of pastel; pink, white and blue.

On the front porch of Miss Hazel's, an orange tabby cat sat chewing its toes. Ransom let himself inside and went to the front bedroom where he placed his derby on the dresser. The leather wallet with the silver clasp lay beside it.

Ransom picked out the letters Elizabeth had written to him. The most recent ones still held the scent of lavender. He put these in the top drawer with his buckeye and took out Elizabeth's photograph. He turned the picture over and again read the message on the back: *To Lieutenant Isaac Pinckney, all my love, forever and always, Elizabeth.*

"Ransom?" Miss Hazel called to him from the hall. "I thought I heard you come in." Ransom gathered his hat and the leather wallet.

When he stepped from the room, Ransom gave Miss Hazel a folded check. "For room and board," he said.

"You look like a *fine* gentleman," she said and quickly inspected the check's amount. "I'm so pleased." Miss Hazel saw the leather wallet tucked beneath his arm and asked, "Where are you going? It's nearly time for supper."

"Now that I'm presentable, I'm going to see Elizabeth." He showed Miss Hazel the worn leather wallet. "These are the letters she wrote to Lieutenant Pinckney. They belong to her."

"Goodness no." Miss Hazel took Ransom by the hand and led him across the hall to the sitting room. "Absolutely not. Elizabeth hasn't recovered from losing Isaac. And it's rude to drop in on a family unannounced at supper time. I won't allow it." She settled in a dark oak chair cushioned with crimson tapestry and motioned Ransom to the sofa across from her. "Sit with me. Have you ever thought I might enjoy your company?"

From his place on the sofa, Ransom sat facing the many photographs on the wall. His eyes fixed on the picture of an engine and rail cars lying on their side, half submerged in mud.

"My father was an engineer with the railroad," Miss Hazel said. "You might remember the crash in Beaufort when the One-Nineteen left the tracks and ran into the marsh." She pointed to the photo of the wreck and looked to him with a hint of expectation, then caught herself. "No, of course you don't, you weren't born yet. Nobody knew how to get the engine out of the mud. My father solved the problem and raised the One-Nineteen in three days. It ran for another twelve years between Wilmington and Jacksonville."

Lucinda entered the room with a tray of coffee in fine china cups and thick cream in a tiny pitcher with gold leaf around the lip. She placed the tray on the table between Ransom and Hazel. Ransom helped himself to a hard cube of sugar, sucking on it until a sip of coffee turned it to syrup. Outside, the orange tabby meowed at the door.

"Lucinda," Miss Hazel said, "let Henry in, would you please?"

The instant Lucinda opened the front door, the cat raced into the sitting room and slipped beneath Miss Hazel's chair. It purred at her feet and rubbed its face against the wooden chair legs. Miss Hazel pressed her knees together and balanced the saucer on her lap. She held the cup precisely, raised it to her lips and took a dainty sip.

"You know, you really are a handsome man," she said. "Has a woman ever told you that?" She could have been his grandmother, but when she spoke to him, her soft gray eyes seemed younger.

"I haven't known many women, just Elizabeth and–." Ransom stopped himself.

"That's a shame," Miss Hazel said. Ransom marveled at the way she held her coffee cup. Her hands were small and the skin as delicate as tissue paper. "A man as good as you should have a woman tell him every day."

She sipped coffee, but Ransom, who had gulped his to a quick finish, held the empty cup and saucer for want of something to do with his hands. Lucinda appeared with a tray of ginger cookies fresh from the oven. Miss Hazel smiled and looked to Ransom as if he were the most charming man on earth. He wanted to believe her.

"Were you ever married?" he said.

"No, I was the school teacher when I was younger. The town wouldn't let me marry. Then I became the postmistress. I still tutor a few children, such as Elizabeth, but you know that." She paused then added, "I wanted to marry, but when I was younger, I didn't understand the truth of the matter."

"The truth of what matter?" Ransom said.

"Don't you know? Goodness, I can't let you pursue Elizabeth if you don't know. All we want, all anyone wants, is to love and be loved. Marriage doesn't necessarily assure that, but friendship does. A lucky few get to have both."

She took the last sip of coffee and returned the china cup to the saucer in her lap, then reached down and rubbed the orange tabby's neck. It raised its chin and purred.

"A cat taught me how to love," Miss Hazel said.

"A cat?" Ransom said, unsure if he had heard correctly.

"I know it sounds preposterous, but it's true. A cat will be itself no matter what. You can kill it, but you can't change it. If you're going to love a cat, you have to love that cat for what it is, fangs and all. It's the same with Elizabeth. You have to love her for who she is, not for who you wish her to be." Miss Hazel tried to smile but looked down at the floor instead, as if reading her fortune in the wood grain.

Outside, the day grew dark and shadows crept into the room. Miss Hazel sat so still and so quiet, Ransom couldn't tell if she was breathing. She looked old now in the fading light, old and weary as though she'd traveled a great distance.

"I should have married," she said. "I should have had a family. When I was a young woman, men found me desirable. Mother wanted me to marry a doctor. Doctors are useful, you see, and they have clean hands."

Miss Hazel rose from her chair. Ransom stood up too and watched as Miss Hazel walked to the fireplace. She looked on a gold framed photograph in the center of the mantel, a picture of a young woman in an evening gown. She picked it up and carried it to Ransom.

"I wish I was this beautiful again," she said. "I wish I was this young."

Ransom looked into the eyes of Hazel at sixteen, maybe seventeen, as ripe and lovely as any woman who ever graced the world.

"I wish I'd taken a lover," she said. "Just once."

"You were beautiful."

"My beauty faded, as beauty does. So did my dreams. I can't even recall what I dreamed of doing with my life. It was so long ago. In forgetting, the mind saves us from much pain. Mother and Father left me this house but little else. They expected me to marry. After all, a pretty girl is born married. By the time I was willing, no one was interested."

Miss Hazel sat again in the cushioned chair. Ransom stood over her, taking in her soft gray eyes, her shapely lips and graceful hands. She remained lovely, not stunning as she once had been, but elegant. Ransom thought he should tell her this, but he didn't.

For a moment, she lowered her eyes. Somewhere in the house, a clock ticked out the seconds. Ransom wanted to say something kind but couldn't find the words. In his heart, he felt the need to gather her delicate fingers in his.

"Well, now," she said, blinking back the sadness that had come over her, "let's get something to eat."

29

THE FOLLOWING MORNING, after breakfast, Ransom walked the boardwalk of Main Street dressed in his new suit. On the edge of the boardwalk, outside the general store, the patent medicine salesman sat on a wooden crate and watched the sky.

"My friend," the salesman said when he saw Ransom approaching. He stood up and straightened his gray suit jacket.

"May I interest you in some of the finest patent medicines ever created on God's green earth?" Seeing that Ransom was heading for the door of the general store, the salesman positioned himself in front of it. "Does your wife feel tired at the end of the day?"

"You're supposed to feel tired at the end of the day," Ransom said, trying to step around the man. "That's why it's the end of the day."

"Is your wife sad and moody and a fright to live with?" The salesman blocked Ransom's every attempt to get around him. "I have something that will make her happy and a joy in your life. It's made by a doctor so you know it's good for you."

Ransom leaned left and grabbed for the door handle, but the salesman countered with a side step. Ransom slipped to the right and was blocked again. He stepped back, resigned to waiting the man out.

"It's a miracle of science and medicine," the salesman said, talking fast. "Science and our brilliant doctors have isolated the very compounds in our brains that make us happy. Unhappy people simply don't have the right brain compounds in the proper amounts. Made from the purist medicinal grade alcohol and the most miraculous herb God has ever blessed us with, cocaine, Doctor Clover's Vitality Booster restores your brain compounds to the precise balance nature intended. It'll help you think more clearly. I personally guarantee Doctor Clover's Vitality Booster will put pep in your every step! Why wait to have a good day when every day can be a good day with Doctor Clover's Vitality Booster? Or, sir, if your children are driving you crazy, perhaps you would prefer Doctor Clover's Baby Silencer, a mother's best friend."

It seemed the man would never stop. He talked faster than a machinegun, spraying words everywhere.

"You told me about the Baby Silencer already," Ransom said and slipped inside the store.

"My stars," the storekeeper's wife said from behind the counter. "Don't you look like a regular dandy?" She dusted the brass speaker horn of a Victrola record player. "You still carry that buckeye?"

"No ma'am, I don't need it anymore."

"I see," she said. "Well, now that you're part of Pocotaligo society, I'm sure you'll be entering the Rose Day competition."

"I'm a businessman," Ransom said, taking his derby off and looking around the store. "I don't have time for flowers."

"Flowers are something you make time for." She placed a record on the Victrola but didn't crank the machine. "Are you here to purchase the brass bed?"

"I just came to look at it."

Ransom heard a motorcar on Main Street and looked out the large display window in time to see Mister Lyttelton drive past in his Model T. Elizabeth sat on the passenger side wearing a large hat. A pink scarf fluttered about her neck.

Mister Lyttelton turned down the alley beside the general store. A moment later, they appeared on the boardwalk. The patent medicine salesman jumped to his feet and began rattling the same machine-gun patter. Mister Lyttelton breezed past without paying him the least bit of attention. Ransom hustled out of sight and hovered at the end of an aisle, behind a forest green pea-sheller and a barrel of fence staples.

Elizabeth entered first, touched the Victrola record player and stood on tiptoe to read the record label. Her father leaned on the counter with his back to the store.

The storekeeper's wife had the credit book out and started going over Mister Lyttelton's account. Ransom tossed a fence staple up the aisle. It struck Elizabeth between the shoulder blades and she turned around, breaking into a huge smile when she saw Ransom.

"Father," she said. "I'm going to look at some fabric."

"Your mother has fabric at home," he said without looking up from the ledger.

Elizabeth walked away from the counter and past the bolts of fabric, her eyes set on Ransom at the end of the aisle. She walked past cans of sardines stacked ten high like fat silver shingles and past the hundred-pound burlap sacks of feed corn, cracked corn, cornmeal and grits.

Ransom ducked behind the pea-sheller. Elizabeth stopped at a shelf loaded with steel double-spring jaw traps. Behind her, Mr. Lyttelton turned away from the counter and cast his eyes across the store.

"Elizabeth," he said. "What are you doing?"

Without facing her father, Elizabeth dragged a finger across a steel leg trap.

"Something caught my attention." She continued walking down the aisle towards the pea sheller.

"Are you going to start running traps?" Her father again leaned over the account book. "That'll be the day."

Elizabeth turned the corner behind the pea sheller. Ransom took her in his arms, felt her warmth, and breathed in the scent of lavender.

"You have no idea," she whispered. "I couldn't sleep and I couldn't stop thinking of you." Her eyes, blue as crystal, gazed into his. Her hair billowed beneath her hat and the cowlick at her temple made her all the more precious. As she spoke, her lips beckoned to Ransom, so red and so delicious, forming each word with a voice that sounded like the song of a wind chime. "I wanted–"

Ransom pressed his lips to hers. She threw her arms around his neck. Her warmth filled him.

"I've missed you so much," she said between kisses. He held her tight and felt the softness of her breasts against his ribs. He forgot to breathe and didn't care. He wanted to kiss her forever.

"Elizabeth?" Her father called from the store counter. But still they kissed, hidden behind the pea sheller. Ransom heard the man's shoes thudding up the aisle, coming closer, but neither of them could stop. Heat and hunger kept them entwined.

"Elizabeth?" Her father said.

"Meet me behind the barn Friday night," she said, her breasts heaving, her cheeks flushed and rosy. "My father will be in Columbia." She pushed Ransom away. He tiptoed up a neighboring aisle, careful not to make a sound.

⟬30⟭

RANSOM STEPPED OUT of the general store in time to see Captain Ace Edwards' yellow biplane circling Main Street. He skimmed the rooftops then banked over the bandstand on the south end of town.

"That's my best customer," the patent medicine salesman said.

Sheriff Pate stepped out of the jailhouse and looked up into the sky. Over the depot, the plane came into view again and nosed down. A block short of where the sheriff stood, the plane touched down. It bounced and careened, spewing a great cloud of dust as it sped toward the sheriff who raced back to the safety of the board-walk, dodging a wingtip at the last moment.

The plane began to slow as it passed the general store. Sheriff Pate ran after it with a dog yapping at his boot heels. The two of them were all but concealed in dust.

With the plane still moving, the sheriff grabbed a wing strut and climbed on. Waving his arms and pointing fingers, he screamed at Ace but the roar of the engine drowned him out. Ace, wearing goggles and a neck scarf, ignored the raging lawman and steered the airplane near the bandstand. He cut the engine and the propel-ler quickly spun to a stop. Suddenly, with the plane's engine quiet, Sheriff Pate's rant filled the air.

"You land here one more time and I'll burn this damn machine!"

The sheriff shouted and waved his arms like a madman, then stormed off the wing and marched back to the jailhouse.

Ace climbed from the cockpit as townspeople gathered around. He waved to the patent medicine salesman who approached with a case of Doctor Clover's Vitality Booster under one arm and an open bottle in his hand. Ace took a swig and corked the bottle which he slipped in his hip pocket. He left the salesman loading the case onto the plane and skipped up on the boardwalk as he headed for the general store.

"Look at you," Ace said as he breezed past Ransom, "wearing a suit like a regular dandy."

"I thought you were too scared to land here," Ransom said.

Ace paused outside of the general store. "When a man needs Doctor Clover's Vitality Booster, a man's got to do what a man's got to do."

Ace yanked the door open and entered the general store like a small explosion. Ransom followed him inside. The pilot moved in fits and starts. No part of the man held still, not even a whisker. There seemed to be a constant humming energy inside him.

"Does the Victrola work?" Ace fidgeted with the brass speaker funnel.

"Of course it works," the storekeeper's wife said. "It's brand spanking new."

"Let's hear a tune," Ace said. "Put some music on."

"Are you interested in buying it?"

"No," he said. "I got no use for a Victrola on my airplane. What I need is some red paint." He leaned on the counter and rocked back and forth. "I'm going to paint my airplane red. I'll be the Red Baron."

"You keep pushing the sheriff and you're likely to be dead," Ransom said from the door where he stood brushing dust from his hat. "I'm just trying to warn you."

"You've come a long way since I dropped you off here," Ace said.

"I'm a businessman now," Ransom said.

"In this town? This town's going to dry up and blow away. I wouldn't waste my time. This town has its eyes on the past and its back to the future." Ace spoke too loud for the confines of the store. Ransom thought the man needed a knock on the head to slow him down a notch, but it wasn't his place to do it.

"This town's fine," Ransom said. "There's nothing wrong with this town."

"This town allows a train to run through it but not an airplane," Ace said. "Trains are as outdated as horses and buggies. Trains need tracks, infinite miles of tracks. Automobiles are a novelty, destined to die a quick death. *Airplanes* are the future. A town without an airport is like Charleston without a harbor, nothing at all. Planes are faster and cheaper and all they need is a strip of ground."

"How much ground?" Ransom said.

"Not much. A quarter of a mile, half a mile would be better. That's what I'm saying. Why build miles and miles of track and roads when all you need is a little strip for planes to land on." Ace drew the bottle from his back pocket and took a sip. Putting it away again, he faced the storekeeper behind the counter. "I'd like to buy some red paint."

"Barn paint?" the storekeeper said.

"Barn paint isn't the right kind of red."

"Red is red," the storekeeper said.

"No. Red is not red." Ace leaned over the counter. The storekeeper's wife slipped away to the stock room. "There are all sorts of reds. Barn paint is dark, like it has some blue in it or maybe purple. The red I want is bright, maybe with a little orange in it, but not too much, maybe a little yellow too, a little sunshine."

"I don't sell sunshine," the storekeeper said, putting some distance between himself and Ace. "But, you can pay me for it, if you want."

"Can you see what I'm thinking?" Ace said.

"I'm not sure I want to. Just pick a color from the color chart and I'll mix it."

At the door, Ransom considered an imagined future with planes instead of trains. He was trying to calculate the expense of clearing and filling in a swamp for a quarter of a mile when the storekeeper spoke to him.

"Ransom," the storekeeper said as he cranked the Victrola to life, "show this man the paint chart in the back. It's beside that brass bed you keep promising to buy."

The storekeeper touched a switch on the Victrola. The record began to spin as he set the needle. A distinct '-*plunk*-' came from the machine then a fuzzy sound spilled from the brass horn that looked like a giant jasmine flower.

Ransom led Ace to the back of the store as the hissing from the Victrola transformed into irresistible music. In that moment, Ransom lost interest in the paint chart and pointed Ace in that direction. For the first time in his life, Ransom wanted to move to music. He wanted to dance.

The storekeeper said, "Do you know this song, Ransom?"

"The Tennessee Waltz," Ace shouted. His voice cut through the music like jagged steel.

"I was asking Ransom," the storekeeper said.

Ace ripped the paint chart from the wall, not caring to remove the thumb tacks in each of the four corners. Small triangles of paperboard remained pinned to the wall where the tacks held.

"Can you make this color of red?" Ace spread the paint chart on the counter beside the Victrola and stabbed a finger on a sample square.

"Most people leave the paint chart on the wall where I had it."

"I'm not like most people."

"Praise the Lord," the storekeeper said.

The Tennessee Waltz played on, a bit scratchy, but in perfect time. Ransom felt the music lift his spirit and swayed side to side, wishing he had someone to dance with.

"I don't have the right base," the storekeeper said. "The formula for the bright red you want needs Viceroy White. All I have is Milk White."

"They're both white, aren't they?" Ace said. "How different can they be? Use the Milk White. White is white. They're obviously made by different companies. Use what you have. Think. Why am I the only one who thinks?"

"If red ain't red," the storekeeper said, "how come white is white? White ain't white. It's chemistry and things happen in chemistry I can't explain. I just know to respect it."

Ace took a swig from the bottle of Doctor Clover's. "Look," he said as he put the bottle away, "I've been to college. I've studied chemistry and know what I'm talking about. Use the white you have, it won't make the least bit of difference."

The music began to drag and the storekeeper gave the crank on the Victrola several turns. The Tennessee Waltz picked up again. As the storekeeper went to the back to mix paint, Ransom leaned on the counter beside Ace.

"If a man had an airfield," Ransom said, "could he make money with it?"

"Hell yes," Ace said. "It'd be like owning a seaport."

31

Friday night, Ransom walked through the fields belonging to Elizabeth's father. It seemed to him that every star burned white-hot. Crickets and frogs sang from the ditches as he passed. Off in the deep cypress swamp, an owl called, lonely and far away.

Ransom wore his fine suit and derby hat. He thought he should have a cane if he was to be a true gentleman. As he walked through the young cotton, he planned a trip to the men's store in Charleston to buy a cane, one with an ivory handle.

Across the field, lights from the Lyttelton house shone from every window. Ansel Deadwilder's touring car stood in the oyster shell drive and Ransom knew he'd have a long wait until Elizabeth came out to the barn. He slipped past the hen house, through the grassy backyard, and around a tangle of muscadine vines growing on an arbor made of cedar posts. From there he hurried through an open place between azalea bushes to the woodpile behind the barn.

He could see Elizabeth in the kitchen window. Ansel stood behind her until she left the kitchen and came to the back door where she looked towards the barn. Ansel followed her. The moment he appeared, Elizabeth ducked into the house again. They seemed to be arguing. Sometimes Elizabeth's mother, moving through the house, paraded past one window after another.

Ransom stretched out on the woodpile to wait and let his mind drift to the heavens. Searching for his star, he studied each one carefully, trying in his mind to change its color. But, these stars would not change for him. He tried harder but he soon lost which star he'd been looking at. There were too many.

Long after the dew had settled on the grass and on his suit, he heard Ansel Deadwilder's car purr to life. He sat up in time to see Ansel back out of the drive and onto the road then head off towards Pocotaligo. A moment later, a light went out in the house.

One by one, the windows fell dark until only a single window was lit. Behind the gauzy curtains, Elizabeth was undressing, though all Ransom could see was a hazy outline of her neck and shoulders as she sat at a dressing table. She raised a brush and drew it through the long strands of her hair, over and over again, like some ritual of the spirit. Ransom could watch Elizabeth brush her hair until the end of time, but she put the brush away and when she did, he felt a loss. A moment later, Elizabeth left the dressing table and the light went out.

Ransom settled back on the woodpile and looked up at the stars, but he'd grown tired of stars and tired of waiting. Where the open lawn met the cotton field, a fox pranced across the dew laden grass, sniffing the ground. It froze and looked in Ransom's direction for half a breath, its nose in the breeze. Watching Ransom, it took a step back, then another, until it melted into the darkness beneath a Catawba tree.

The screen on the back door bumped. His wait was over. Elizabeth crossed the yard wearing slippers and a chiffon robe. Strands of blond hair fluffed loosely about her head and neck.

"Ransom," she said and threw her arms around his neck. "I thought Ansel would never leave."

"I would have waited all night." Ransom pressed his face against the softness of her shoulder and breathed her scent. Her hair drifted over his cheeks as he gathered her closer, his arms around her waist.

"Hold me," she said. "I get so lonely and so frightened. Hold me."

They stood behind the barn with their arms around each other, breathing as one. Elizabeth curled against him, warm and soft.

He scooped her up in his arms and carried her to the woodpile. Ransom marveled at her lightness. He could feel her body naked beneath the robe and night clothes with none of the barriers of daily dress, no buckles or ties or infinite layers.

He sat down on the woodpile with Elizabeth in his lap. Blond hair tumbled wild down her shoulders. She took his derby and pressed it on her head.

"What were you doing out here all this time?" She held to his neck with her face so close he could feel her breath on his lips.

"Looking at the stars," he said, easing his lips closer to hers. "When I was in France, I had a favorite star. I could talk to it in my head and will it to change colors."

"How peculiar," she said, frowning at the notion. "I suppose it was the stress of war that caused you to think such things."

He kissed her. Her breath became his breath as they tasted each other and could not get enough. Ransom slipped a hand beneath her robe and felt the softness of her breast. The derby fell from her head and rolled away across the wet grass and neither of them cared.

"I've missed you so much," she said between kisses. "It's been unbearable without you. I want to see you every night. You must never go away again."

The bow holding her robe together came undone and the folds of light fabric melted away from her breasts and belly. Ransom kissed the tender hollow of her throat and felt a shiver rise from deep within her. She moaned and let her head fall back as his lips explored the warm place between her breasts. Her hand found the nape of his neck and she pressed him closer. He kissed her breast through the gown and breathed in the fragrance of her skin. Heat engulfed him and he wanted more.

He thought to take her inside the barn and lay her down in the new hay and touch his lips to every fold and every curve and every delicate place on her body. Still holding her close, he stood up.

In his arms, she felt on fire. Her robe lay open. He could see her breasts through the slight gown, each dark nipple raised against the fabric. The cotton belt that had tied it all together dragged across the ground, gathering dew. To have a woman so open to him thrilled Ransom beyond intoxication.

They heard the screen door bump.

Elizabeth gasped. Ransom's heart stopped cold.

"Put me down."

Elizabeth gathered the robe and cinched it with the cotton belt. She pushed him towards shadows at the corner of the barn.

"Elizabeth?" her mother called. "Are you out here?"

Rising up on tiptoe, she pecked Ransom on the lips. "Meet me at Little Muddy Baptist Church tomorrow at noon," she said. "I'll bring a picnic. We can be alone there."

"Elizabeth?" Her mother followed the footprints through the grass to the woodpile. "Elizabeth?"

Ransom's body still burned with desire and, even at a distance, with a breeze passing between them, he could sense her passion too. He hungered for her. He hungered for her skin against his lips and the scent of her. He looked back and saw his derby on the grass at her feet.

"My hat."

Elizabeth snatched it from the ground and took a step towards the dark corner where he hid, holding the derby in her outstretched hand. Ransom reached for it, but couldn't grab it before Elizabeth's mother appeared. He pressed himself against the wall and stood perfectly still in the shadows. If the woman looked close enough, she'd see him.

"Elizabeth," her mother said, "I thought I heard you go out, and then, you weren't in your room. What on earth are you doing out here at this hour?" When she saw the derby, her tone grew sharper. "Whose hat is that?"

Elizabeth placed the derby on her head.

"It's an old one of Father's." She hooked her arm behind her mother's elbow and they walked away, arm in arm.

"But, what in the world were you doing out here?"

"Looking at the stars," Elizabeth said. They crossed the lawn, following her footprints back to the house. "I thought I might talk to a star in my head and try to make it change color."

"Oh, Elizabeth," her mother said, "you are so peculiar."

32

THE NEXT DAY AT NOON, Ransom waited on the steps of the
Little Muddy Baptist Church, a modest structure built of cypress
and painted white. In the churchyard, a single table, sixty feet
long and sheltered with a tin roof, stretched through a grove
of pines. Although he had never attended, Ransom figured any
church with such a monument to food was a church where he'd
feel welcomed.

The Little Muddy River meandered behind the church grounds.
Below a clay bank, a sand beach stretched a hundred feet along
the river where a lazy current flowed, black as boiled coffee. There
was no far bank, only a dense jungle of cypress trees standing like
columns holding up the sky. Feathered strands of Spanish moss
dripped from each limb. Briars, dense and lethal as barbed wire,
tangled at the base of every tree.

Ransom had tied the buggy in the shade at the edge of the
woods so the black mare could graze. He missed his hat and rubbed
a hand through his hair as he walked to the road and looked in the
direction of town. Maybe Elizabeth would bring it.

He did not see Elizabeth on the road, but he did see the sheriff
racing towards him on the Indian motorcycle, a cloud of dust bil-
lowing behind him. Ransom withdrew to the steps of the church

and sat down to wait. The sheriff slowed, turned the bulky motor-cycle into the sand yard and rolled to a stop where Ransom sat. The lawman planted both feet on either side of the Indian while the engine idled between his legs, popping and cracking until he turned it off.

"Cooter said I'd find you out here." The sheriff pushed the goggles above his forehead. "The check you gave Cooter for the horse and buggy ain't no good. The bank won't pay it."

"What?" The news brought Ransom to his feet. "Of course it's good. I have a line of credit at the bank. Sterling and Sterling is backing me."

"I don't know about that, but Cooter wants his horse and buggy back. I'll give you a day to make it right. If you don't, I'll haul your butt in and lock you up. Should've done it the first time I seen you. I knew you weren't no good."

Elizabeth appeared on the road, driving a buggy by herself. She wore gloves and a broad-rimmed cartwheel hat. Her horse had been trotting but slowed to a walk as it turned into the churchyard.

"I'll leave you two love birds alone," the sheriff said, pulling the goggles down over his eyes. "Get square with Cooter." He kick-started the Indian and rolled out onto the road, turning back towards town. The engine revved as he gained speed and roared out of sight. Watching the sheriff ride away, Ransom caught Elizabeth's mare by the bridle and led it into the shade.

"What did the sheriff want?" Elizabeth said when he helped her down. She had his derby and pressed it on his head.

"Nothing." Ransom reached up and adjusted the derby so it cocked slightly to one side.

Elizabeth reached into the buggy and pulled out a blanket and a white oak picnic basket.

"I'm actually a very fine cook," she said. "You'll see." Ransom took the heavy basket from her. Elizabeth held his elbow as they walked across the church grounds to the river. "I've always thought this beach was so romantic. This is where they baptize their converts."

"Will the sheriff tell your daddy we're here together?" Ransom said.

"He'll tell Ansel and Ansel will threaten to tell my father. He's so jealous, but I can handle him." She raised her chin and straightened her spine. "I have all day and I intend to enjoy myself."

They stepped down to the sandy beach where Ransom spread the blanket near the edge of the water. Elizabeth sat in the middle of it, straightened a corner that had tucked under, then took off her hat and set it aside. They sat below the bank and out of sight of anyone passing on the road.

"There was a skirmish here between Union and Confederate cavalry," Elizabeth said as she tugged at the fingers of her glove. She pulled it off and gave Ransom an inviting sideways glance. Her blue eyes stirred something within him and sparked a gentle burning. "The walls of the church are covered with bullet holes," she said. "I'll show you later."

Ransom sat beside Elizabeth and moved the picnic basket out of the way so they could touch. He pressed his thigh tightly against hers and put an arm around her. They sat on the blanket and watched the black water creep past. A leaf twirled on the invisible current. At the water's edge a small alligator, less than a foot long, paddled by, chasing a school of minnows.

"Why was the sheriff here?" She leaned her head on his shoulder. "He upset you. I can tell."

"It's nothing," he said and pulled her closer.

"Don't say that. Something's worrying you. You just don't want to talk about it."

Although the sun shone bright on the water and the towering cypress, the air in their small hiding place was cool and refreshing. The warmth where they touched kindled a burning hunger. Elizabeth's cheeks flushed crimson. She raised her head just enough to smile into his eyes.

"You don't have to tell me." She put her head on his shoulder again. "Is it bad?"

"I don't know."

Ransom placed a fingertip beneath her chin and kissed her thoroughly. Above them, out on the road in front of the church, he heard the rumbling of a finely tuned internal combustion engine. When it faded to a hum, he peered over the embankment to see Ansel Deadwilder's touring car idling in the churchyard. The top was down and Ansel sat at the wheel. For a moment, the man stared at the two buggies parked in the shade, then looked around before climbing out of the car.

"Elizabeth," Ansel called.

"My god." Elizabeth covered her mouth with her hand. And then, as if realizing how compromised she appeared, she sat up and shoved on her hat.

Ransom rolled away from her and watched Ansel Deadwilder standing at his automobile.

"Elizabeth," Ansel called. "Sheriff Pate said you were here with Ransom."

She hurried to put on her gloves and adjusted her hat only to cause more hair to tumble loose.

"Ransom and I were about to enjoy a picnic," she said as she stood up. The fingertips of her gloves hung loose as withered teats. Her large brimmed cartwheel hat was cocked backwards on her head. She tried to adjust it, but the effort merely caused more strands of hair to fall along her neck and shoulders. A wayward curl dropped over her forehead and into her eyes. She had the appearance of a woman discreetly mauled.

"There you are," Ansel said, smiling like a shark. He drew an envelope from the inside pocket of his jacket and flicked it with his fingers, making the envelope snap. When he joined them at the river, he glanced at the blanket spread out on the sand and raised an eyebrow. Ransom stood beside Elizabeth.

"Looks like a cozy, out of the way place," Ansel said, "unseen from the road, perfect for a treacherous young man who cares not a fig about a woman's reputation."

"It's not like that," Ransom said.

"Of course not." Ansel stood on the bank and looked down on them. "I'm sure you were studying Bible verses. Anyway, thank goodness, I arrived in time. Although, I doubt anyone will appreciate the sacrifices I have made." He handed Elizabeth the envelope. "Out of duty to your father and my supreme love for you, my dear Elizabeth, I beg you to read this letter."

"Ansel, what have you done now?" She took the letter and read aloud the return address. "The War Department?"

"Yes," Ansel said, smiling.

Elizabeth glared at Ansel then opened the envelope and began reading. Her face grew waxen. Her eyes flared. Leaning into the letter, she gasped a horrid little sound. Her hand and the letter began to tremble.

"What is it?" Ransom said. "What does it say?"

Elizabeth looked over the letter to Ransom. Her eyes burned with anger and began to tear.

"Your charming suitor has syphilis," Ansel said. "Syphilis," he said again, trailing each syllable as it rolled off his lips. "That's an official document of the United States Army. It states clearly in the second paragraph the conditions of Private Ransom James MacTavish's discharge from service, syphilis. He has syphilis."

"It's just syphilis on paper," Ransom said. "I don't really have it. I had to get home and the British wouldn't let me. I wanted to see you."

"Ransom," Elizabeth said, "how could you?" Her eyes were piercing. She shook her head as if somehow that would help her understand. A tear surged down her cheek. She stepped away, opening space between them that chilled Ransom as thoroughly as a plunge into ice water.

Looking to Ansel, Elizabeth said, "Who else knows?"

"Just your father," Ansel said. "I was duty bound to tell him. And the sheriff, of course, I had to tell him why I so urgently needed to find you."

The letter slipped from Elizabeth's fingers and twirled a dizzy pinwheel to the ground. She staggered as if she might faint.

"For God's sake, Ansel," she cried. "Don't tell anyone else."

"It's only on paper." Ransom reached to hold her steady, but she jerked her arm away.

"Don't touch me," she snapped.

"It's only on paper!" Ransom tried again to grasp her arm. "You have to believe me."

"It's an official government document." She pointed to the ground where the letter had fallen. "I read it myself. I don't have to believe you. I don't even know you."

"Precisely the point I've been trying to make from the

beginning," Ansel said as he knelt to pick up the letter. He folded it and slipped it back inside his jacket. "You have no idea who this man is."

"What will people think of me?" Elizabeth said.

With a damning look at Ransom, Elizabeth knelt and grasped the corner of the blanket. Ransom stepped onto the sand an instant before she yanked the blanket out from under him. She gathered it in a wad and snatched the heavy picnic basket on her way up the river bank.

"Elizabeth," Ransom said to her back. She kept walking. "Please listen to me. It's not real. I don't have syphilis. Doctor Lafitte can check me out, he'll tell you."

Elizabeth marched on. "I'm not stupid," she called over her shoulder. "I read the letter. What will people think?"

"Now that you've come to your senses," Ansel said, following Elizabeth across the churchyard, the basket heavy in her hand. "It's time to be reasonable. Marry me. I'll buy you the biggest Charleston house on Murray Boulevard. You can entertain as freely as you wish."

Elizabeth stopped so suddenly, Ansel nearly bumped into her. She turned on him with venom in her eyes. The blanket fell to the ground. With both hands, as though gripping a pipe wrench, she grasped the handle of the white oak basket laden with food. She swung it with all her strength and with all her anger.

The basket caught Ansel on the side of his head and knocked him off his feet in an explosion of food and napkins and utensils. Fried chicken skidded off the hood of the touring car, leaving greasy streaks. A red and white checkered table cloth landed on the front seat. Plates and forks and spoons clattered across the back. Yeast rolls arched through the air as though launched from a catapult. A jar of pickled okra cracked the windshield and the juice leaked on the polished green metal, while far beyond the car, a quart of lemonade rolled through the sand.

Elizabeth stood over Ansel. He knelt at her feet and pressed a palm to his left ear. Blood seeped between his fingers. Boiling with rage, Elizabeth's shoulders quivered as she raised the empty basket for another blow, but Ansel reached up and took it from her hand.

Choking on her fury, the veins in her neck strained to the bursting point, Elizabeth snatched the letter from the inside pocket of Ansel's jacket. Sobbing as she staggered back, she tore the letter to bits.

"Ansel Deadwilder," she said, spitting tears as she ripped the letter into smaller and smaller pieces, "if you tell another soul, I will scratch out your eyes and feed them to the crabs."

33

"Your check's no good," Cooter said as he came out of the livery. Ransom reined the buggy to a stop beside the gas pump and climbed down.

"I'm going over to the bank now," he said.

"Everybody's crying." Cooter rubbed the nose of the black mare. "It's on account of the cotton market crashing. We're in for hard times."

"Cotton market?" Ransom staggered back.

"Lord, yes," Cooter said. "They said it'd happen."

Ransom began running towards the bank. Cooter called after him. "There's a redheaded girl about to bust with a kid asking for you."

Ransom stormed through the front door of the bank, shocking the teller who pointed to the bank manager's office. Out of breath, Ransom braced himself against the manager's desk. Before he could speak, the man pushed a telegram across the desk for Ransom to read.

We hereby withdraw any and all authority and liability regarding the credit account of Ransom James MacTavish. Any loans Pocotaligo Farmers Bank extends regarding this account are the sole responsibility of Pocotaligo Farmers Bank.

"Sterling and Sterling pulled your credit." The manager pushed a second and more official looking document across the desk. "This is the amount you owe."

"Eight hundred dollars?" Ransom said. "How am I supposed to pay? I didn't make two dollars a week with Froggy. My daddy made less than that farming on shares. Without cotton, I got nothing."

"You have thirty days before we take a legal action."

Ransom folded the paper itemizing his debt and walked out into the sun. He couldn't think. His mind had frozen as surely as if someone had poured concrete into his skull. It was hardening by the second. His feet had more sense than his head and managed to take him to Miss Hazel's. He let himself through the gate and past the roses then stumbled in a fog up the walkway to the porch.

"Ransom," Miss Hazel called from the sitting room when he entered the house. "You have some explaining to do."

Miss Hazel sat in her favorite chair. Cookies, coffee, sugar cubes and the cream pitcher with gold leaf trim filled a tray on the center table. Across from Miss Hazel, Amelia Rose sat on the sofa with her belly dominating the room. She fed herself bites of ginger cookie with one hand and gripped a coffee cup with the other. The saucer lay on the floor beside her feet where the orange tabby licked cream from it.

"First," Miss Hazel said, "the bank wouldn't honor the check you gave me for your room and board. Second, I'd like you to explain your relationship with this young lady."

"Ransom," Amelia Rose said. "I didn't have no where to go. The old lady died and her nephew come down from Columbia and run me off. I ain't going to have this baby back in the woods by myself."

Ransom felt suddenly weak and flopped down on the far end of the sofa. Outside, from the direction of Wanda's boarding house, he could hear Froggy hawking shrimp and crab.

"Give her my room," Ransom said. "I'll pay for the doctor too."

"You're broke," Miss Hazel said. "You can't pay anyone."

Ransom nodded, unable to speak the truth.

"Ransom," Miss Hazel said. Her voice was so soft and so kind it hurt. "You know the cotton market collapsed. We're in for a long bad spell. I've seen this before."

The concrete in Ransom's head had hardened into stone and still it spun. Nothing made sense. He reached across the sofa and touched Amelia Rose's hand and gathered her fingers into his. Her familiar warmth gave him comfort. For the first time since Elizabeth had read the letter from the Army, he felt a small, stable point of reference.

"What do you intend to do?" Miss Hazel said.

Ransom had no answers. He released Amelia Rose's hand and stood up.

"I'm coming with you," Amelia Rose said.

"You better stay here."

"Yes, dear," Miss Hazel said, "for the baby."

Ransom hurried from Miss Hazel's and went directly to Dr. Lafitte's. He asked the doctor to check on Amelia Rose and promised to pay when he could. When Froggy rolled past on the wagon, Ransom ran out and climbed aboard.

"See what I mean about cotton?" Froggy looked Ransom over from head to toe and took in the Charleston suit, shoes and derby. "Fine clothes don't mean nothing," he said.

They passed Mr. Roebuck's pretty little train in silence. They passed the great ditch and the old house with hay on the porch and that sunbaked stretch of land that couldn't grow a weed. Joe Broke-shoulder stood in the yard and watched them pass as though witnessing an execution.

At the pier, Ransom retreated to the shrimp boat. On the berth in the cabin, he found a ball of hardened clay, shards of green and blue and brown glass were pressed into it like irregular windows and hawk feathers splayed out in all directions. He climbed into the berth, stretched beside the feathered Gullah charm and closed his eyes.

Shadows and light drifted through the cabin as the sun slipped across the sky. Ransom felt the tide return from the ocean, flushing the shrimp back into the muddy creeks and lapping against the hull. Wind combed through the marsh grass and rippled across the water. It breathed through the open windows of the shrimp boat, hushing over Ransom's body, but he didn't want even the wind to find him and turned his back to it.

When Ransom finally opened his eyes, darkness had settled on the earth. On this night, there was no moon. Frogs and crickets and a chorus of insects sang loud the pulse of the marsh. Out the window he could see the glow of Froggy's fire up on the bluff. He forced himself to leave his hiding place and dragged his shame up the hill.

On the bluff, he found Amelia Rose seated on a tea crate at the fire, tending to several croakers roasting on sticks over the flames. Her great belly ballooned beneath her thin dress. Cornbread cooked in a black iron frying pan nestled in the coals and the coffee pot steamed.

"Who brought you out here?" Ransom said as he drew close to the fire, his shoulders slumped.

"I brought my own self. Miss Hazel's cook told me where to find you."

"You walked?"

"Just like I walked from Miss Annie's and slept in the woods at night. I don't need nobody to do for me."

"Ain't she something," Froggy said from the door of the shack. He grinned with bare gums and his two creosote teeth. "She come out here and just started cooking. Life just got a whole lot better. Sheila likes her fine."

"It's about ready to eat," Amelia Rose said.

But Ransom wasn't hungry. He turned away from the fire and trudged to the pier. Amelia Rose went after him.

"Where are you going?" She reached for his hand but snagged only his little finger. It was enough. "All that mess about cotton and the bank don't matter," Amelia Rose said. "You were broke when I met you and I don't care one bit if you're broke now."

Ransom looked at her and took in the scabby legs, spotted red where the bedbugs and mosquitos had gotten to her, the summer dress that draped across her huge belly, eyes that looked out from a soul stronger than the whole damn world, and red hair that sparkled like nothing else when it caught the sun. He wrapped his fingers securely over hers.

Together they walked the length of the pier. When they came to the ladder leading down to the crab boat, Ransom sat and dangled his feet over the side. Amelia Rose sat beside him, her leg pressed against his. She hung her feet over the edge and kicked them back and forth, fluffing her dress in a most unladylike manner, cooling her belly and thighs.

"I've been a fool," Ransom said and looked out at the night.

"You got a good heart." Amelia Rose leaned into him. "I've seen your heart. I know."

"I don't have a brain. Not one worth using. All the time I thought I was making a life, I was just making a mess." He lowered his eyes to the water and the crabbing boat. The outgoing tide pulled the flat-bottom boat away from the pilings. It tugged on its tether, jerking against the current.

They watched a one-legged cricket kick off from the pier and launch itself into the air. It did a slow roll, tumbling forward with its single leg kicked out until it landed on the water and drifted away. It kicked and created a tiny ripple. When it kicked again, a fish sucked it beneath the surface.

"My life got as far as the shit house and just sat down." Ransom reached for the ladder and descended to the crab boat.

"You've done enough fool things for one day," she said. "Promise me, you won't do no more, not today."

"I can't promise anything," he said from the boat. He pressed the derby on his head. The stench of the boat soiled his Charleston suit. Dark water soaked the knees when he untied the line and released the boat into the current.

"I'll wait right here 'til you get back," Amelia Rose said.

"I might not get back." Ransom drifted into the darkness.

"Then I'll just wait right on forever," she said. When he didn't answer, Amelia Rose called to him, "Ransom?"

He pretended not to hear and gave himself to the current, putting distance between them. When some time had passed, he raised the brim of his derby and saw Amelia Rose seated on the edge of the pier, swinging her legs and growing smaller as he drifted away.

The current carried him past the first jug on the crab line and past where he had learned to cast a shrimp net. He drifted around a corner of marsh grass and could no longer see Froggy's fire or the pier. A pair of dolphins rose in the black water beside him, breathing a sigh.

"Talk to me," he said, but the dolphins, swimming side by side, only smiled and slipped beneath the surface.

Ransom surrendered to the voice inside his head that told him how stupid he had been. Like that one-legged cricket, he wished to throw himself into the ocean and make it take him. He slumped to the bottom of the boat until foul water soaked through his fine suit. A rotten croaker, half eaten by gulls, pressed against his leg.

"Lord," Ransom said to the stars, "why was I made to be so miserable? Give me to the ocean. Feed me to a whale. Strike me dead with a bolt of lightning." He lay still, letting the tide take him as he tied his brain into ever tighter knots, each knot cinched with shame and self-loathing.

Drifting beneath the stars, the current took him far from the pier and familiar tidal creeks until Ransom heard voices and laughter and smelled the smoke of a hardwood fire. He sat up and pushed the dead fish away. The foul water drained from his clothes as a mild breeze pressed the boat against the marsh grass. The tide had stopped and at the water's edge, a fat raccoon picked through oyster shells.

On the island, fires burned in the Gullah village. A woman squealed and a wave of laughter filled the air. When the laughter quieted, he heard a steady voice that sounded like the narrative of a storyteller, although he couldn't discern the words and didn't know the language.

Bullfrogs began to croak, deep and resonant. Smaller frogs and insects joined with higher notes until the chorus was complete, loud and pulsating. At the edge of the water, the raccoon squatted and fed herself with both hands. On the island, the Gullah sang a soulful melody that came to him on the wind. The words were unknown to Ransom, but he didn't need words to understand. And the stars, the stars were everywhere.

The tide reversed and the current flowed in from the ocean, carrying the boat and Ransom back towards the pier. The raccoon moved on to yet another dinner. Distance grew between him and the village. The song of the Gullah faded until all he heard was an occasional far away chorus.

He drifted. Soon marsh grass blocked his view of the Gullah fires and he could no longer hear them at all. The current carried him through the place where the dolphins had looked into his eyes. It carried him past the last jug float on the crab line and past the place where he'd learned to shrimp. Alive beneath the stars, the infinite stars, he rode the current back to the pier, back to the fire, back to Amelia Rose.

34

"Miss Hazel!" Ransom called as Froggy reined the mule to a stop beside the roses at the gate. Amelia Rose sat doubled over between them. "Miss Hazel!" Ransom called again, louder than before.

"What the hell's going on?" A man shouted from the neighboring house. "It's the middle of the night. Are you drunk or just stupid?"

Miss Hazel came to the door holding a lamp. "What on earth?"

"She's having the baby." Ransom jumped from the wagon and reached back to help Amelia Rose down. "She's having the baby!"

"Lord, help us." Miss Hazel ran out the door and down the steps in her night gown, the lamp flickering in her hand. Then, realizing how she was dressed, Miss Hazel scurried right back into the house and called from the door. "Get her inside!"

Amelia Rose staggered between Froggy and Ransom, who held her up by her elbows. Halfway to the porch she gasped and leaned hard against Ransom until the pain subsided. By degrees they got her up the steps and into the front room.

"Crack a window," Amelia Rose said once they had her in bed. She dripped with perspiration. Froggy opened the window looking out on the front porch and a cooling breeze passed through the room. Amelia Rose dropped her head back on a pillow.

"I'll get the doctor." Ransom touched Amelia Rose on the arm. "You'll be all right."

Amelia Rose looked up at Ransom and their eyes met as she swallowed hard against the pain. Pulling away, Ransom hurried from the room and out the front door, letting the screen slam behind him. He sprinted down the alley and across town to Dr. Lafitte's office where he banged on the door until someone opened it.

"Amelia Rose's baby's coming," he said to a figure peering out.

"Is this her first?" a woman said, surprising Ransom.

"Yes ma'am."

"The first always takes longer," the woman said. "I'll just be a minute." She drew back and the door closed behind her.

Ransom paced the boardwalk, stopping occasionally to look through the glass window fronting the office. Figures moved in the dark interior, embraced, then separated. When the door opened again, the woman appeared with a satchel.

"Where's Dr. Lafitte?" Ransom said.

"I'm the midwife. A woman prefers another woman. Believe me."

At Miss Hazel's, the midwife banished Froggy and Ransom to the front porch where they sat on the steps.

"While you were off getting the midwife," Froggy said, "Miss Hazel sent for Preacher Heygood. He's in there now, sleeping on the sofa.

"A preacher?" Ransom said.

"He's a good man, keeps me in Bibles."

"Does he know you smoke 'em?"

"It ain't a sin if you read it first," Froggy said.

"I got to see what's going on." Ransom went to the open window and looked in. "Breathe," the midwife said, dabbing a folded cloth over Amelia Rose's brow. "Breathe now. You got to keep breathing."

Amelia Rose whispered something to the midwife and pointed to the window where Ransom stood. The midwife drew the curtains, shutting him out. He went back to the top step and sat beside Froggy.

"This is going to throw us off for in the morning." Froggy took a Prince Albert tobacco tin from his pocket and began rolling a cigarette. "We'll miss the tide if she don't hurry up." He struck a long kitchen match with his thumbnail and lit the cigarette, blowing an easy stream of smoke. "Hope it's a girl," Froggy said. "I'd love to have a little girl running around my place. Wouldn't that be something?"

The curtains parted and lamplight spilled across the porch.

"Ransom?" The midwife leaned from the window. She sounded frightened. "You got to marry her or she won't have this baby." Amelia Rose made a sound and the midwife ducked back into room.

"She can't stop a baby from coming," Ransom said. He looked to Froggy. "Can she?"

"I wouldn't want her to try."

"Don't I have a choice?"

"Sure," Froggy said. "You can choose. But when it comes to women, a man don't know what he's doing 'til he's too old for it to matter." Froggy turned to Ransom smiling bare gums and ragged dark teeth. "I was married once. When I lived in San Francisco, I took up with this crippled China woman. She was small, like a child and had this bad leg so she couldn't get around too good. Her own people didn't want her, but she suited me just fine. At night I'd sleep all wrapped around her, best damn sleep I ever had. She was my best friend. I didn't know I loved her 'til she burned up in the fire of '06." Froggy looked again at the stars. "My life ain't been worth spit since I lost her."

"I slept like that once," Ransom said, remembering the night he slept with his arms around Amelia Rose as they lay beneath the pines. She had kept him warm and pressed so close he could feel her heart beating against his. "Froggy, when you were married, were you happy?"

"It ain't about that." Froggy eyes glistened like he was recalling more than he was telling. He gazed out into the night and spoke softly, so as not to be heard inside the house. "It's your own damn life," the old man said. His stringy beard twitched with each word he spoke. "She's a good woman, as good as you're likely to ever find, but you ain't got to marry her."

Ransom nodded and looked at the stars, hoping for an answer.

"But," Froggy said. That single word, accented with all the depth of his crusty old soul, carried enormous weight.

"What?" Ransom said.

"You ain't got to do nothing." Froggy's attention drifted away, then he looked to Ransom and added, even more softly than before: "You say you can't make babies 'cause of what happened to you in your war?"

"That's right."

"Maybe…" Froggy paused, weighing his words. "Maybe this baby's the only baby you're ever going to get."

A shrill whistle pierced the night, long and loud, announcing a train approaching from the north. It barreled into town and passed the depot without slowing, filling the night with a rush and roar. Railcars and passenger cars clacked and rattled. The train sped south, trailing its noise and clatter. It cried one more time before leaving in its wake a silence more fragile than before.

"The Palmetto Limited," Froggy said. "It must be midnight."

"The town lets trains come through here all the time," Ransom said. "But not an airplane. And planes are the future."

"They ain't got the room for airplanes," Froggy said. "That's the riddle."

"Yeah," Ransom said, "that's the riddle. They'd have to fill in a swamp to make a place for planes."

"Or drain it," Froggy said, "like the Yamassee Hunt Club did out at Joe Broke-shoulder's place. It'd cost more than anyone around here's willing to pay."

"That's it!" Ransom sat up. He recalled the old house on Joe Broke-shoulder's land and the half mile strip of sunbaked clay. "We don't have to fill in a swamp and we don't have to drain it either. It's right there at Joe Broke-shoulder's. It's been right there all along, just waiting for me to see it."

His mind seized on that promise and began to put the pieces together while the two men sat on the top step of Miss Hazel's porch and waited for Amelia Rose's baby. Neither spoke again for what seemed to Ransom to have been hours.

Above them, stars journeyed across the summer sky. The house grew quiet. He couldn't hear the midwife in the bedroom, nor anyone else. In that quiet spell, a plan began to form in Ransom's mind. Against the night, he saw a vision of a life he'd never dreamed. The suddenness of this understanding took his breath away.

Finally, when night had settled deeply on the town and the air had grown still, Ransom stopped thinking. His thoughts leveled out and all the searching and weighing and counter-weighing feathered into silence. In that moment, the pieces of the riddle fell into place. Savoring the clarity of his plan, Ransom drew a breath and went inside to find the preacher.

35

WHEN HE ENTERED THE HOUSE, Preacher Heygood sat up on the sofa, wiped sleep from his eyes and gathered his Bible from the end table. Ransom opened the door to the room where Amelia Rose lay exhausted beneath sweaty sheets. Someone had turned the lantern down and the room was dark as a cavern. The midwife lay on top of the sheet beside Amelia Rose, holding her hand. Ransom felt as if he stood at the edge of something sacred, something that would forever exclude him.

He hesitated, reaching for the midwife without touching her. His hand hovered for a moment over the sleeping woman. Beside her, Amelia Rose overtaken with exhaustion, slept just as soundly. Ransom paused to witness their serenity then touched the midwife on the shoulder and nudged her awake.

"I'd like to marry Amelia Rose now," he said, "if you think it'd be all right."

"I think it'll be just fine." The midwife gave Amelia Rose's hand a gentle squeeze. Amelia Rose opened her eyes and drew a deep breath. It frightened Ransom to see her so weak. He felt guilty because of it and didn't know why. Her eyes found his and her lips curved into a timid smile.

The preacher entered the room with Miss Hazel who looked worn out. Froggy waited in the hall, hovering just outside the bedroom door. The midwife turned the flame up in the lamp, filling the room with amber light.

Ransom rounded the bed until he stood between the wall and the side where Amelia Rose lay. Her belly, a mound in the middle of the room, pressed high beneath the sheet. Against the wall, the preacher stood close behind Ransom and looked over his shoulder.

Amelia Rose stretched and grimaced. She sucked in her breath and the midwife hurried beside her, pushing between Ransom and the preacher.

"You're too late," the midwife said. "This baby's coming whether we're right in the eyes of the Lord or not."

"No," Amelia Rose said and motioned the midwife away. She sucked in a breath and seemed to find some place to rest between the pains.

"Take her hand," Preacher Heygood said. Ransom reached for it, but Amelia Rose snatched it away.

"I don't know if I want to marry you now," she said. "I did a while back, but I don't know now. I shouldn't have to beg a man to marry me."

Ransom couldn't think of a word to say. He turned to the midwife but found no clue. He turned to Froggy standing at the door, who looked just as stunned. Ransom took a hasty step backwards and bumped against the preacher who was too dazed to move.

"I'm sorry," Ransom said. "I'm sorry I woke y'all up." The room filled with pity. He couldn't look at them.

Ransom retreated. Once, he glanced back at Amelia Rose, but on seeing her stern expression, he determined not to look at her again. He was headed out the bedroom door when Miss Hazel caught him by the arm.

"Just one minute." Miss Hazel steered him into the hall.

"She's not going to marry me." Ransom wanted to run. He wanted to get out of that house and out of that town and never look back. He pulled away from Miss Hazel and headed for the front door, but she grabbed him again.

"She still wants to marry you," Miss Hazel said. "She just wants you to propose to her. Every woman wants to be proposed to. She's no different." Miss Hazel pushed something into Ransom's hand. "And give her this."

Ransom looked down into his palm where a slight gold band glittered in the lamp light.

"It was my mother's," Miss Hazel said. "I have no daughter. I'm sure my mother would be pleased if Amelia Rose wore it."

Ransom took a deep breath and considered his options. He stood in the hall, halfway between Amelia Rose and the front door. He should run, he thought. He should stay. Run. Stay.

He stepped back into the bedroom and wove his way past the midwife and around the foot of the bed, squeezing between the preacher and the wall until he again stood over Amelia Rose. For an instant, her gaze fell on the gold band Miss Hazel had given him. Then she looked up at Ransom.

"I want you to marry me," he said.

Amelia Rose lay silent. Ransom could tell by the way she squinted that she was thinking hard about something.

"No," Miss Hazel said, "Ransom that will never do. Come here."

The preacher stepped away, clearing a path for Ransom. Miss Hazel pulled him out to the hall.

"I'll get him back to you in just a moment," Miss Hazel said through the door.

The midwife joined them in the hall and said, "If you're going to be so slow about this, it'll have to wait." Behind her, Amelia Rose moaned and writhed beneath the sheets.

"There's time," Miss Hazel said. "We have to make this something she'll remember."

"I promise you," the midwife said. "She'll remember tonight."

"She should have flowers on her wedding day." Miss Hazel led Ransom through the front door and into the yard where her roses gave the night air an exquisite sweetness. Ransom reached for the first one, but Miss Hazel stopped him.

"Not the roses," she said. "I can't bear to see them picked, not before Rose Day."

"That's two weeks off," Ransom said. "Why'd you bring me out here?"

"The poor child should have roses on her wedding day," Miss

Hazel said, "but I can't let you pick my babies. I thought I could, but I can't."

All but unnoticed, at the corner of the yard, wild pea vines climbed the fence pickets. Their tiny delicate blossoms held the slightest hint of pink and blue, like lace in a watercolor.

"Pea blossoms," Miss Hazel pointed to the vines, "give her pea blossoms."

"I take one step to get married," Ransom said as he picked an array of blue and another bunch of pink, "and all of a sudden, everybody's telling me what to do and running my life."

"This is her wedding," Miss Hazel said. "The only one she'll ever get. Some women never get married. I know. I know how special it should be. Ransom, it's about making memories. There'll be times when a good memory might be all that holds you two together."

She turned Ransom around and pushed him back towards the house. At the steps Ransom hesitated and Miss Hazel jabbed a finger in his back. "Keep marching, soldier."

Ransom made his way into the house on his own steam. He marched down the hall and through the bedroom door and around the bed until he again stood over Amelia Rose. The preacher pressed close behind him.

"Get down on one knee." Miss Hazel pressed close behind the preacher and reached over to push Ransom to the floor. "And humble yourself," she said. "Amelia Rose will take care of you for the rest of your life. If that doesn't humble you, you don't deserve her."

Beside the bed, Ransom sank to one knee. Preacher Heygood shuffled closer.

"Take her hand," Miss Hazel said.

"Amelia Rose," Ransom said and passed her the bouquet of pea blossoms. The lines on her face softened, but still, she did not smile.

Amelia Rose gathered the flowers over her heart and looked at Ransom. He could see himself reflected in her eyes. Something else shone in her eyes as well, but he couldn't name it. It seemed more real in his heart than in his mind. He knew he could build a life with this woman. And he knew no matter how much time passed, no matter how old she became, he would always see her as young and beautiful.

"Look her in the eye," Miss Hazel said and reached around the preacher to poke Ransom again.

"I am looking her in the eye." Then he said to Amelia Rose, "Tell Miss Hazel I'm looking you in the eye."

"He's looking me in the eye."

"Amelia Rose." Ransom's chest swelled. "Marry me."

"Don't answer," Miss Hazel snapped. "Not if he can't ask any nicer than that." She pushed past the preacher and grabbed Ransom. "You have to ask her, not tell her. You're supposed to say, '*Will* you marry me?' Give her a choice. Say it that way, so she can decide."

"The preacher wouldn't be here if she hadn't already decided," Ransom said.

"Don't get smart with me," Miss Hazel said. "I'm just trying to help."

"Damn it," Ransom said over his shoulder. "Let me do it my way. It's my wedding too."

"Well!" Miss Hazel backed away and slumped in the overstuffed chair in the corner, crossing her arms over her chest. "I was just trying to help."

"Amelia Rose," Ransom said. His knee hurt from kneeling on the hardwood floor, but the tenderness in Amelia Rose's eyes soothed his spirit and gave him strength. "I never dreamed I'd find someone like you. I've seen how quick life is over and how lonely it can be too. I'm stronger with you than without you and no matter what comes our way, I know we'll get through it as long as we stick together."

He tightened his hold on her hand and looked directly into her eyes. Her eyes fixed on his. In that moment, he felt joined inside with her. His soul touched her soul.

"Amelia Rose," he said. "It'd make me proud to be your husband and a daddy to your baby. I humbly ask, will you marry me?"

A labor pain seized Amelia Rose. She lay grimacing to keep from screaming, her knuckles clinching white as she gripped the pink and blue pea blossoms to her heart. Her other hand felt sticky in Ransom's. When the pain had passed, her eyes searched his eyes. He felt the strength of her spirit and did not turn away.

"Yes," she said. "I will." A broad smile spread across her face, and in that moment, life filled her eyes.

Ransom shook her hand.

"Preacher," the midwife said. "Get on with it. There's a baby waiting to be born."

The preacher pressed into the narrow space between the bed and the wall.

"Friends and neighbors," he began, "we are gathered this day to unite in Holy matrimony Amelia Rose Prescott and Ransom James MacTavish. A man shall leave his father and his mother, and shall cleave unto his wife: and they shall become as one flesh."

Amelia Rose's face flushed and contorted as she fought a wave of pain. A moan came warbling from deep within her. She clamped her lips together but the pain would not be stopped and burst from her in a scream that shocked them all.

"You better get to the 'I do's," the midwife said.

Flustered, the preacher quickly turned a page in his Bible and said, "Do you, Amelia Rose Prescott, take this man to be your husband until death do you part?"

"Yep," she said with a grimace. "I do."

"Do you, Ransom James MacTavish, take this woman to be your wife, until death do you part?"

"Yes sir, I do."

"Give her the ring," Preacher Heygood said.

Ransom slipped the band on the finger of Amelia Rose.

"What God has joined together, let no man put asunder. I now pronounce you man and wife. You can kiss her if you want."

Ransom looked at the preacher and the midwife. Froggy beamed from the open bedroom door. Miss Hazel, seated in the corner, wiped her eyes. Ransom thought he might wait for a more private moment to kiss his new wife, but Amelia Rose pulled him down to her and kissed him long and hard on the lips.

36

WEEKS LATER, ON THE MORNING OF ROSE DAY, Ransom wore his freshly cleaned and pressed Charleston suit. With his derby tilted just enough to denote a man of confidence, he leaned on Miss Hazel's gate and watched the house. At Ransom's elbow and all along the fence, Miss Hazel's rose bushes had been stripped of every bloom and every velvet petal. There was not a rose to be seen. Not even on the ground where careless feet had trampled through the pine needle mulch.

The front door opened, and Amelia Rose stepped from the house for the first time in weeks. In her arms, she held their baby wrapped in a soft blue blanket. The brass thunder of a marching band striking up resounded from Main Street.

Miss Hazel waited behind the screen door. At the top of the steps, Amelia Rose looked out on the day and filled her lungs with fresh morning air. She wore a cotton dress with a springtime print of yellow flowers. Her hair was held back with a tortoise shell comb and draped beneath a straw hat graced with a sunflower that made the gold highlights in her hair all the more dazzling. Under Miss Hazel's care, Amelia Rose had grown shapely. Her green eyes flashed bright. Happiness filled her to bursting. Weeks of nurturing and good food and care had softened her skin into the thing Ransom most loved to touch.

She was beautiful.

Looking out on the stripped rose bushes, Amelia Rose gasped. "Miss Hazel, what happened to your roses? They're gone."

"I felt horrid that I hadn't let Ransom pick a rose for your wedding." Miss Hazel stepped from behind the screen door. "I had to find a way to make it up to you. Memories are so important. You'll see."

"What about the contest?"

"It's time someone else won." Miss Hazel touched Amelia Rose on the shoulder. "You should go. Show off your new baby and your new husband."

Amelia Rose left the porch and followed the brick walk to where Ransom waited at the gate. They kissed over the baby and Ransom took her hand.

"We can buy the brass bed now," he said as they walked toward town. "It'll be our marriage bed forever."

On Main Street, Cooter Acorn pedaled by on a bicycle and rang a bell fastened to the handlebar. Everyone in the county was in town. The crowd carried them along like a surging tide as they walked hand in hand. They passed a man from Tennessee selling Waynick sewing machines and they passed an internal combustion engine churning three tubs of ice cream at once.

A bright flash, blue and quick as lightning, caught Ransom's attention. Nearby, white smoke rose above a wooden box camera perched on top of a tripod.

"Fine classical photography framed and permanent!" the photographer shouted. "For generations your descendants will admire your artistic sensibilities. Priceless at any cost. Who'll be next?" He spotted Ransom and Amelia Rose. "What a lovely couple." The photographer motioned them closer.

"We should have a picture made," Ransom said. "But after we get the brass bed. With all these folks in town I don't want it to get away from us."

They moved through the crowd of townspeople, farmers, their wives and strings of children. The air was awash with heavenly smells of roasting peanuts, baked pies and buttered popcorn. Kids shouted and screamed and chased each other.

At the general store, Ransom took Amelia Rose all the way to the back where bedframes leaned against the wall. But, then he stopped so suddenly, he caused her to jostle the baby. Where the brass bed had been Ransom saw only an iron frame.

"A lady bought it this morning," the storekeeper said. "Paid cash. I had to sell."

"But."

"It's okay." Amelia Rose tugged at Ransom's hand. "We got lots of other good things."

"But." He looked back as Amelia Rose pulled him away. "That was our marriage bed."

Leaving, they saw Elizabeth and her father at the counter. Her father tipped his hat to Ransom who tipped his derby in return.

"You're the girl in the picture," Amelia Rose said, pressing close to Elizabeth and showing her the baby. "You were engaged to Lieutenant Pinckney."

"Yes." Elizabeth smiled politely and nodded. She cupped her palm over the baby's head, feeling the sparse, silky threads of hair.

"I named him Isaac," Amelia Rose said, "after *your* Isaac. He's who brought me and Ransom together."

"He's perfect." Elizabeth pressed a kiss to baby Isaac's forehead. A tear formed in the corner of her eye, but she brushed it away as she put an arm around Amelia Rose and hugged her. "May I hold him?"

Amelia Rose passed Isaac into Elizabeth's arms.

On the counter, the storekeeper wound the Victrola. A scratchy hiss sounded from the machine, rising and falling as the record turned, until violins sounded a chord and 'The Tennessee Waltz' spilled into the air.

"Dance with me," Ransom said and took his wife's hand.

"I don't know how."

"I don't either. Just pretend."

So, she pretended to waltz with him down the aisle as he held her close. They waltzed, in their own make-believe way, around the stacks of paint cans and sacks of chicken feed then back to the counter again. The Victrola sang out, the melody rising and falling and moving them together in three-quarter time. People gathered at the door and crowded inside.

Amelia Rose laughed at their awkwardness and Ransom laughed too. He leaned her to the left and stood her up again, then leaned her to the right and spun her about. Her simple dress billowed and whirled. They followed the waltz and every step they took, they took together. He was strong for her and she was soft for him. He forgot the people watching. He forgot the store and the aisles and the smells of turpentine and tobacco. He forgot everything except the music that filled his ears and Amelia Rose who filled his heart.

The Victrola wound down to a dragging, distorted end, but Amelia Rose and Ransom continued to dance, lost in each other until the people at the door began to clap. This broke the spell, but not completely. A bit of magic lingered in Ransom's heart and when he looked into Amelia Rose's eyes he could see the magic there too.

That evening, Ransom took his family home in a buggy rented from the livery. Amelia Rose held baby Isaac sleeping in her arms. A framed photograph of their family lay in her lap. Colors burned the sky. A dark wash of magenta and every shade of orange touched the small clouds scattered across the horizon. A biplane droned over a distant stand of pines, its silhouette black against the multi-colored sky.

They came to the house Joe Broke-shoulder had once used to store hay. The house was newly painted white and a lamp glowed behind blue-shuttered windows, inviting them home. Two shiny black biplanes parked off the clay runway in what had once been a couple acres of Joe Broke-shoulder's cotton. Golden letters flowed along the length of each new plane and read 'Roebuck Airlines.'

"Welcome to Pocotaligo International Airport," Ransom said, reining to a stop. "You can go anywhere in the world from right here."

"I want to go to Paris," she said.

"Okay." Ransom tied the reins to the brake lever. "Someday, but right now we're just getting started."

"It feels like a dream," she said.

"It might feel like a dream, but it's real. When I told Mr. Roebuck an airplane can go places a train can't and get there faster and cheaper, he listened. I told him I could make a place for planes to land right here so anytime he needed a contract signed, he'd just have to hand it to a pilot."

"And he gave you the money just like that?" Amelia Rose said.

"It took a while to work it out, but, yeah, he's backing us. Someday there'll be planes flying all over the place. They'll be taking off and landing right here, and every time they do, they'll put money in our pocket."

On the horizon, the sun had set and thrown back a band of glorious color in a final farewell. Ace's biplane came low across the trees. It crossed over the cotton fields and slowed to the point of stalling.

"It's pink," Amelia Rose said. "That airplane is *pink*."

"It was supposed to be red, but something happened with the paint." Ransom stepped down from the buggy. He reached back to take Isaac and cradled him in his arms. "Ace is now the Pink Lady Mail Courier and Aerial Service."

The airplane slowed even more, all but falling from the sky. The wings rocked, teetering on the edge of a stall, as the Pink Lady turned toward the buggy. Amelia Rose and Ransom stood shoulder to shoulder and watched it approach.

"Ransom," Amelia Rose said. "Something's wrong with it. It's wobbling. And it's coming right at us."

Barely higher than the house top, the plane came straight at them. Seated in front of the pilot, a woman passenger waved then raised a bushel basket. The moment the plane passed over, the passenger dumped the contents of the basket over Amelia Rose, Ransom and Isaac.

"My God," Amelia Rose yelled and tried to run.

Ransom grabbed her arm. "Rose petals," he said. "It's just rose petals. Miss Hazel sent 'em."

A fluttering cloud billowed in the air and drifted down on them like delicate, sweet-smelling snowflakes. He felt them touch his brow but couldn't take his eyes off Amelia Rose. She raised her face to the sky and savored the exquisite touch of rose petals falling on her cheeks, sweet and light and lovely. Petals gathered in her hair and tickled her ears as they tumbled past. Some landed soft as kisses on her closed eyelids, others dribbled tender down her throat, slipping beneath her dress and into her bosom. She threw her head back and spread her arms to the sky, laughing as she breathed the wild perfume.

Amelia Rose was still giddy when the Pink Lady landed. Ace and Wanda hurried up to the buggy. After a quick round of hugs and handshakes and a few tears, Ace and Wanda took the buggy back to town.

"I'll never forget today," Amelia Rose said as they stood on the porch of their house, watching Ace and Wanda go. Petals lingered in her hair and all the world smelled of roses.

With baby Isaac in her arms, Ransom scooped up Amelia Rose and carried them both across the threshold. Down the hall, a single lamp burned in the bedroom. Something gleamed in its light and caught Ransom's eye through the half opened door.

With his wife and baby in his arms, he nudged the bedroom door open with his shoulder. It swung wide to reveal a brass bed, fully dressed with quilts and pillows, and littered with deep red velvet rose petals. On either side of the headboard, tea crates served as night stands. A note card lay angled in the center of the bed. Ransom gently placed his wife on the rose covered mattress and took the card to the light. Leaning toward the lamp's glow, he began to read the card aloud.

"It says '*Live long and love longer*, Captain and Mrs. Charles Augustus Guignard.'"

"Who's that?" Amelia Rose said.

"Miss Wanda and her dead husband."

Ransom put the card away and, as Amelia Rose prepared to nurse baby Isaac, he slipped out into the hall. Except for the bedroom, the house was empty. They would have a lifetime to grow into this place. In the front room, he found the photograph of his new family and placed it on the mantel. For a moment, in the dark with only moonlight spilling through the windows, he stood looking at the image. Baby Isaac lay almost undetectable in his mother's arms. Time would bring more photographs. One day, when they were old and worn out, the walls would be covered with pictures of their life together.

Ransom went outside, careful not to let the screen door slam. Bullfrogs croaked from the drainage ditch and far away a dog barked. Stepping down from the porch, he stood beneath the night sky and searched the heavens for the star he had known in France. He could not find it. It didn't matter, not now. The star had brought him here. A breeze cooled the air and touched his face. It carried the scent of freshly plowed earth and salt marshes. With a last look at the heavens, Ransom went inside.

In the bedroom, Amelia Rose put sleeping Isaac in a bassinet and covered him with a light blanket. At the foot of the bed, she rummaged in a wooden chest until she found two long tapered candles and a pair of crystal holders. She placed an unlit candle on each tea-crate nightstand.

"Get in bed," she said as she changed into a night gown. Outside, crickets droned like invisible machinery.

In his long johns, Ransom climbed beneath the covers, scattering rose petals on the floor.

Amelia Rose turned down the lantern wick until the flame pressed out and darkness filled the room. Only the faint glow of moonlight entered through the windows. Moving through the shadows, she bent over Ransom and pressed warm lips to his. He stopped breathing until she pulled away. Then, standing beside the bed, she lit a match and filled the room with light.

Without a word, she touched the burning match to the candle beside Ransom. More light filled the room as the wick caught fire. She lit the candle on her side too. Amber light filled every corner and, above each candle, a puddle of gold shimmered on the ceiling.

Amelia Rose climbed into bed and rolled to face her husband. She kissed him lightly and drew back. They lay face to face in a cocoon of linen warmed by the heat of their bodies. He saw in her eyes the miniature flame of a candle. There was no end to the goodness inside her. Her soul lay deep and pure as all creation.

"Like two candles," she said from some place far away, just short of dreaming. "I don't know where my light ends and yours begins." She stroked the outline of his face. "Are you scared?"

"No," he said, but something in his tone betrayed his lie. He could feel it and so added, "Maybe just a little."

"Me too," she said, touching him. "But I know we'll be alright as long as we stick together."

"I want to be a good husband and a good daddy too, but I don't know what I'm doing."

"You're a good man Ransom James MacTavish," she said, breathing the words. "A good man can figure out the rest."

"I hope so, but we sure got off to a rocky start."

"Rocks make a good foundation." Beneath the covers, she took his hand in hers. "Why didn't you run off this time?"

"Because..." He tried to answer, but a knot cinched in his throat and choked him. He closed his eyes to find the words. When he opened them again, he saw her face across the pillow. A single rose petal lay tangled in her hair. "Because you're my best friend."

Amelia Rose snuggled close and drew his hand to her heart.

"You're my best friend too."